SCANDINAVIAN CLASSICS
VOLUME XXX

. .
.

SWEDEN'S BEST STORIES

An Introduction to Swedish Fiction

SELMA LAGERLOF
Courtesy of Dr. Henry Buergel Goodwin

SWEDEN'S BEST STORIES

AN INTRODUCTION TO SWEDISH FICTION

TRANSLATIONS BY
CHARLES WHARTON STORK

A Selection of Short Stories by

TOPELIUS · STRINDBERG · AHLGREN
GEIJERSTAM · HEIDENSTAM · LEVERTIN
LAGERLÖF · HALLSTRÖM · MOLIN
SÖDERBERG · BO BERGMAN · ENGSTRÖM
NORDSTRÖM · ELGSTRÖM · SIWERTZ
SILLÉN

EDITED BY HANNA ASTRUP LARSEN

46472

NEW YORK
THE AMERICAN-SCANDINAVIAN FOUNDATION
W · W · NORTON & COMPANY, INC.
Publishers

CONTENTS

* Translated by Velma Swanston Howard.

INTRODUCTION

THE demand that literature should take up problems for debate, formulated by Georg Brandes, gave an impetus to the development of fiction. Before that time, most of the great masters in Sweden wrote chiefly verse. Literature meant poetry. The new fashion of using literature as a means of presenting new ideas and arguments craved the medium of prose, and fiction even more than drama gave scope for discussion and for that wealth of photographic detail which became the accepted style of the day. While the lyric strain so characteristic of Swedish genius has continued uninterrupted, it has for the last fifty years been accompanied by a rich vein of creative prose. Several writers of the first rank have chosen fiction as their chief if not their only means of expression.

It is true, the modern novel had not been without forerunners. As early as 1839, the erratic genius, C. J. L. Almquist, had startled his contemporaries with his innocent-appearing little story *It Can Be Done* (translated into English under the title *Sara Videbeck*) which was nothing less than a plea for a form of companionate marriage. Still earlier, Fredrika Bremer had initiated the domestic novel. Her *Sketches from Everyday Life,* published in 1828, was the first attempt to describe the ordinary middle class home from personal observation. Her novels had a great vogue, not only in the Scandinavian countries, but in England and America. Viktor Rydberg, poet, philosopher, and historian, wrote some historical fiction in which, under the veil of a distant time, he dealt with modern tendencies. Of entirely different caliber are the historical romances of the Swedish Finn, Zacharias Topelius, who wrote in the pure delight of telling a good story, though with a wholesome moral pleasantly mixed with entertainment in the good old fashion.

In the seventies and eighties of the nineteenth century, new ideas and discoveries in the fields of political thought and physical science reached Scandinavia, and were at once made the subject of literary discussion. The ideas of Darwin, Spencer, Stuart Mill, Buckle and others were launched in novel and drama before they had become familiar to the people through any other channel. Evolution, higher criticism of the Bible, democracy, social reform, new theories of education, the emancipation of women, divorce and free love were the topics around which discussion seethed.

At the same time, the naturalistic fashion in

Introduction

literary style was introduced in Scandinavia, though much tempered by Northern reserve. Ibsen once indignantly repudiated the comparison between himself and Zola, saying, "I go down into the sewer to cleanse it; Zola goes down to take a bath." Strindberg, too, denied the influence of Zola on his novel *The Red Room* (1879), which is generally regarded as opening the realistic era in Sweden, while he acknowledged his debt to Dickens and, in the matter of style, to Mark Twain.

August Strindberg was the greatest genius of the new era in Sweden, and was indeed the very incarnation of its revolt and restless seeking. His unhappy childhood and youth had bred in him that passionate resentment which later he carried into his attack on tyrants in high places. His cry for social justice came from his own quivering nerves and suffering spirit. His own struggle to get a start in life enters directly into his novel *The Red Room,* which has for its subtitle *Pictures from the Lives of Artists and Authors.* It describes the unequal fight which these young Ishmaels of the pen and brush were waging against the speciousness of the powers who guarded the approaches to the academy and the press, the stage and the publishing houses. In the attack on everything smug and established, Strindberg found opportunity also to pay his re-

Introduction

spects to the government Circumlocution Offices,
to the Riksdag, to organized charity, and organized evangelism. The atmosphere of the book is
Bohemian. The name is taken from the red furniture in the room of a Stockholm café where the
young men used to gather and discuss the problems of the universe as well as the immediate and
pressing problem of where to get their next meal.
The types and characters were new. The milieu
was new, and so was the style with its easy, con-
versational tone and its intimate descriptions
based on minute observation.

In *Married,* two collections of short stories,
Strindberg went even further in using the problems of daily life as subjects for literary treat-
ment. The work was directed against Ibsen's
A Doll's House—which is cleverly parodied in
one of the stories—and in general against the
whole movement for the emancipation of women.
Strindberg's woman hatred had not at that time
grown to the fantastic proportions it attained
later, and *Married* is not so much an attack on
women as a plea for nature and natural conditions. Amid much that is preposterous, it con-
tains some common sense. There is both sanity
and sweetness in his insistence on the child as the
center of the marriage relation. How he recon-
ciles his defense of prostitution with his concern
for the welfare of the coming generation is not

so clear; but what interests us here is not so much Strindberg's theories as the shifting of emphasis from the great romantic feelings to the practical problems which so often make or mar happiness: —the rent, the meals, the amusements; the daily toil and anxiety of the job; the encroachments of the wife's family; the struggle between love and the certain knowledge that more children will mean complete pauperization; the sordid miseries of a summer in the city when moving to the country is financially impossible. No one has ever described the tortures of genteel poverty more vividly than Strindberg.

Owing perhaps to the antidote furnished by *Married*, the literary woman cult never reached the same height in Sweden as in Norway. Nevertheless, the preoccupation of literature with the problems of marriage and the family naturally appealed to women. At the same time, the literary fashion of the day, with its stress on first-hand observation and on the details of daily life, is one in which women excel. Therefore it was no accident that two of the cleverest writers of fiction in the realistic period were women, Anne Charlotte Leffler and Victoria Benedictsson (pseudonym Ernst Ahlgren). Especially the latter has retained both critical approval and popular interest. Fru Leffler, a member of the upper class, described the conflict in the life of a gifted woman between intellectual interests and domestic duties. Fru Benedictsson also wrote stories of married life, but is at her best in her pictures of life among the common people in Skåne. With her sober truthfulness, enlivened by humorous comprehension, and her eye for the characteristic even when ugly, her contempt of mere prettiness, she is a realist of the purest water.

Far darker are the pictures of peasant life drawn by Gustaf af Geijerstam, the most prominent of the men writers who followed the lead of Strindberg. He made a laudable attempt to study "the people" close at hand, and even tried to live as a peasant. Proclaiming the great Russians as his master, he was perhaps prone to see the Swedish peasant through Russian spectacles. At any rate, he seems to have reached the conclusion that the lives of the very poor were reduced to the elemental cravings of hunger and sex. The struggle for existence he saw as so terrific that it killed all softer feelings, even the primitive affection of children for aged and helpless parents, and as a natural result led to crimes of appalling brutality.

This phase of Geijerstam's production, so characteristic of the era, was short-lived, and he afterwards turned to the writing of domestic novels about people of his own class. The naturalistic principle held sway in Swedish literature only

Introduction

a scant decade, from which the school takes its name, the School of the Eighties.

II

The last decade of the nineteenth century witnessed a flowering of fresh young talent the like of which has rarely if ever been seen in Sweden. Heidenstam, Selma Lagerlöf, Per Hallström, Levertin, Pelle Molin, and the poets Fröding and Karlfeldt were young with the decade. Different in other respects, they were all alike in chafing under the restraints of realism and seeking the wider vistas and freer paths of poetic imagination. The school they formed has been called Neo-Romanticism or Symbolism, but in Sweden is more frequently known simply as the School of the Nineties.

The liberating word was spoken by Verner von Heidenstam, who had recently made his début as a poet, and who, in 1889, published a pamphlet entitled *Renascence*. If Strindberg's opinions had been shaped by his early sufferings, Heidenstam's attitude toward life had been determined by singularly fortunate circumstances. He had just returned from years of foreign travel. The beauties of Italy and the Orient, seen with the artist's eye and comprehended with the poet's mind, were still vital and glowing in his consciousness. He was supremely fitted to perform what he regarded as the function of the poet, to create beauty and joy, to inspire and uplift. The "shoemaker realism" and the "cellar air" prevalent in the literature of the time were repugnant to him. He wanted to reinstate the great emotions and fervid enthusiasms as subjects fit for the poet, while he repudiated the utilitarian philosophy of the preceding decade, which he summed up as follows: "He (Strindberg) does not say, do good, for therein is ecstasy. No, he says, begin every day with some little good deed; then the water will run in the kitchen, and the electric lights will not get out of order, and you won't have any tiresome visitors."

Heidenstam preached the joy of living, but he never conceived it as sensuous ease. Rather, he thought of it as an effort of the will. Therefore there was no break with his past, but a natural transition, when he turned from the worship of form and color to the worship of moral beauty as seen through a great personality. Characteristically, he chose as his hero Charles XII, the king who, judged by utilitarian standards, did his country endless harm, but who left his people a great spiritual heritage.

Strindberg had been Heidenstam's forerunner in the imaginative historical tale, and it is interesting to compare the two. Strindberg, in his

Swedish Fates and Adventures, had turned away
from the pageant of lords and ladies that used
to occupy the old romanticists, to follow the fate
of the victims: the peasant who had his grain
ridden down by the hunt; the young priest stifled
by the rules of his order; the disinherited young
nobleman unequal to the struggle for existence.
Heidenstam, in *The Charles Men,* writes of the
poor and lowly: the soldier in the ranks, the aged
stewardess, even the silly clown who develops into
a hero; but he sees them all as taking part in the
great struggle of which the king is leader. The
light that shines around him falls also on their
humble path. If it were not idle to sit in judgment, we might say that the deeper human pity
is Strindberg's and the higher ideal is Heidenstam's.

To Heidenstam, Charles XII is neither the
cruel tyrant nor the Nietzschean superman treading down others by the right of his own great-
ness. He is the strong spirit pouring his strength
into the weaker wills of his fellows and forcing
them to be their best selves. Such a man, he in-
sists, cannot be measured by ordinary standards.
"Sometimes we put a man in one side of the
scales and all our wisdom in the other, but still
the scales do not move. Do you know what that
means? It means that in that man there is a
drop of the eternal righteousness; for that drop

is heavier than gold or lead, and we have no scales with which to weigh it."

The study of the great leader who must follow his star at whatever cost has always been supremely interesting to Heidenstam. In discussing the character of Charles XII, he once said that the very essence of tragedy was the conflict between opposing moral demands. If the conflict were soluble, it would not be tragedy. In *The Bjälbo Heritage,* the moral conflict is clearly marked. Magnus, the born ruler, must depose his weak brother, Valdemar, before he can get the chance to do his lifework, to pacify the land and lay the foundations of a new Christian state. He loves Valdemar and suffers agonies of remorse, but when the devil appears and offers him peace of mind if he will undo what he has accomplished, he bids the tempter begone, saying, "Take me, but leave my work." The problem of the great leader is uppermost also in *The Pilgrimage of St. Birgitta,* the only finished portrait of a woman Heidenstam has ever drawn. He touches lightly on St. Birgitta's happy married life to follow her on her career as saint and prophet.

While Heidenstam revitalized his country's past, Selma Lagerlöf drew her inspiration from the folk life of her immediate surroundings. She has herself told how she conceived the idea of writing a book about the quaint characters who

used to gather at her father's house and about
the legends with which the neighborhood teemed;
how she struggled vainly to conform with the realistic standards of the time; and how Heidenstam's pronouncement gave her courage to let
the material shape itself as it would. The result
was *The Saga of Gösta Berling,* published in
1891. It was a book so at variance with everything known before, that the critics were puzzled,
though it must be said to the everlasting credit
of Georg Brandes that he—the high priest of
realism—recognized its importance and hailed
the young rising genius. The reading public was
soon won and has never swerved from its alle-
giance.

Selma Lagerlöf opened a world of romance
and legend, of mysticism and the supernatural.
Superstition is the warp and woof of her stories.
It is true, she never drags superstitions out in the
light of day where they would be exposed to the
reader's sceptical gaze; she is too good an artist
for that. But these strange beliefs are always
there just beneath the surface, living in the minds
of the people with whatever reality faith can give
them. Unseen forces take sides in the battles of
humanity, aiding the good, confuting the evil.
Sometimes she reveals the terrors of nature, as
in the storm in *Jerusalem.* We do not know
whether it is only a terrific thunder-storm, or

whether the hell-hounds are really unleashed; we are only conscious of the terror that nature can strike in the minds of people who live in the shadow of its overpowering might. Nature with her is not merely a world governed by scientific laws as the realists told us when they sent fairies to limbo and asked us to love nature soberly for its own sake. With Selma Lagerlöf everything in nature is endowed with personality. Trees and rocks are loosed from their background; they speak and gesticulate and take part in the human drama.

Although she draws freely on old legends, Miss Lagerlöf's romanticism is not dependent on distance of time or place or on the trappings of romance. It can mould the clay of Dalecarlian peasants and gild the madcap adventures of feckless Värmland cavaliers, because it is an attitude of mind. It is her intimate absorption in things and people close at hand, combined with the bold flight of her imagination, that gives her books their inimitable charm.

Other distinguished writers of the Neo-Romantic period are Oscar Levertin and Per Hallström, who both began as realists. Levertin found his most congenial subject in medieval or rococo times. Hallström takes his themes from many ages and places, from modern Philadelphia, from revolutionary France, from medieval Flor-

Introduction

ence or Don Juan's Sevilla, or from an imaginary island in the sea, but he is not interested in picturing any milieu for its own sake. He simply uses an exotic background, or the wilderness of his native land, to liberate his imagination and provide the wide sweep of horizon which gives a single human fate universal significance. It is only the spiritual essence of a situation that interests him, and he is prone to think that character is best revealed in sorrow and renunciation, as life takes on its deepest significance with approaching death.

The period of the nineties has found a sympathetic interpreter in Ruben G:son Berg and an aggressive champion in Fredrik Böök. Both these critics have helped to crystallize its meaning. The literary movement takes on added significance from the fact that it was a part of a general movement of peaceful nationalism. It coincided with the effort of the Swedish people to study their own history, traditions, and racial characteristics—in short, with their effort to know themselves and be themselves. Heidenstam and Selma Lagerlöf have both created types that have been regarded as the quintessence of the national character, Gösta Berling impersonating its love of romance and festive glamor; the "Charles man," its patriotism and power of unselfish devotion. Naturally, such types, created by two

great artists, do more than reflect the national
character. They shape it.

III

The realistic period initiated by Strindberg was
short-lived, but it stands to reason that a movement of such momentum—a part of a world-wide
revolt—could not spend itself in a single decade,
and if we look to the writers of to-day, we shall
find more threads going back to Strindberg than
to Heidenstam and the poets of the nineties.
The connection with the eighties of last century
is very marked in Hjalmar Söderberg, the senior
in age and still the central figure in the group of
prose writers whose work falls entirely or almost
entirely within the present century. He acknowl-
edges it in his autobiographical novel, *Martin
Birck's Early Days,* which states the same problems of religion and sex that were uppermost in
the eighties. He does not attempt to solve them,
but he asks, with pointed address to the romanticists, why this sudden insistence on the joy of
living, when all the old problems are still
unsolved, and the world wags on as wearily as
ever.

Söderberg is a pupil of Anatole France, an ad-
mirer of the Danes, J. P. Jacobsen and Herman
Bang, resembling the latter in his disillusionment

and pessimism. He writes in a detached, delicately ironical style, disclaiming all serious import, but while he declares his unfaith and amorality, he is always trying to draw aside the veil that separates man from the unseen. Behind his light, frothy humor there lurks a terror of existence. Akin to Hjalmar Söderberg, but less negative in spirit, is Bo Bergman.

The passion for social justice which characterized the realistic period in the nineteenth century is not so marked to-day. Many of the reforms then urged have been effected, and for those remaining there are other methods of attack. Literature has less reason to concern itself with causes, and there is no longer the fervent belief in the immediate results to be gained. Yet something of the spirit of the old "indignation literature" is still with us, notably in the women writers. In the work of Anna Lenah Elgström a passionate sympathy with the weak and suffering is one of the strongest elements. Elin Wägner's clever stories of business girls and professional women have been distinct contributions to the cause of feminism. Marika Stjernstedt, a novelist of considerable power, has taken up the problems of the unmarried woman and of divorce.

The complex currents of modern life are reflected in the works of Sigfrid Siwertz, whose recent books deal with the moral dissolution following the World War. A master of the short story, he has been compared to Hallström, whom he resembles in the ability to take a single incident and make of it a window from which we look out upon the world. In style and manner of approach he is very different. Where Hallström is classic and romantic, Siwertz is modern and realistic.

Like Hjalmar Söderberg and Bo Bergman, Sigfrid Siwertz is a native of Stockholm, and like them he describes the city's highways and byways—and waterways; for he often uses the harbor and skerries as his background. Other writers have cultivated each his own locality. Henning Berger is most at home in the cities. Hjalmar Bergström has recreated a whole province in Bergslagen with small towns, farmhouses, and manors. Ludvig Nordström portrays the villagers and fishermen in northern Sweden.

In the present volume we have wished to give not only a cross section of literature, but also a picture of life as it is lived in Sweden. The limited space and the great wealth of material have rendered choice difficult. Swedish readers will miss the old masters, Rydberg and Almquist, who are not included because they have not left us any short stories that would give an adequate idea of their merits. For similar reasons we have been

Introduction

obliged to omit many writers now living whose work would otherwise have been represented. The greatest space has, naturally, been given to the writers who are at their best in the short story. We hope the volume will give some idea of the great wealth and diversity of Swedish fiction and that it will point the way to further reading.

The translator, Mr. Stork, and I wish to express our thanks to Mrs. Velma Swanston Howard who has been kind enough to let us use her translations, revised by her for this volume, of three stories: *The Legend of the Christmas Rose* by Selma Lagerlöf, *The Stone Man* and *Half a Sheet of Paper* by Strindberg.

HANNA ASTRUP LARSEN

ZACHARIAS TOPELIUS

THE PITCH BURNER
WHO ALWAYS GOT TO THE TOP

ZACHARIAS TOPELIUS (1818–1898) is known to every child who ever studied a Scandinavian school reader. His delightful children's stories and fairy tales have been read as much in Norway and Denmark as in Sweden, and some of them have recently been translated into English and published in the United States. Equally dear to somewhat older readers are his historical romances, *The Surgeon's Stories,* which won the distinction of high praise from Theodore Roosevelt. Although Topelius was born after Finland had been subjugated by Russia, he dwelt with particular affection on the time when the history of Finland was intertwined with that of Sweden. *The Surgeon's Stories* are romances of the campaigns of Swedish kings from Gustavus Adolphus to Gustaf III, and stress especially the honorable part taken in these campaigns by the Finnish regiments. They are based on sound historical knowledge. Topelius was professor of history in Helsingfors for more than twenty years and remained professor emeritus till his death. Though himself a Swedish Finn, writing in Swedish as a matter of course, he was broad-minded enough to sympathize with the *fennoman* movement which had for its object the development of a Finnish culture. Topelius has also written verse of fine poetic quality.

Zacharias Topelius

The Pitch Burner
Who Always Got to the Top

BESIDE the old red church in my native town was a plot of greensward which in former times had been a burial place. This abode of the dead had, in the course of time, been pushed more and more to one side by the living, who prefer to conduct their business on the surface of the earth untroubled by sorrow before they go beneath it. The doctor affirmed that this shifting of the dead was in the interest of health, since life does not go on well cheek by jowl with death. I don't know, it is very possible. What is certain is that our revered forefathers first had their resting-place under the floor of the church, then were hoisted away to the slope in front of the steeple, and from there were passed on to an enclosed churchyard in a corner of the town, to find their asylum at last in a field some versts beyond the gate. The slope near the steeple was now a grass meadow where the sexton cut hay, in which process a bone would now and then be caught in the teeth of the rake; but no monument or gravestone, not even a half-mouldered corpse aroused

[3]

the new age to any respect for the bygone generations which lay buried under the velvet turf.

Since the dilapidated schoolhouse was near the church, the schoolboys found it handy to use this slope as a playground at the time of year when the snow had melted and the ground had dried in the rays of the May sun. Now a ball sailed merrily skyward, now roller-skates rattled, now the noisy band divided into Turks and Christians, who, without the slightest consideration for the repose of the graves, battled together on the formerly hallowed ground. Old Sexton Vik did not approve of these pranks, but as long as the grass still resembled the first down on a sixteen-year-old lad's chin, and no harm was done to his prospective harvest, he let many things pass that were contrary to rule, with the reservation that he would complain to the schoolmaster if such disorder continued on into midsummer. This zealous servant of the church had in his youth belonged to the militia, and although no chronicle recorded his campaigns, there may have been something of the soldier left under the old man's gray jacket, because for all his religion he could not refrain from watching with secret enjoyment the battles between the Turks and the Christians. When, therefore, one of the boys succeeded in performing any notable act of valor, such as storming a camp or knocking down a whole group of enemies, the sexton could be heard shouting from the belfry door, "Look at him, boys! He's a real man, he always gets to the top like the old pitch-burner."

Boys like being praised for heroic deeds, but they had never heard of pitch-burners making themselves particularly famous for great achievements. It seemed to them decidedly odd that a black fellow, such as they had often seen covered with tar and soot stirring with his long stake in the great pitch kettle over by the river, should be held up to them as a model of manhood. They assailed the old man with questions as to what this meant, but always received the snubbing answer that it was none of their business; let them see they knew their catechism at the summer examination, that was all they needed to know in this world.

Now the sexton had a favorite, Kalle Videstrand—if I may be so bold as to mention my own name. Fourteen I was, small in stature but quick with my fists and a master in the art of tripping; it was therefore I who usually came out on top in the war and threw down fellows who were a head taller. Poor boy as I was, in summer I used to row Vik out on fishing trips, and managed my oars so well that a pike could seldom resist his shining hook.

Now I got it into my head to find out once for

all what was at the bottom of this remarkable expression of praise. I therefore began slyly one evening when Vik was sitting in the stern with his line and I was rowing in front of him just opposite the pitch factory. "Was it there he lived in the cabin on the slope?"

"Yes, there it was he lived," replied the sexton abstractedly.

"And he became a general?"

"What's that?"

Vik gave his line a jerk, for he thought he felt a bite, but it was only the tug of some water-weed.

"Yes, the one who got to the top," I continued ingenuously.

"He was no soldier," came the rough answer.

"But was he terrifically strong then?"

"Not that either, as far as I know."

"I have heard so from Mrs. Anderson," I assured him. "He is supposed to have hoisted down the big church bell all alone when it got cracked and had to go to the foundry. And when it was recast he hoisted it back all alone to the beam in the tower."

"What the mischief! It was Master Freytag did that. The pitch-burner was a little fellow. I've seen him, I have, though he has lain dead more than a hundred year."

I was crushed, but still determined to hold on

[6]

to the thread as obstinately as the sexton held his line. After a while, when we had turned back up the river, there was a heavy jerk, as if the hook had stuck in a floating log. The sexton pulled in his line carefully, and I managed my oars so deftly that, despite his desperate resistance, a twenty-pound pike was pulled into the boat. It flapped about mightily, until the lucky fisherman flung himself upon it and after a hard struggle finally subdued it.

"See, now you've got to the top, like the old pitch-burner," I exclaimed, gripping the thread of my purpose as the pike had taken the line.

"God forbid!" responded the sexton after a short silence, when he could free his thoughts from the exhilarating capture.

"What can there be bad in always getting to the top?" I asked.

"Listen here, Kalle," the sexton resumed, visibly softened by his unexpected luck, "that expression of coming out on top like the old pitch-burner was a saying when I was a boy, and it's well that it will soon be forgotten. One shouldn't wish one's Christian fellowmen something that one ought not to wish to one's worst enemy. But since we're in front of the pitch works again, we might put ashore a few minutes to tar my line. It's beginning to get frayed."

We laid in alongside the bank and went up to

the brown pitch works. It smoked like a kiln; thick bitter fumes swept down to the ground and clung like oil to whatever they touched. The whole shore was as if paved with thick asphalt; every step left an imprint, and here and there tufts of wool in the pitch showed where some unlucky sheep had stretched itself out in the warm sun on this treacherous bed and had only escaped by the partial loss of its hide. The building was highly inflammable, having burned down about once a generation, and was now constructed of light boards so as to be consumed quickly next time with as little damage as possible. It was a tallish structure with a high chimney and no window but with wide doors on all sides, so that no matter what the direction of the wind, the smoke could always escape. Inside there was nothing to see but the bare brownish-black walls and the enormous copper kettle, the pitch retort, where the furnace beneath converted sixty hogsheads of tar into pitch at every boiling. The process had now been going on for several days under constant supervision. The familiar black fellow went about stirring with his stake in the black broth, which could not be allowed to catch fire or to boil either too much or too little, before at the right time it was run off into the barrels. We were above the earth, but I recalled what I had read

somewhere about Charon and the Styx. How a
human being could live in air that made one's
eyes smart so was hard to comprehend. As seals
pop up from time to time above the surface to
breathe, this panting martyr to his useful calling
had now and again to feel his way out to the
open door to gasp for a mouthful of fresh air.

"Well, Kalle," inquired the sexton, "should you
like to become a pitch-burner? It's a paying
trade; pitch brings in good money and gives a
man a livelihood."

"No, thank you," said I, "not if I come to the
top a thousand times. What would money do
for me without eyes and lungs?"

"But look at that fellow there! He has stood
it for fifteen summers. Every morning he comes
here he may expect to see the shanty burst into
flames over him, and if he gets near the fire,
he's like tow, he's done for in a twinkling. Or
what do you think if he should happen to doze
off when he's watching here alone at night?
Wouldn't he be dragged out in the morning suf-
focated with smoke? But look! that doesn't
trouble him in the least. When a good fellow's
doing his duty he doesn't think of life and limb."

"But what if he should fall into the kettle?"
I asked, with a shiver at the thought of such a
horrible event.

"I think we clean folk have had enough of

this," Vik announced, drawing me out with him into the fresh air. "A shoemaker would soon be able to lacquer boots with us. Sit down on the stone here and I'll tell you about the old pitch-burner while I'm tarring my line."

I felt like a seal when it crawls out on an ice-floe in spring, and pricked up my ears as the seal does when he hears the tones of a flute in the distance. We sat down on the handiest stone, where the breeze blew the smoke away from us, and I heard how a man gets to the top in this world.

.   .   .   .

It's not worth the trouble, Kalle, to listen to simple folk talk about former days. Give that Anderson woman a fly's leg, and she'll make it into an ox. But what's pitch should be pitch, and what's a lily-of-the-valley should be a lily-of-the-valley. I have the story from my grand-father, who was ninety-six when he left the world. He had heard it as a boy from Peter Smeds, and Peter Smeds was a lad of sixteen when he started fetching wood to the first pitch-works. That's as good as a bank-note in your other hand.

The pitch-burner was a fine boy in his younger years, Peter said. Hans was his name, and Master Hans he was called by those who wished to stand well with him, but that's forgot now, and indeed 'tis a small thing if a name's forgot, if only the poor soul wins rest in heaven.

This same Hans—whatever his name may have been besides—was a poor boy, small of build but nimble in the head, as you are, Kalle. Take warning: A nimble head shames nobody, but it must be used with understanding and not for evil. Hans with his white skin and his red cheeks looked just like a girl, poor as he was; I think it was his ruin, since he thought he was born to be something great in the world. He was always wishful to get on, and I say nothing against that; a man may well set that before him, but Hans wanted to get ahead too fast. He always wore flowers on his well-brushed jacket and set himself off with a cock feather in his cap as if he was a courtier. Folk saw to what that pointed and said: "Oh, Hans will get on, he'll come to the top for certain."

As sure as he lived, Hans would have liked to serve as a soldier among the king's men; that was the quickest way to get on in those restless days. But for that he was too small. Instead for his fine manners he got service as page with the provincial governor, Count Tott, who lived then in his splendid castle on the other side of the river, where the Residence grounds are now, but of the castle there's no more to be found than

[11]

a little brick dust here and there in the sand. Gentlefolk looked down on simple folk as a mast on a ship's rat in those days; but Hans was determined to get up, and up he got. From page he grew to be chamberlain; he stood in a coat of gold lace in the back of his master's carriage on the way to church, and had his place with the count's cloak on his arm in the noble's pew next to the altar. After that he became seneschal, was called master like the priests, and next to the governor was the chief man at all entertainments. He received guests on behalf of his master and was considered such an important man that no one dared undertake any errand to the castle without first getting into the good graces of Master Hans.

It seemed now almost come to fulfillment, what folk had said, that Hans would get to the top. But there was still a thumb's breadth wanting, for however high Hans was, the governor was higher; and if one carried the thing through, the king was higher than the governor. When, therefore, Count Tott went away on a journey, and Master Hans followed him, one could hear folk say, "Hans will come back as governor or else as king; anyway he'll get to the top."

Hans came back after many, many years, but neither as governor nor as king; rather as a poor masterless man, thin of body and purple under the eyes, yet just as arrogant and ambitious as before. Nobody knew where he had flitted about in the world, but something must have gone wrong with Fortune's wheel. Never trust Fortune, Kalle; she's like Brunberg's cartwheels: if the felloe holds, the spoke is bad; and if the spoke holds, the axle breaks. Some people thought that Hans had gambled away his wealth, others considered it more likely that he had squandered it in striving for higher position. Peter Smeds knew nothing of that; that was guesswork, nothing more. What everyone did know was that Master Hans brought with him from Germany a strange customer by the name of Captain Svart. He too must have been a fine fellow, Peter said, a bit darkish, a bit cross-eyed, so that he never looked people in the face, but always insinuating, always grinning at everyone as if he wanted to be everyone's best friend. The captain never set his foot in a church, but it was said he was skilled in many arts, especially in that of turning copper into gold and, what was even more necessary, of winning the confidence of all those who reach out after the yellow metal.

These two clever heads, Master Hans and Captain Svart, worked out a plan together. The town was then in its beginning and so unprogressive that its citizens could only distil tar and not pitch, and pitch at that time was worth a lot of money. Master Hans conducted the captain to the most prominent of the townsfolk and explained to them how the city and they themselves might soon achieve great prosperity if they turned to boiling pitch. Captain Svart, he said, was particularly adept in that art and would, under the supervision of Master Hans, undertake the management of the new pitch works. Hans would keep for himself only a dollar per barrel, the owners of the factory should have three, but what was left over was also to go to Hans. What was that but turning tar into gold?

Now the townsfolk might well have asked why Captain Svart could not with less trouble have made straight into gold the great copper kettle which was needed for the pitch works; but nobody thought of that, they all bit on the hook. Well, Kalle, there are worse hooks to bite at than a useful industry which improves a raw material; one should only look to it that there is no cloven foot behind. The pitch factory was built where it stands now, with a cabin on the wooded slope. Thither went Master Hans with his captain to become the first pitch-burners. You may guess people wondered how such fine gentlemen could condescend to such exacting work, wherein the finest and grandest person would soon look as if dipped in tar. But Master Hans and the captain well knew why for a time they let themselves be so deeply humiliated. They would wash themselves clean when the proper moment came, and the folk who had previously thought themselves deceived in their expectations when Hans did not come back as governor began again to whisper among themselves: "He gets a dollar a barrel, he'll come to the top safe enough."

Aye, whom will not money bring to the top? Hans boiled pitch; many hundreds, many thousands of barrels. The bitter smoke lay over the river night and day like a cloud, the cheap tar ran in from the great woods, the precious pitch rolled out in its receptacles to the merchant ships. Master Hans got his dollar per barrel, he got much more; on that he had counted, he knew the prices. Not in vain did he stand on the furnace floor in the smoke; he grew rich and built a cellar under his cabin for all the silver coins he guarded there. If Captain Svart did not make gold, at least he knew how to coin silver. But he was disinterested, he kept nothing for himself; he increased the pitch-burner's hoard, continued to squint, and continued to laugh with a strange evil grin, which was always playing about the corners of his mouth.

At this time Peter Smeds was working as woodcarrier at the pitch works and had the job of keeping up the furnace. There were only the three of them living at the cabin: Hans, the captain, and Peter; but in the woods lived an old witch woman, Martikay, who came every day to clean up and cook. Martikay was of the sort that priests and magistrates used to burn at the stake in those days, but she wasn't complete in her trade—she needed to take lessons from Captain Svart. The two used to revile each other so that it set one's hair on end, but then Master Hans would come between them and say, "Quiet, quiet, so the boy won't hear!" Peter heard more than he cared to, and thought to himself: "I can't keep on here, I'll run away."

While he was thinking this over, he lay awake one night in the loft, where he had his sleeping quarters, and heard them talking in the cabin below. Peter was inquisitive—as you are, Kalle —and had noticed that a board was loose in the middle of the floor on which he lay. He softly lifted it and could then hear what they said to each other in the dark of the night.

The captain said, "To-morrow the thirteenth quarter is up."

"That's good," said Hans. "Then I'll burn the pitch works, go over to Stockholm, be a gentleman again, and come back as governor of the province."

"If I so choose," said the captain.

"That doesn't depend on you," said Hans.

[16]

"In the contract it stands 'thirteen after thirteen.'"

The captain answered, "So it stands. You have now been a pitch-burner for thirteen years, and after thirteen years the thirteenth quarter is done."

"No," said Hans; "that means that after the thirteenth quarter I have still thirteen years before our contract is fulfilled."

Peter thought he heard the captain laugh, but he could see nothing. He wondered what they could mean by "thirteen after thirteen," and while he was wondering he heard Hans say again, "That was thirteen years *afterwards;*" but the captain said, "That was thirteen years *before.*" With that they began to revile each other, and Peter began to feel it was too uncanny for him alone in the dark of the loft. He stole barefoot down the stairs and was going to run away in good earnest. But he had forgot his boots in his sleeping quarters. Turn back he dare not, and leave his precious boots he could not, so he crept under a woodpile and waited for the dawn.

A little after daybreak he saw Hans and the captain go from the cabin to the pitch works. To Peter's surprise Hans was now washed clean and dressed in such fine clothes as Peter had never seen before. He walked in front with haughty steps, and the captain followed him, grinning, in his usual tarry things just like a servant. When they had gone into the building, Peter bethought himself whether now wasn't the time to get his shoes and be off. But he could do that later, and he was curious to see how Hans in his fine clothes would behave at the pitch kettle. "I can just ask whether I shall feed in more wood," he thought to himself.

Peter cautiously opened the door and saw the great kettle boiling up to the brim. There stood the captain alone stirring with his stake in the kettle. Every time he moved it, it seemed as if the pitch wanted to spout up to the stake; it hissed, it spat, the seething waves whirled up like the eddies at the river mouth; it seemed as if a great beast were swimming in the kettle and trying to get to the surface. Never had Peter seen the kettle so near to boiling over; and when that kettle boils over, everything is on fire. But the captain didn't seem to regard the danger; he kept on stirring and grinned the while more horribly than he had ever grinned.

"Where is Hans?" Peter took courage to ask.

"He is in my element," said the captain, and struck with his stake into the kettle so that the black boiling pitch splashed high up toward the roof.

Peter was not the lad to ask a second time. He ran to the cabin and met Martikay.

"Has it happened? May I fly off now?" she asked.

Had what happened? Peter did not answer. He rushed up the stairs, found his boots, and ran to the town without looking back. Never in all his life had he felt such a cold shudder run up his back.

What had happened was soon revealed. Next day a barge put in by the pitch works, and the crew went ashore to fetch their cargo. Where was the pitch-burner, Master Hans, who always used to stand with his tablet by the storehouse to enter every barrel and for every barrel earn his round dollar? He wasn't to be seen, Captain Svart was not to be seen, the fire under the great kettle had gone out, the cabin where they had lived was abandoned, and in the high fir by the gully in the rock sat a laughing magpie. Some there were who believed that the magpie was Martikay, and that she had now taken her opportunity to fly. There's no need to credit all that simple folk say about old women.

When the fire was kindled again, and the half-congealed pitch began to boil, something floated up in the kettle. A black lump it was, and that was the pitch-burner. Not much use he had now of the fine clothes he had put on when he meant to burn the pitch factory and go to Stockholm. But Hans it was and no other. The boatmen fished out the poor wretch, turned over their tobacco quids, and stirred in the kettle again to see if by chance they might come upon the captain too. No, you may depend upon it, Kalle, he was not there; it wasn't hard to guess where *he* was. Then the burgomaster and the public prosecutor came to take charge of the silver tithes, and what do you suppose they found in the cellar? Kindling wood they found, kindlings and sawdust, but not so much as a six-styver piece. There was a great hue and cry as to where the silver dollars might have betaken themselves. As if it wasn't enough to be drowned in a kettle of boiling pitch, here was nothing left behind but kindling wood. Some thought the captain had cleared out to Sweden with the silver. There was a hearing, but what could they make of it? Svart was gone, Martikay gone, and the boatmen knew nothing except that the pitch-burner had come floating to the top. There was only Peter that knew anything, but Peter had not gone to his first communion and so could not be put upon oath. At the hearing he related only what he chose; never did he dare tell a soul except my grandfather what he had heard through the floor. Fear sat hard on him; he was so deathly afraid of the captain that it was a shame.

Ah well, all that was as might be, but the most remarkable part came later. Everybody knew that the pitch-burner had wanted to get up in the world; why shouldn't he then float on top in the kettle? He was to be buried, naturally, but the question was whether, like other Christian men, he should have a grave under the church. The priests said flatly no, and nobody could blame them; there didn't seem to be any principles in Hans's catechism, and still less in Svart's, that they could hold with. In those days, let me tell you, it was a strict question, this of church discipline; not every cockerel could crow on the church grounds. However it came about, the priests gave in so far that the pitch-burner could be buried under the floor of the vestibule by the north door of the church. There he lay forty or fifty years, I don't rightly know just how long, when the old church was torn down to make room for a new one. Some of the dead that people cared about were moved and put under the floor of the new church, others were dug up and taken to a charnel house. Among these was the pitch-burner. Folks would have forgotten about him already, if he hadn't been found under the floor of the vestibule just the same as when he was dragged out of the pitch cauldron. Not a hair was changed except that the pitch had dried and fallen away in places, so that he could be better recognized.

Then came a time when people died in great numbers and were buried, and the charnel house was filled over and over again with the old bodies that had to make room for the new. Every time the charnel house was opened, the pitch-burner always lay on top. There was no magic in that, although it seemed so. I believe it came about in this way, that all who were laid above him mouldered away and fell to ashes, but he stayed unchanged. So time and the generations went their way, names were forgotten, ancestors were forgotten, good or bad were no longer called to mind, but still the pitch-burner came to the top. I have seen him many times, though he might have been my great-grandfather's grandfather. When I was a youngster like you, we used to peep in through the cracks between the thin boards, and when the sun shone in through the wall in the middle, we could see him as plainly as I see you. We had courage enough in the bright daylight, but not for fifteen silver farthings would any of us have cared to peep into the darkness on an autumn evening.

With that there came a dean who didn't like that the pitch-burner after his death should be a public spectacle, and he had him buried in a corner of the churchyard slope. Do you imagine he stayed there? How could he be kept down? In fifteen or twenty years he was at the surface again, a spring pushed him up as straight as a stone. He was buried again, and again he came up. Then the old dean had him buried seven yards under the earth. There he may be kept for my time and yours, but whether he stays there till doomsday is more than I know.

He wanted to come to the top, and to the top he came. It's so with mortals, that where their treasure is, there will their hearts be also. If the soul longs for heaven, the body will follow it there in good time. If the soul's desire is for what seems the highest place on earth, it will draw the body after it. Never did the pitch-burner imagine that he would always come to the top after that fashion. God preserve a sinful mortal from such a grim honor and such a terrible immortality! No, Kalle, let us live our span contented with the simple lot that is assigned to us. Let earth have its part and God His, and all will be as it should in this transitory existence.

Now that the line is fixed, let us row home. See how wondrously the sun is shining over there by the river mouth! Can you tell me why it doesn't shine so red when it stands highest in the heavens? I will tell you. It stands there in its time of greatest toil and fulfills its master's will, but when it is born in the morning and dies in

[23]

the evening, it shines with deep adoration. It is a hard task to stand high. Exalt not yourself, rather be lowly, think of the pitch-burner! Why should we want to be highest in this world of trial? Why should we not rather shine with adoration of God?

AUGUST STRINDBERG

AUTUMN

THE STONE MAN

HALF A SHEET OF PAPER

AUGUST STRINDBERG (1849–1912) was primarily a dramatist, the only dramatist of world dimensions that Sweden has produced, but the rejuvenating force of his genius was felt also in the domain of fiction. When only twenty-two years old, he wrote the historical drama, *Master Olof,* which with its ease, flexibility, and naturalness created a new technique. Thirty years old, he initiated the era of realistic fiction with the Stockholm novel, *The Red Room.* A few years later, he discovered the skerries with their fishing population as a field for romantic fiction, and wrote *The People at Hemsö.* Once more he struck a new note in his *Swedish Fates and Adventures,* a collection of short stories actually treating modern themes under the veil of historic fiction.

In *Married,* two volumes of short stories, Strindberg took issue with the literary woman cult which had emanated from Ibsen. His hatred of women later grew to be an obsession, and had much to do with turning him from a democrat and champion of the common people into a believer in Nietzsche's doctrine of the superman. He came to regard women as biologically inferior. This idea dominates his naturalistic dramas, *The Father, Miss Julia, Creditors,* and *The Link,* and in spite of masterly technique and keen psychology, these works suffer, even artistically, from the author's intense bias. All Strindberg's works mirror to a greater or less degree his own experiences, and he has besides left us a group of frankly autobiographical books, *The Bondwoman's Son, Confessions of a Fool, Inferno,* and *Legends.*

In the latter part of his life Strindberg entered upon a mystic-religious phase, and to this period belong the dramas *To Damascus, Easter,* and *The Dream Play.* His admirers built in Stockholm a small intimate theatre seating only a hundred and fifty people as a workshop for trying out his dramatic ideas.

August Strindberg

Autumn

From *Married*

THEY had been married ten years! Happily? As happily as circumstances had permitted. They had pulled along as smoothly and steadily as two bullocks of equal strength, each at its place in the team.

In the first year, naturally, many illusions about marriage were dispelled, that of absolute bliss, for instance. With the next year children began to arrive, and the drudgery of life did not leave much time for reflection.

He was very domestic, extremely domestic, one might say; finding in his family his miniature world, of which he was the middle point. His children were the radii, and his wife sought likewise to be a middle point but never in the centre of the circle, since that was where the husband was; for which reason the radii sometimes ran to him, sometimes to her, intersecting each other.

In this tenth year the husband was appointed a secretary of prison inspection, and had therefore to travel about. This was a blow to his domestic habits, and he felt a genuine repugnance at the thought that now he would have to be away a whole month. He could not tell for sure whether it was his wife or the children he should miss most; perhaps it was all of them together.

On the evening before his departure he sat on the sofa watching his wife pack his portmanteau. She was on her knees on the floor putting in his linen. She then dusted off his black clothes and folded them carefully so that they should take as little room as possible; he wasn't very handy at that sort of thing! She had not taken a place in the house as his maid-servant, scarcely as his wife. She was mother, mother to the children and to him. She never felt humiliated at darning his socks and never asked for thanks. Nor did she consider him indebted to her for such things, when he in return gave her and her children both stockings and many other things which she would otherwise have had to go out and get, while her children were left at home alone.

He sat in the corner of the sofa watching her. Now that the departure drew near, small intimations of regret began to stir in him. He surveyed her figure. The shoulder blades had grown more prominent, and the back was bent with work over the cradle, the ironingboard, and the stove. He too was bent with work at his desk, and his eyes needed the help of glasses.

But just now he was really not thinking of himself. He saw that her hair was thinner than formerly, and that the part between the braids was growing brighter. Was it for him she had lost her beauty, only for him? No, it was for the little community which consisted of them all, for she had worked for herself too. And his hair had also become thinner on the crown in the fight for them all. He would perhaps have had more youth if there had not been so many mouths to feed, but not for a moment did he wish he had been alone.

"It'll do you good to go about a bit," said his wife; "you that have always sat too much crouched up in the house."

"You're glad to be quit of me, you are," said he, not without a touch of bitterness; "but I shall be missing you a lot."

"You're like the cat, you'll miss your warm corner, but I don't believe you'll miss me so dreadfully."

"And the children?"

"Oh, when you're away; but when you're home you're always picking at them; not seriously of course, but still picking. Oh, you're really fond of them, I believe; I don't mean to be unjust."

At supper he was very gentle and felt in low spirits. He did not read the evening papers but wanted only to talk with his wife. She, however, was so busied with chores that she did not give herself much time to chat, and besides her feelings had been pretty well blunted by her ten years' campaign in the nursery and the kitchen.

He was more emotional than he cared to show, and the disorder about him made him restless. He beheld bits of his daily life, of his existence, tossed higgledy-piggledy on chairs and bureaus, and the black open portmanteau gaped at him like a coffin. White linen was wrapped about black clothes, which still retained the shape of knee and elbow, so that it seemed to him as if he himself were stretched there in his white laying-out shirt ready to have the lid put on and be carried off.

Next morning—an August morning it was—he hurried out of bed, dressed breathlessly and was very nervous. He went into the nursery and kissed all the children, who were rubbing the sleep out of their eyes, and after embracing his wife sat himself in a cab to go to the railway station. The journey in company with his chiefs diverted him, and he felt it was really a good thing to stir himself up a bit. His home behind him seemed like a stuffy bedroom, and he was thoroughly glad when he got to Linköping.

The rest of the day was taken up with a fine prison dinner at the big hotel, where they drank the health of the provincial governor, but not that of the convicts, for whose sake the trip was made.

But then came the evening in his lonely room. A bed, two chairs, a table, a wash-stand and a tallow-candle which spread its feeble light on the naked wall-paper. The secretary felt ill at ease. Everything was lacking: slippers, dressing-gown, pipe-rack, desk; all the little things that were the constituents of his life. And his children and wife. How were things with them? Were they well? He grew restless and extremely depressed. When he was going to wind up his watch, he could not find the key. It hung at home on the watch-frame his wife had embroidered for him when they were engaged. He went to bed and lighted a cigar. But then he had to get up and hunt for a book in his portmanteau. Everything was so neatly packed that he was afraid to disturb it. But as he dug about he found his slippers. She thought of everything! And then he got hold of the book. But he did not read. He lay and thought of the past, of his wife in the last ten years. With that appeared the picture of old times, and the present vanished in the bluish-brown cigar smoke which rose in spirals toward the rain-splotched ceiling. He was conscious of an infinite remorse. Every hard word since those days came back to him, and he regretted every bitter moment he had caused her. At last he went to sleep.

On the following day, work and another dinner, with healths to the prison governor, but still none for the convicts. In the evening, loneliness, desolation, chill. He ached with the need of talking to her. He therefore got some paper and sat down at a writing-table. He paused at the first stroke of the pen. How was he to address her? It was always "Dear Mama" when he sent home a note to say that he should be out for dinner. But now it was not to mama he wrote, it was to his former fiancée, his sweetheart. So he wrote "Lily, my darling," as he used to. At the start it went laboriously, because so many words of endearment had vanished from the dry, dull speech of their common everyday life; but soon he grew ardent, and with that the forgotten melodies rose up in his remembrance: waltz-beats and bits of novels, lilacs and swallows, evening moments of sunset across the mirroring bays; all of life's vernal memories danced out amid golden clouds and grouped themselves about her. At the bottom of the page he put a star, as lovers do, and wrote beside it—just as of old—"Kiss here!" When he had finished and read through his letter, he felt a glow on his cheeks, and was somewhat embarrassed. Why, he could not exactly say. It was like giving out his innermost thoughts to some one who might perhaps not understand them.

Still he sent the letter.

A couple of days passed before the answer came. During the interval of waiting he went about with a feeling of childish discomfort and bashfulness.

But then the answer came. He had struck the right note, and from cooking smells and children's din rose a song, bright and harmonious, warm and pure as that of first love. From now on there began an interchange of love letters. He wrote every evening and sometimes would also send a post-card in the course of the day. His companions did not recognize him. He began to give such attention to his clothes and the details of his outward appearance that he was suspected of a love affair. And he was in love, afresh! He sent her his photograph without spectacles, and she him a lock of her hair. They were childish in their expressions, and he bought tinted writing-paper with doves upon it. But at the same time they were persons of middle age not far past forty, though the struggle of life had made them feel older. In the past year he had also given up his conjugal privileges, not so much from coldness as from respect, for he saw in her always the mother of his children.

The end of his trip drew near. He now began to experience a certain unrest at the thought of the reunion. He had corresponded with a sweetheart; should he rediscover her in the mother

[33]

and the housewife? He feared to find himself disappointed at the homecoming. He did not want to see her with a cook's apron on or with the children at her skirts when he was to embrace her. They ought to meet at another place, alone. Could he bring her into tune with him at Vaxholm, for instance, in the inn where they had spent so many happy hours in their engagement time? That would be an idea! To recapture there in memory for a couple of days the first glad period of their springtime, which would never return.

He sat down and presented his plan in a long glowing letter, which she answered by return mail with her assent, delighted that he had lit upon the same thought as she.

Two days later he was in Vaxholm putting in order their room at the hotel. It was a beautiful day in September. He ate his dinner alone in the big hall, drank a glass of wine, and felt himself young again. It was so bright and airy here. Outside the bays spread shining and blue; only the birches on the shore had changed their color. In the garden the dahlias were still in full bloom, and the mignonette breathed its perfume from the borders. Now and then a bee would still visit the withering blossoms, but would turn back to its hive in disappointment.

[34]

In the channel there were sailing-boats passing in and out before a light breeze. As they came about, the sails would flap and the sheets thresh, while the frightened gulls flew screaming away from the herring-fishers, who sat in their skiffs with rod and float.

He took his coffee on the veranda and began to look forward to the coming of the steamer, which was due at six o'clock.

Restlessly, as if he were going toward an uncertain event, he promenaded up and down the balcony, looking out across the bay and the channel in the direction of the city to catch sight of the boat.

At last a puff of smoke rose across the fir woods of Tenö. His pulse quickened and he drank a liqueur. Then he went down to the shore. The smokestack now appeared in the middle of the channel, and soon he could see the flag at the bow. Was she there, or had she been prevented from coming? It would only need that one of the children should be ailing to keep her at home, and then he would have to spend the night alone at the hotel. The children, who had been in the background during the past weeks, now came forth as something that stood between him and her. In their last letters they had spoken but little of the children, as if they

[35]

wished to keep out a disturbing element, something they did not want as witness to their present state of feeling.

He paced the landing, which creaked under his feet, till he finally paused irresolutely near a pile, gazing continuously out at the boat, whose hull grew ever larger, while her wake spread a flood of molten gold across the rippling blue expanse of water. He could now see people moving on the upper deck and sailors busy with ropes at the bow.

Then something white flutters beside the pilot house. As he is alone on the dock, no one can well be waving to anybody but himself; and no one can be waving to him but she. He takes out his handkerchief and answers the signal. But he notices that his handkerchief is not white, for he has long since changed to colored ones from motives of economy. . . . The steamboat whistles, and the engine slows down. On up to the landing the vessel glides; and he catches sight of her. They greet with their eyes but cannot as yet exchange words because of the distance. The boat is warped in, and he sees her quietly leaning forward over the gangway. . . . It is she, but it is not she. Ten years are between! The style has changed, the cut of dresses is different. Formerly he saw her dark delicate features half enclosed in the then popular bonnet, which left the forehead free; now it is shaded by a poor imitation of a man's hat. Then her pretty figure was outlined in sportive curves under the graceful drapery of a cloak, that roguishly hid and revealed the roundness of the shoulders and the motions of the arms; now her entire form is distorted by a coachman's ulster which displays the dress but not the figure. And as she takes her last step on the gangway, he sees her little foot, which he had been so fond of when it had been in a buttoned boot that followed its shape, now prolonged in a pointed Chinese slipper which prevents the ball of the foot from rising in those dancing rhythms that had formerly enchanted him so.

It was she, but it was not she! He embraced her and kissed her. They asked each other how they were and how the children were. Then they went up on the shore.

Words came broken, dry, forced. So strange! They were as if shy before each other, and there was no allusion to their correspondence.

At last he took courage and said, "Shall we take a walk before the sun goes down?"

"I should love to," she answered, and took his arm.

They went up the street into the little town. All the places of summer amusement were closed and shuttered up, and the gardens were despoiled. An apple or so that had hidden behind the leaves was still left on the tree, but the beds were stripped of every flower. The verandas, which had lost their awnings, looked like skeletons, and where faces and happy laughter had been all was silent.

"It has an autumn look," he remarked.

"Yes, it's forlorn to see the summer amusements like this."

And they strolled on.

"We ought to go and see where we used to lodge," she said.

"Yes, that will be nice."

They went along the row of bathhouses.

There lay the little cottage wedged in between the gardener's and the chief pilot's places, with the red fence around it, the veranda and the garden plot.

Memories of the past sprang up. In that room their first child had been born. Jubilation and festivity, song and youth! There stood the rose-bush they had planted. There was the strawberry bed they had laid out; but it was there no more, for it was grown over and become a grass plot. There in the cinders were the traces of the swing which had hung there, but was no longer to be seen.

"Thanks for your lovely letters," she said, and pressed his arm.

He blushed and made no answer. Thereupon they turned back to the hotel, while he related the details of his trip.

He had had the table set in the big hall where they used to eat in the old days. They sat down without saying grace.

There they were tête-á-tête again. He took the bread tray and passed it to her. She smiled. It was not yesterday that he had been so polite. But it was very novel and pleasant to eat away from home, and soon they started an eager conversation, as in a duet, each in turn bringing out a memory, and in these memories they lived. Their glances shone, and the little wrinkles were smoothed away. Oh, the rose-and-golden times which we live but once, if live them we may, and which many, many never live! At dessert he whispered . to the waitress, who straightway brought in a bottle of champagne.

"My dear Axel, what are you thinking of?" said his wife half reproachfully.

"Of the spring that is gone but will return."

But he did not think of it exclusively, for disturbed by his wife's reproach as if a cat had gone through the room, he had a dark vision of the nursery and the porridge dish.

However, things brightened up again, and the rose-red wine touched again the strings of memory, until they threw themselves once more into the magic intoxication of the past.

The hours flew swiftly. They got up and went into the parlor, where the piano stood, to drink their coffee.

"I wonder how my little ones are," said the wife, awakening for the first time from the enchantment.

"Sit down and sing!" he bade, opening the piano.

"What shall I sing? You know I haven't sung for ever so long."

Oh, he knew that, but now he would have a song.

She sat down and played a prelude. It was a shrill hotel piano that sounded like loose teeth.

"What shall I sing?" she asked, turning around on the stool.

"You know, Lily," he replied, not daring to meet her look.

"Your song! Yes. If I remember it."

And so she sang, "Where lies the happy country Where my true lover dwells."

But alas! the voice was thin and sharp, and emotion made it untrue. At times it was like a scream from the depths of a soul which feels its noon is over and the evening drawing near. The fingers which had been busied with heavy work

[40]

did not easily find the right keys, and the instrument was played out, the cloth on the hammers being worn so that the bare wood clacked against the metal strings.

When the song was done, she did not dare to turn around for a while, but sat as if waiting for him to come to her and say something. But he did not come, and there was silence in the room. When she turned around on the stool, he was sitting in a corner, weeping. She wanted to run to him, take his head in her hands and kiss him as of old, but she remained sitting motionless, her eyes on the floor.

He held an unlighted cigar between his thumb and forefinger. When he heard that all was quiet, he bit off the end and struck a match.

"Thanks, Lily!" he said, and lighted the cigar. "Will you have coffee now?"

They drank their coffee and talked about summer amusements in general and where they should go next year. But the conversation soon began to lag and repeat itself.

Finally he said in the middle of a long unsuppressible yawn, "I'm going to bed."

"I'll go too," said she, rising. "But I'll go out a little while first—on the balcony."

He went into the bedroom. His wife stopped a while in the dining room to talk to the landlady about pickled onions, from which they digressed into washing woollens, so that the conversation lasted half an hour.

When she returned, she stood at the bedroom door and listened. Everything was quiet within, and her husband's boots were outside. She knocked, but there was no answer. Then she opened the door and went in. He was asleep.

He was asleep!

Next morning they were at coffee together. The husband had a headache, and the wife looked uneasy.

"Bah! what coffee," said he with a grimace.

"It's Brazilian," said she.

"What shall we do to-day?" he asked, taking out his watch.

"You ought to take some bread and butter instead of fretting over your coffee," opined his wife.

"Yes, I'll do that," said he, "and a little nip to finish with. That champagne, brr!"

He got a bread and butter tray with a brandy flask and brightened up.

"Now we'll go to Pilot's Hill and see the view."

They got up and went out. The weather was splendid, and the promenade went well. But when it came to climbing the hill their pace was slow; the wife was short of breath and the husband stiff in the knees. They drew no comparisons with former times.

They then went out into the meadows.

The fields had been mown long since and afterwards grazed over, so that not a flower was to be seen. They sat down each on a separate stone.

He began to talk about the prison inspection and his work, she about the children.

Next they went on a bit further without talking. He took out his watch.

"It's three hours to dinner," he observed.

At the same time he thought, "I wonder what we shall do to-morrow."

They turned back to the hotel. He began to look for newspapers. She smiled and sat by him without speaking.

Dinner was quite silent. Finally the wife broached the subject of servants.

"Oh, for heaven's sake don't let us start on servants," he burst out.

"Yes, we haven't come here to quarrel," she replied.

"Have I started quarreling, I'd like to know?"

"Or I, either?"

Then came a fearful pause. He would have been glad now if there had been some one to come between them. The children? Oh, by all means. This tête-á-tête began to be tiresome.

But with that he felt a pang as he thought of the bright hours yesterday.

"Let's go to Ekbacken and pick wild strawberries," she suggested.

"There are no strawberries this time of the year, my good lady; it's autumn."

"Let's go, anyhow."

So they were walking again. But they found nothing to say to each other. He sought with his glance for an object, a place on the road that they could talk about, but everything was dried out, talked to death. She knew all his opinions on every subject and disapproved of many of them. Furthermore he was now longing for home, home with the house and the children. It was too silly to go about here like a pair of idiots liable any moment to get into a quarrel. At last they stopped, for the wife was tired. He sat down and began to trace on the ground with his stick, only wishing she would give him some opening for an outbreak.

"What are you thinking?" she asked finally.

"I?" he responded as if released from a weight; "why this is what I think: we're old, mama; we've played out our play, and we'd best be content with what has been. If you agree, we'll go home by the evening boat. Eh?"

"That's what I've been thinking all along, dear old boy, but I wanted you to say so first."

"Well, come along, we'll go home then! It's not summer any more, it's autumn."

"Yes, autumn it is."

They went back with lighter steps. He was somewhat abashed at the awkward prosaic turn matters had taken and felt the need of giving a philosophic interpretation to the situation.

"You see, mama," he explained, "my I. . . ." (the word was too strong) "my affection for you has in the course of years undergone an evolution, as they put it nowadays. It has developed, amplified itself, so to speak, so that from concentrating on an individual as in the beginning, it has now broadened itself to include in the family, as it were, a collective object. It refers not to you as a separate person, or to the children, but to the whole combination. . . ."

"As uncle always says, the children are lightning-conductors."

After his philosophic exposition he had become himself again. It was good to get out of the frock-coat attitude and into a dressing-gown again.

And as soon as they got back to the hotel, his wife started on the portmanteau, and then she was in her element.

When they boarded the steamer they went down at once to the dining room. To save his face he had first asked if they should watch the sunset, which she had declined. As they ate supper, he helped himself first, and she asked the proprietress what the bread cost.

When he had eaten to his heart's content and was about to put the beer-glass to his mouth, he could no longer restrain a thought that had been amusing him for some time:

"Old fools, eh?" he exclaimed, smiling at his wife, who looked up at him in the middle of a bite.

But she did not smile back at his shining fat face. On the contrary, her eyes flashed like lightning for an instant, and then assumed an expression of such withering dignity that he became embarrassed.

The enchantment was now broken, the last trace of the sweetheart had vanished; he was sitting only with the mother of his children, and he felt himself crushed.

"Because I was silly a while, you needn't forget to respect me," she said severely. "But there's a good deal of contempt in a man's affection; it's a funny thing."

"And in a woman's?"

"Much more, that's true. But then she has greater provocation."

"Lord knows, it's about equal, though in different ways. Probably they're both in the wrong. A thing one has over-estimated because it is difficult to get may easily become an object of contempt."

"Why should it be over-estimated?"

"Why should it be hard to get?"

The steamer's whistle above their heads interrupted the conversation.

They had arrived at their destination.

When they were back in their home, and he saw her in the midst of the children, he soon felt that his "affection" for her had gone through a transformation, and that hers for him had flowed over and been distributed among all these little cry-babies. Perhaps it was only as a means to these that he possessed her affection. His rôle then was transitory, and he therefore felt himself set to one side. If he was not necessary to provide bread, he would now presumably have been discarded.

He went into his work-room, put on his dressing-gown and slippers, lighted a pipe, and felt at home again. Outside the wind-gusts lashed the rain, and there was a whistling in the stove-pipe.

His wife came in when she was done with the children.

"This is no weather for strawberry-picking," she remarked.

"No, old lady; the summer's done, and autumn's here."

"Yes, it's autumn," she responded, "but it isn't winter yet, that's one comfort."

"That a comfort! Not much comfort when we only live once."

"Twice, when one has children; three times, if one lives to see one's grandchildren."

"But after that it's really all up."

"Unless there's another life after this."

"There's no being sure of that. Who can tell? I believe in it, but my faith is no proof."

"Yes, but it's nice to believe it, so let's believe, let's believe there may be another spring for us! Let's believe it!"

"All right, we will believe it," said he, putting his arm around her waist.

The Stone Man

IF one stands by the harbor where the steam-boats lie, and looks out toward the sea, one sees to the left a mountain covered with forest green. Behind the mountain stands a large house built in the shape of a spider. From the main building eight wings project, just like the legs on a spider's round body. Those who enter that house do not come out again at will, and some stay there a lifetime. It is the prison house.

In the old king's time the mountain was not green, but gray and barren. Nothing grew there then, not even moss or heart's-ease, which usually thrive on rocky ground. There were only gray stone and gray men, who looked stony and who quarried stone, broke stone and carried stone. Among these stone people there was one who looked more stony than the others.

He was but a youth when, in the reign of King Oscar the First, he was shut up in this prison because he had killed a human being. He was a prisoner for life, and on his gray garb were the letters L. P., in black.

Winter and summer he tramped the moun-tain breaking stone. In the winter there was little to see. The harbor was bleak and empty of boats, and the semicircular pier with its piles yawned like a mouth, exposing a row of teeth. Now he could see the woodshed, the riding school, and the two stark gigantic lindens. Sometimes an ice yacht would sail past the island; now and then a few boys on skates would pass. Otherwise the place was quiet and deserted.

It was livelier in summer time, when the harbor was lined with fine boats, newly painted and decorated with flags, and the lindens were green —the lindens under which he had sat when he was a little chap, waiting for his father, who was an engineer on one of the finest boats. And now he had not heard, in many years, the murmur of the wind in trees, for none grew on his mountain. But the rustling of the leaves in the lindens of Riddarholm lived in his memory, and to hear it once again was the only thing he longed for.

When on a summer's day a steamer passed the island, he heard the splash of waves and perhaps the blare of a band. And he saw bright faces that darkened at sight of the gray men on the mountain. Then he cursed heaven and earth, his fate and the cruelty of man.

Thus he cursed year in, year out, and he and his fellow prisoners tormented and cursed each other day and night; for crime severs while misfortune unites sufferers.

Life at the prison was at first needlessly hard;

the guards punished the prisoners arbitrarily, unmercifully. Then, one day, there was a change; the food was better, the discipline less severe, and every man had a cell to himself.

It was the king who had eased the prisoners' bonds a trifle. But as hopelessness had hardened the hearts of these unhappy men, they were incapable of any feeling of gratitude. Now they thought it preferable to be together in one room, where they could talk at night. And they complained of the food, the clothes, the guards, as before.

One fine day all the bells of the city were tolling, Riddarholm's loudest. King Oscar was dead, and the prisoners had a holiday. They were allowed to speak to each other now, and they talked of how they would kill the guard and escape. They even talked of the dead king, and spoke ill of him.

"If he'd been just, he would have set us free," said one.

"Or else he'd have shut up all the crooks at large," said another.

"Then he'd have had to turn jailer himself, and jugged the whole nation."

It is the way of prisoners to regard all men as criminals and to think that they themselves were caught only because luck was against them.

It was a hot summer's day, and the Stone Man

walked along the shore, listening to the tolling of the bells for Oscar the Mild. He looked under the stones for sticklebacks and bullheads, but found none. Out in the water neither roach nor albacore was visible; consequently no gulls or terns appeared. He felt now that a curse rested on the mountain, since not even fishes or birds would come near it.

He thought of his fate. He had lost his name —both Christian and surname—and was merely number 65, a name written in figures instead of letters. He was not registered; paid no taxes; did not know how old he was. He was only a gray object moving on the mountain, which the sun burned terribly—burned on its clothes, on its head with the close-cropped hair, which once had been curls combed and brushed by a mother's soft hand. That day he was not allowed to wear a cap because it would have rendered less difficult an attempt at escape. As the scorching sun beat down on his pate he remembered the story of the Prophet Jonah, to whom the Lord gave a gourd that he might sit in its shade.

"Then what did he get!" sneered he; for he believed in nothing good, positively nothing.

Just then he saw a big birch bough rocking in the surf; it was quite green, with a white stem, and probably had fallen off a pleasure boat. He dragged it ashore, shook the water off, carried it

[52]

some distance to a crevice in the rock, and put it up securely between three stones. Then he sat down under the bough and listened to the wind blowing softly through the leaves, which wafted a scent of finest resin. After a little, in the cooling shade of the birch, he fell asleep.

And he dreamed: The mountain was a greenwood with lovely trees and fragrant blossoms. Birds were singing; bumble bees and honey bees buzzed about the flowers, and butterflies fluttered. But quite by itself was a tree which he did not know. This tree was the loveliest of all. It had many stems, like a bush, and the branches were intricate and fine as lacework. Under the smooth, shiny leaves sat a little black and white bird that looked like a swallow, but wasn't.

And in the dream he could interpret birdnotes, therefore he heard and understood fairly well what the bird was singing. It sang:

Dirt, dirt, dirt there,
Heave, heave, heave here,
In dirt, in dirt, in dirt died you,
From the dirt, the dirt, the dirt rose you.

It was about dirt, death, and the resurrection—that much he understood. But the dream went on.

He was standing on the mountain in the blasting heat consumed by hunger and thirst. His fellow convicts had turned against him and threatened his life, because he would not help them set fire to the prison. They pursued him with stones up the slope until he was stopped by a high wall. To scale it was impossible, and so, in sheer desperation, he determined to end it all by dashing his brains out on the stones. He made a rush for the wall, when, lo; a gate opened, a green garden gate—and then he woke up.

When he saw that the beautiful greenwood had dwindled to a birch branch, he muttered in disgust:

"If at least it had been a linden!"

He listened. . . . So it was the birch that sang so loudly; it sounded like the sifting of sand and gravel, while the linden had soft, velvety heart-tones!

Next day the birch was faded and gave but little shade. And the day after, the leaves were dry as paper, and rattled like chattering teeth. Finally, there was nothing left but a thick birch-rod, which reminded him of his childhood. Again he thought of the Prophet's gourd, and cursed as the sun burned his pate.

There was a new king and new life in the country's government. New waterways were to be made in the city, and the convicts were sent out in barges, to dredge.

It was the first time in many years that the Stone Man had been away from his mountain. Once more he traveled by water and saw much that was new to him in his native city—saw the railway and the locomotive. It was below the railway station the men began dredging.

They brought up all the refuse that lay bedded on the lake-bottom. Up came drowned cats, old shoes, decomposed fats from the tallow candle factory, chemicals from the dye works, tanner's bark from the tannery, and all the human filth which washerwomen had rinsed out of the clothes in the public wash house for the last hundred years. There was a stench of sulphur and ammonia so insufferable that only convicts were expected to stand it.

When the barge was full the prisoners wondered where their cargo of mud was to be dumped. They got their answer when the boatman steered for their own mountain.

There the filth was unloaded and spread, filling the air with the vilest odors. The men waded in mud; their clothes, hands, faces were covered with it.

"This is hell!" said the prisoners.

For several years they dredged and unloaded

on the mountain, and eventually the rock disappeared entirely under its cover of dirt.

The pure white snow fell winter after winter, and threw a clean white blanket over all the impurity. When the spring came once again and the snow melted, the bad odors were gone, and the mud began to look like mold. That spring, since the dredging was over, the Stone Man was sent to work at the forge—and never went near his mountain. But once, in the autumn, he stole out, and then he saw something wonderful.

Plants were growing in the filth! Sappy, ugly plants, to be sure, mostly brownwort, not unlike nettle but with brown flowers, which are ugly; for flowers should be white, yellow, blue, or red. There were real nettles, too, with a green flower, and burdock, sorrel, thistle, pigweed—all the prickly, stinging, evil-smelling plants which people detest but which spring up over night on dustheaps, burned lots, and mud dumps.

"We cleaned out the lake and got the dirt," said the convict. "That's gratitude for you!"

Then came a time when the Stone Man was transferred to a cliff where a fort was to be built, and again he worked in stone, stone, stone. There he lost an eye and was flogged now and then, and there he remained so long that meantime the new king died and was succeeded by another.

On coronation day a prisoner was to be released; the one who had conducted himself the best, and had also come to a full realization that he had sinned, was to receive a pardon. The other prisoners regarded this as unfair to them; for in their circles a man who repented a thing he could not help doing was a poor wretch.

And so the years passed. The Stone Man was now very old, and being too feeble for heavier work, he was sent back to his mountain and put to sewing sacks.

One day the chaplain on his round paused before the Stone Man, who sat and sewed.

"Well," said the clergyman, "are you never to leave this island?"

"How would that be possible?" the Stone Man replied.

"When you see that you did wrong."

"When I find a human being who does more than right I'll believe that I did wrong. But I don't think I ever shall."

"More than right—that would be mercy. May you soon find it!"

One day the Stone Man was sent out to break roads on the mountain, which he had not seen now in twenty years, perhaps. It was again a warm summer's day, and the pleasure boats, gay as butterflies, steamed noisily by. Coming out on the headland, he found, not a bare cliff but a lovely green wood, where myriads of leaves shimmered in the breeze like ripples on a lake. There were tall white-stemmed birches and trembling aspens and along the shore grew alders. It was as in his dream. At the foot of the trees the grasses whispered, the flowers nodded, the bumble bees buzzed, and the butterflies fluttered. Many birds sang there, but he did not understand their songs, so he knew that this was not a dream.

The Mount of Damnation had been transformed into a Mountain of Blessing, and he could not help thinking of the Prophet and his gourd.

"This is grace and mercy," said something within him, a voice or a prompting—call it what you will.

And when a steamer passed the island, the faces of the passengers did not darken, but brightened at the sight of the lovely green. He fancied he saw some one wave a handkerchief, as people do when they sail past a summer resort.

He stepped forward under the rustling trees. There were no linden trees among them; but now he did not dare to sigh for lindens, lest the birches should turn into rods. He had learned that much.

Walking down the leafy avenue, he saw at the end a white wall with a green gate, and he heard something playing which was not an organ; for its movements were quicker and merrier. Above the wall there was a glimpse of the bright roof of a villa, and a blue and yellow flag fluttered in the breeze.

He saw a ball of gay colors rise and fall on the other side of the wall, and heard the high, thin-voiced chatter of children. The clinking of china and glass told him that a table was being laid.

He went and looked through the gate. The lilac was in full bloom, and the table stood under the shrubs. Children were romping, and there was singing and playing.

"This is paradise," said the voice within him.

He stood there a long while, watching, so long that at last the broken old man drooped with fatigue, hunger, thirst, and all the misery of life.

The gate opened, and a little girl dressed in white came out. She carried a small tray on which stood a glass of wine, the reddest he had ever seen. The child went right up to him, and said:

"Here, nice old man, is some wine for you."

The old man took the glass and drank. It was rich man's wine, and had come a long way, from sunny lands, and it tasted like the sweetness of a good life when at its best.

"This is mercy," said his own old broken voice.

"But child, you never would have brought me this if you'd known who I was. Do you know what I am?"

"Yes; you're a convict," the little girl replied.

"You knew—and yet— Aye, this is mercy."

When the old convict turned back he was no longer a man of stone, for something had quickened in him, too. He had just passed a steep hill when he saw a lovely tree with many stems, like a bush. It was a crab-apple tree, but this the old man did not know.

In the tree fluttered a restless little black and white bird which some folk call "tree-swallow;" but the name is something else. He settled at last deep in the foliage, and sang sweetly, but mournfully:

In dirt, in dirt, in dirt died you.
From the dirt, the dirt, the dirt rose you.

It was just as in the dream. And now the old man understood what the tree-swallow meant.

Half a Sheet of Paper

THE last moving van had gone; the tenant, a young man with a mourning-band around his hat, wandered through the empty rooms to see if anything had been left behind. No, nothing had been forgotten, nothing. He went out into the corridor, determined never to think again of all he had passed through in this apartment. But there, on the wall, near the telephone, was a slip of paper covered with writing. The entries were in several handwritings; some quite legible, in black ink; some, pencil scrawls in black and red and blue. There stood recorded the whole beautiful romance that had been lived in the short space of two years. All that he had resolved to forget was written there—a bit of human history on half a sheet of paper.

He took the sheet down. It was a piece of sun-yellow scratch paper that casts a sheen. He laid it on the mantel of the fireplace in the living room, and, bending over, he began to read.

First stood her name: *Alice*—the most beautiful name he knew, because it was the name of his sweetheart. Beside it was a number, *15,11*— It looked like a chant number on the hymnboard in church.

Underneath was scribbled: *The Bank.* It was

there his work lay, the sacred work which for him meant bread, home, family—the foundations of life. A heavy black line had been drawn across the number, for the bank had failed, and he had been taken on at another, after a short period of much anxiety.

Then followed *the livery stable* and *the florist*— That was when they were engaged, and he had a pocketful of money.

The furniture dealer—The decorator—They furnish their apartment. *Express Bureau*— They move in. *Opera House Box-Office,* 50,50. —They are newly married and go to the opera on Sunday evenings. Their most delightful hours are those spent there, sitting quietly, while their hearts commune in the beauty and harmony of the fairyland on the other side of the footlights.

Here followed the name of a man (crossed out) a friend who had risen high, but who fell —dazzled by prosperity—fell irremediably, and had to flee the country. So ephemeral is that will-o'-the-wisp, Success!

Now something new came into the lives of the couple. Entered with a pencil in a woman's hand stands *The Sister*. What sister? Ah! the one with the long gray cloak and the sweet, sympathetic face, who comes so softly and never goes through the drawing-room, but takes the corridor way to the bedroom. Below her name is written: *Dr. L——*

Here first appeared on the list a relative—*Mother*. That is his mother-in-law, who had discreetly kept away so as not to disturb the newly married. But now she has been called, and comes gladly, since she is needed.

Then came some entries in red and blue pencil. *Employment Agency*. The maid has left, and a new one must be engaged. *The Apothecary*—H-m! It begins to look dark. *The dairy* —Milk is ordered, sterilized milk. *The grocer, the butcher*, and others. The household affairs are being conducted by telephone. Then the mistress of the house is not at her usual post? No. She is confined to her bed.

That which followed he could not read, for it grew dim before his eyes, as it must for the drowning man at sea who would look through salt water. But there it stood recorded, in plain, black letters: *The undertaker.*

That tells enough!—a larger and a smaller casket. And in parenthesis was written: *"Of dust."*

There was nothing more. It ended in dust, the way of all flesh.

He took up the sun-yellow paper, kissed it,

[63]

folded it carefully, and put it in his breast pocket.

In two minutes he had relived two years of his life.

But he was not bowed down as he walked out. On the contrary, he carried his head high, like a proud and happy man, for he knew that to him it had been given to hold for a little the best that life can bestow on man. How many there were, alas! who had not had this.

ERNST AHLGREN

MOTHER MALENA'S HEN

VICTORIA BENEDICTSSON (1850–1888) writing under the masculine pseudonym ERNST AHLGREN, is regarded by Swedish critics as the best of the realistic writers who appeared in the 1880's. Her private life was tragic. To escape from oppressive conditions in her home, she married Mr. Benedictsson, a man much older than herself, but though she devoted herself to his house and her step-children, she failed to find personal happiness. Under the influence of the new ideas about freedom for women, she attempted to break away, but was soon disillusioned. Made desperate by disappointed love, failing health, and adverse criticism of her work, she took her own life.

Fru Benedictsson first attempted with poor success to write in the highflown romantic manner of the preceding era, but after Strindberg had pointed the way in realistic fiction, she learned to write in her own style, simply and naturally, taking her subjects from the plain people in her native province, Skåne. She is at her best in the short stories of which *Mother Malena's Hen* is a good example. She has also written novels dealing with the problems under discussion in Scandinavian literature at the time. *Money* describes a young girl who marries, as she herself had done, without any idea of what marriage means. In *Fru Marianne* she has, if not changed her opinions, at least shifted the emphasis. The book shows how an idle young woman is transformed in marriage with a sensible kind man. The book was regarded in radical circles as a falling from grace, and was adversely criticised in *Politiken* of Copenhagen, where she was then living. This criticism affected her profoundly.

Ernst Ahlgren's biography has been written by Ellen Key.

Ernst Ahlgren

MOTHER MALENA'S HEN

ALTHOUGH Mother Malena lived at the poor-house, she still kept possession of her hen, and that was a terrific luxury; it was usurping the good things of life at the expense of others, it was exalting oneself above those less fortunate. Mother Malena was acting above her class at the poor-house.

This hen was a seed of continual dissension. When Pernilla's youngsters broke anything, it was immediately blamed on the hen, though, Lord knows, the hen was so clever and intelligent that Pernilla's youngsters might have given thanks on their bare knees if they had been half as sensible as she. And if there was anything on the table that ought not to be there, at once "it must have been the hen." This though Mother Malena knew on her soul and honor that the hen was the cleanest animal that could walk the ground; and that if it came to that one might rather pick up the hen in one's bare hands than one of Pernilla's brats with the tongs. On such occasions Pernilla turned up her eyes like a saint and said that she knew for sure it was a slow death to be devoured by chicken lice, but it would be her fate just the same. Whereupon Mother Malena would answer with a malicious grin that it was a still slower end to be pecked to death by geese, but she didn't intend to go that way, so it wasn't worth their trouble to try—the geese that is, by which in other words she meant to indicate Pernilla and her progeny, together with Stina and Stina's half-grown girl.

As Mother Malena was large and sturdy, with fists that harmonized strongly with her verbal expression, it followed that the hen kept her place, which was in a corner of her mistress's bed, at the foot, where she had her accommodations in the bed straw. There she might sit on the days when she was to lay, having burrowed herself in so that she was hardly visible, blinking with wide-open eyes, now and then staring at some object on the quilt, dropping her beak and picking up what she could find—all with the most profound seriousness that a hen could properly possess. In between times she paraded about on the floor, nodding her head at every step; cackled *sotto voce,* not without a sentimental tone, probably from the feeling of being alone and misunderstood; then suddenly let out and began to scratch with her strong, gray-scaled legs in both directions with a superior skill that showed she was of good extraction.

But Pernilla had a boy, a tow-headed, unkempt youngster with a thin neck, dressed in an old outgrown jacket which did not come down far enough, and a pair of slippery moleskin trousers which had been cut off to fit him but whose upper part was of a size for a grown man. This promising adolescent seldom stuck his nose round the corner of the house, because he inevitably roused the delight of the public by the upper part of his trousers, and he did not care for publicity. He was too delicate-minded for such a thing. Let it not be said, however, that he was lacking in talent, for on the contrary he possessed a gift quite eminent in its way—and it was, too, the only one he possessed: he could mimic the hen. He took his place in the middle of the floor, and whatever the hen did he did after her. In especial he had mastered the faculty of scratching.

He had a pair of long shoes, dry from lack of grease, and with broad, split toes where his own would have peeped out if they had been long enough. It was with these shoes that he scratched. It was a miracle that they stood it, but they did. When he stuffed his hands into his formless trousers' pockets, swung his body, and scraped the floor with his long slippers, there came into his very expression and the stretching of his neck something which in a strikingly shameless manner resembled the hen. Furthermore, when she moulted and had no erect tail-feathers, it came about that even his figure had a likeness to hers. However it was, he could make the other youngsters double up with laughter, perhaps not only at his efforts but even more because of the vexation they believed they could rouse in the hen's owner. She gave him only her silent disdain, but with hate in her inmost heart. It is possible, though, that what Mother Malena took as insult was nothing but his instinctive youthful joy of life or a guileless form of pastime.

He, meanwhile, made capital of all the hen's little weaknesses and ridiculed them. At times she would give a quite inept cackle and begin to run around the room in a foolish way which really was hardly suited to a worthy old matron of a hen. The urchin could imitate this with finished mastery, running about like mad in his half of the room and uttering loud shrieks.

But there is no perfection without its shortcomings, and in spite of her good qualities the hen had one real defect of character to which not even Mother Malena could shut her eyes. This was a most frivolous passion for society. When she was let out on sunny days—and it was necessary that she should have a chance to roll in the sand and pick up worms; her health demanded it, and otherwise the purchasers complained that her eggs were too white—she needed but to hear the chickens' cackle and the cock's crow in Nils Matson's yard, to forget duty and gratitude for her support, and to creep through the first good hole in the fence and vanish till somebody fetched her.

It was no pleasant task to go into Nils Matson's yard and demand one's property. Nils Matson was an old childless widower, cross as a chained dog and stingy as a wolf. Every time Mother Malena came to fetch her pet he consoled her by shouting loudly that the next time he'd "knock the arms and legs off the d—— beast." That was his regular threat against Pernilla's youngsters, who along with other children stole his apples, and he could not make any change in his wording on account of a hen. He always said beast, wishing thereby to indicate the greedy and coarse nature of the said hen. She was a monster that he ought to put an end to.

One day in the late autumn, just as he stood scattering corn for his own chickens, he saw Mother Malena's hen come running into the yard, happy and sociable, mingling with the flock as if she belonged there. Anger rose in his breast with such violence as almost to stifle him. He picked up a stone and threw it viciously at the hen. The flock dispersed, shrieking, but instead of setting off home Mother Malena's hen ran to the feeding trough. That was an unheard-of impudence. Nils Matson flung another stone, bigger than the first, after the fleeing bird.

It struck her.

Now it was a peculiarity of Nils Matson that he could be as nasty as possible to human beings, but towards animals he was extremely tender. If it was only a beetle which had fallen on its back and was clutching at the air with its thin legs, he had to lean down with a long, groaning "Oh!" and help it to its feet again with his stiff dexter finger. When this time he aimed at the hen, he had Mother Malena in his mind; but when he hit her, she was nothing but a misused animal. It had all been the work of an instant, and before he could do anything about it, the hen, flapping her wings and with her broken leg dangling beside her, had fled to a big pile of brush which lay in the corner of the yard, in which she squatted dumbly and without a complaint. Thence, if she could and would, she might creep out under the fence and go home again. So far it was all well and good, but Nils Matson was in reality ill at ease, and with the thorn of remorse in his heart he went into his house.

Towards evening, when Mother Malena came to inquire after her hen, he looked assured enough, however, as he stood in the yard and smoked his pipe.

First Mother Malena only peeped through the

gate, and he pretended not to see her but stood still on a millstone which constituted one of his doorsteps, considering what he should say.

Mother Malena was tall and big, but through the irony of fate she always happened to get skirts that had been made for small women, which caused them mostly to be pulled up half a yard on her legs. And what legs they were! They showed neither calf nor narrow part; they were timbered of good material, straight up and down, without unnecessary flourishes, sound for going, though not decorative to look at. From a distance it looked as if she were walking on stilts, especially as her wooden shoes had a peculiar shape, worn down almost to the ground at the heels and yet like new as to the toes. The latter were therefore higher, so that the foot had the appearance of being merely a part of the leg, flattened out hurriedly and turned up to order, nothing more, no unnecessary fuss about the ankle or anything of that sort.

She now came into the garden.

"I wonder if my hen hasn't come in here," she said with a guttural sound like the note of a duck. When she felt abashed, she always croaked worse than usual.

She was now for the first time honored with a look.

"Aye, that she has. And I've knocked the leg

offen 'er. She's lying in that pile of brush, where you can hunt for her yourself."

Mother Malena looked at him dumbfounded a moment; it was almost impossible to believe him.

He kept on standing there indifferent, smoking as before, except that a glance of spiteful enjoyment stole out at her from under his half-lowered eyelids.

"No, if you've ta'en the life, you can take the carcass," she then answered with the high majesty of grief, and left the yard.

The seed of dissension removed, there should now have been peace in the poor-house. Peace, indeed, there was, but it was the desolate calm of melancholy. Mother Malena talked to no one; with bitterness of spirit she bore her sorrow alone. The boy in the slippery trousers went about purposelessly and didn't know what to be at; he had lost his favorite society. It was as if a member of a formerly cheerful family had suddenly descended into the grave. This member may have been only a source of unnecessary trouble, but still one day he may chance to leave behind him a void which nothing can fill. It was so with the hen. Nobody had thought what she was to them all, before she was gone. She had been the sole diversion of their lives. The thunderstorms she had provoked had cleared the air; now it hung about them heavy and dead. And however it may have been, she had also brought hours of sunshine. They were first reminded of it afterwards. How many times had not Mother Malena gone away with half a score of eggs to sell, and come back with coffee and sugar, and in a good humor. She herself had thawed, and she had invited the others to join her. And they had sat there at their warm cups, drunk healths from the coffee-pot, and talked of all that was happening out in the world: how John Johnson's Kristina had gone to America, or how Peer and Katy had taken out their banns, and everything else of the sort that had happened and ought not to have happened, which was naturally the most interesting of all. And so they had forgotten the years and ailments and the evil way of the world and had been heartily content for awhile. But now this was over. Malena went about unchanging; she looked surly, was silent, and coffee was not to be thought of.

At first it was believed that in a fit of vexation Mother Malena had gone and sold her hen, but little by little the truth leaked out. It was no flattering certificate of character that Nils Matson got in the poor-house.

"The rich can do just as they please," was the verdict given in a ferment of indignation. There was a rumbling to the lowest foundations of the community.

But strange are the ways of fate; this time there was no revolution.

One day when Nils Matson stood feeding his chickens, there crept from the brush heap a phantom, disheveled and thin, with a breastbone like the blade of a carving knife—the veritable ghost of a hen.

What Nils Matson felt at that moment cannot be described: pity, remorse, and a fervent desire to make atonement. He was completely overpowered, had tears in his eyes, and said to himself in a maternal tone: "Good Lord! the poor thing, the poor miserable thing." Thereupon a whole handful of corn rained out toward the brush heap.

Lying on one side and scrambling forward with her one leg as with an oar, the hen began to peck. That delighted Nils Matson's old heart, but he told nobody what he had concealed in the brush heap.

In a short time, however, the hen was in such good condition that she came limping forward to the other fowls, wry in the leg, which had taken on a peculiar swinging motion, but cheerful and communicative, glad to have survived her affliction and to accept her injury.

This could not, of course, continue. Nils Matson's sense of justice rose against his keeping the hen; besides which she would surely not be badly off in the poor-house, and if sometimes she should come into his yard, it wouldn't be such a life-and-death matter. He wouldn't be beggared by what the hen ate.

Towards evening, when the chickens had set themselves to rest, and the lame hen had disposed herself in a corner of the chicken-house—for she was too weak to sit on the perch—Nils Matson's maid was ordered to carry the hen home but was to keep mum about her, or else——. Here followed certain words suited to the occasion.

It was almost dark in the poor-house when the girl entered.

"I'm to give you Nils Matson's compliments, and here is yer hen, and here's a twist o' corn wi' her, so ye may perhaps the better keep her to home."

Mother Malena was struck speechless with surprise.

"Thanks," she finally got out, "compliments and thanks."

With that the girl departed.

Mother Malena was so much moved that she had to strike three matches before she could get a light. There were then many pairs of eyes that were fastened upon the hen, for the youngsters had waked from their early sleep, and Pernilla was sitting at the window knitting a stocking in the dusk to save a candle.

The hen limped, to be sure, but was fat and in good condition.

"If we haven't had a coffee-party before, then by golly! if we don't have it now," cried Mother Malena, who was coming to herself again and had found her voice.

What a light came into all the faces at those words.

"And we'll have cakes, too. Run down and buy sixteen farthings' worth of rolls,—no, that's not enough, here's ten pence, and you can get some coffee thrown in, I'm certain."

Not in a year had anybody seen Mother Malena in such a good humor. There was life in the house. Peat was laid in the fireplace, there were flames and warmth; the folks felt thawed out and eager for talk, the children were on their feet.

The coffee was drunk, the cakes eaten, dipped or dry, and contentment was universal; one might have thought they were having Christmas Eve inside. Mother Malena's placability even rose to such a height that in her mildest and least guttural tones she said to the boy with the slippery trousers, "Martin, show us how the hen does."

And Martin stood forth on the floor, stretched out one foot so that the leg took on a sort of careless swing in his skirt-like trousers, limped

[78]

off to the porcelain stove and spread himself out as if he was sitting on something, for the hen had already sat herself in the opposite corner and was asleep.

GUSTAF AF GEIJERSTAM

KARIN

GUSTAF AF GEIJERSTAM (1858–1909) threw himself enthusiastically into the new naturalistic movement of the 1880's and made a brave attempt to hold together the group of writers known as "The Young Sweden." In his own writing, he wished to find types that should be natural and unspoiled by artificial conditions, and with this in view he went out to live among the peasants of Öland and the skerries. The tales he published in the collections *Poor People* and *The Sheriff's Stories* often deal with criminal instincts working out from some mysterious sub-stratum in the soul. That he could also see the finer types of Northern peasant is shown in *Karin,* from the volume *Poor People*.

Beginning with *Medusa's* Head, published in 1895, Geijerstam turned to describing domestic life among more sophisticated people, as in *The Book about Little Brother, Woman Power, Dangerous Forces,* and *Karin Brandt's Dream.* He was still fascinated by the secret forces that corrode affection, and sometimes these forces border on the pathological. In the peasant novel, *Nils Tufveson and His Mother,* describing the incestuous love of a woman for her son and the consequent doing to death of the son's wife, he has treated his subject with daring frankness. Usually, however, he is so discreet that the unsophisticated may enjoy his novels simply as pleasing domestic stories, and as such they have had a great vogue. The student will be interested in tracing out Geijerstam's intuitive understanding of complexities that are now being defined by modern psychology.

Gustaf af Geijerstam

KARIN

IT was spring in the year 1825. It had come
late; for weeks people had been going about
impatient for the time when the farmer could
begin to set his plough in the earth. But cold
rain-weighted clouds had massed themselves above
the plain; time after time they had shaken quantities of snow down over the earth, and time after
time the ditches had frozen over again, and the
slushy debris had piled up in the woods where
the water had risen after the heavy spring freshet,
so that it stood high above roads and footpaths.
The bog-myrtle was bent by the snow, and the
water had risen above the ice which had fastened
on the lower boughs of the alders and willows.

There lay outstretched the heavy, melancholy
plain. As far as the eye could reach, nothing was
to be seen but the flat expanse of field and soil,
broken by innumerable intersecting fences, with
here and there a streak of unmelted snow behind
a straw-rick or in the shadow of some high ditch
crest. Far away, solitary and gloomy above the
level roofs, the church steeple rose in the little
town which lay in the midst of the plain; and on

the other side, in a deep curve, stretched the sombre fir woods, where isolated birches stood out to break the monotonous ring of dark green needles.

Over this picture hung a gray heavy sky, and the cold blast from the north twisted around the corners in Greater Hoagby, which lay at the edge of the woods, as if it sought shelter from the terrific gale which had free play out on the plain. The wind rattled the doors and windows, scattering broken twigs and last year's leaves. The great clouds took the wind along with them; heavy cold clouds, which opened out in snow or rain here and there, while the plain lay stiff and lifeless under the first days of May. The birches in the hedges whipped with their pliant naked twigs as if buds and leaves would never come; and the oaks, bare, gnarled, and unmoved by the wind, stood in the mounds of half-moldered leaves which in the course of years had fallen and been buried at their feet.

It looked dreary in the farmyard, and dreary beyond; cold, dismal, and wintry. In the barn and kitchen the men went about with nothing to do, and the beasts stood within chewing submissively at what was left of last year's musty straw.

Then one day there came from the south a strong warm wind, which breathed on the ice and melted the snow. The work of liberation had begun long since in the marshes which lay out in the plain as in a bay. It was only near at hand along the edges and in narrow pits that winter still prevailed. But the southerly wind came, splashing the water over the ice and making holes in it from below, tossing the cakes one upon another and carrying them slowly in larger masses out into the lagoon, while it bored small holes around the reeds, which began to straighten up and work themselves loose. Then the sun came and helped. It melted the snow, softened the ground, and coaxed last year's grass and grain to lift once more their rows, which had been stiffened by the winter frost. What was old and useless it burned away, and the young shoots came up, delicate, fresh, and full of promise.

The larks had come. In the sunlight high above the fields one could hear a lively twittering sound. Looking up thither at the risk of being blinded by the sun, one might discover at last a little brown object which stayed ever in one spot of the blue, looking as if it was composed entirely of fluttering wings. The swallows came, sought out their old nests, and flew around in sharp curves, while they looked for new material to furnish their homes for the pleasures of the summer. Ducks and mergansers descended upon the marshes either to rest or to settle permanently. Every once in a while a great wedge of gray geese would voyage by on their way to the north, and a noble swan or two with long neck outstretched would make its questing flight across the wide plain.

A few days later there was life and activity at Greater Hoagby. The cows were to be let out to pasture, not to come in again before winter should return. Madam Berg herself was out on the steps to watch with a smile of satisfaction, as her sixteen cows, not to mention the yearling bulls and heifers, passed across the farmyard and out of the gate. Karin the serving-maid, a girl of somewhat over twenty, and madam's eldest son, a bachelor in his twenties who was working in the stables, together with her boy of twelve, followed along to guide the cattle out into the pastures or down to the great marsh, where they were to spend the spring, the summer, and a good part of the autumn.

It is a day of rejoicing on a farm when the cows can be driven out to graze. There is no longer the trouble of foddering them indoors and of cleaning up the barn. Furthermore, when the cows are let out, everyone knows that summer is at hand and that the evenings will be long and bright. Dark winter is past, the time when the monotonous evenings beginning at four o'clock must be spent inside with whatever work may chance to turn up, with coffee-drinking, talk, or sleep; but now one can go outdoors to work. The actual labor may well be heavier, but it is gayer, fresher, and pleasanter, especially when Saturday evening comes round with dancing, drinking, and love-making.

Madam Berg was a caustic woman and a sturdy woman, with broad shoulders and hips, and a smile that was both cheerful and a trifle haughty. Well on in her forties, she was stout and thick-set, with large coarse hands and a somewhat wrinkled face. Pouches of flesh on either side of her mouth bore witness to good living and a hearty appetite. She surveyed the cattle as they passed one by one, counting them in her mind so as to enjoy their number. Suddenly she called to the boy, who showed an inclination to start the cows on the run with a switch, "Stop that, Jonas! What are you up to there, beating the cows? Can't you leave them alone? Don't run along with them, I tell you.—The blessed boy doesn't hear a word I'm saying—. What makes you so pesky?"

Jonas made no answer, he merely gave a hitch to his trousers and walked more slowly, thinking over the chance of making the cows jump when they had come out on the country road. When the cattle were out, Madam Berg looked once again at the sky to see whether the wind was holding, after which she went back into the house, while Karin and Jan Nils remained where they were to close the gate.

"Well, Karin, shall we have a kiss now?" said Jan Nils as they stood alone outside. He was a tall fellow with a face rather old for his years, broad across the cheek bones, with handsome light-blue eyes, a short thin beard around a kindly smiling mouth, and light smooth hair above a well-shaped forehead, which was already furrowed by a couple of parallel grooves.

"Just try," said Karin, putting herself in the right position. Her lip curled a little, and a small defiant wrinkle came between her eye-brows.

Jan Nils jumped forward directly and caught the girl around the waist. She defended herself with all her might, twisting about in his arms like a snake, throwing her head from one side to the other, and finally by a sudden turn knocking off his cap. He glanced aside, clutching instinctively after his cap, which was already on the ground. In an instant Karin wrenched herself free, gave him another slap on the neck and sprang behind a post. With a "You little devil!" he picked up his cap, put it on again and ran after her around the post, stopping, turning and trying to get hold of her by leaning across it. But she sprang away from him and kept herself protected all the time. In the end he got her by the arm. She gave a little scream and hit him in the face with her free hand. He breathed fast from exertion but was laughing inwardly all the while It was just play and fun, and a kiss was neither forbidden nor uncustomary. He had kissed her many times, and she was at heart very fond of him. But still she wouldn't kiss him. No, she wouldn't. It was so jolly to show him he couldn't have everything he wanted or when he wanted it.

"Ugh, how mean you are, Jan!" she said. He was now leaning toward her and she felt his lips on her cheek.

With that she tore herself free again and stood still quite a way off from him. Her bosom was panting and her eyes gleaming.

"You are the horridest ever," she said.

"Yes, but I kissed you though," said he.

"Oh," she cried gaily, rubbing her hand across the place where his lips had touched her, "that was only on the cheek."

Jonas meanwhile had succeeded in getting the cows into a run on the road. He finally tired of chasing them and now followed them quite peacefully, except that from time to time he would set up a halloing that died away far off in the woods.

He soon vanished up a slope on the far side of the gateposts, so that Jan Nils and Karin, who followed along unhurriedly, were left alone. They walked a long while side by side, smiling. Sometimes Jan looked to the side and met her glance, which rested on him shiningly. There was in the air a scent of moist earth and fresh birch buds, and high over their heads the larks were trilling in the sunlight. They looked about them joyously, breathing in the warm spring air, while Karin proceeded softly beside him with slow and wavering steps. Then she would stand still for long intervals looking about her. She sang the whole time:

> *"If all the bushes were salted meat*
> *And all the brooks were soup here,*
> *I'd take a piece of bread to eat*
> *And dip it when I'd stoop here."*

When she stopped, he too would stand still to look earnestly and thoughtfully over the plain which basked in the warm vernal monotone hue of the sunlight.

He walked ever closer and closer to her. At length he laid his arm around her waist and drew her gently to him. She made no resistance and sometimes for a brief moment would lean her head against his shoulder, shutting her eyes the while. After a little she looked up into his face and smiled. He bent down and kissed her many times.

"I'm getting to kiss you after all," he said.

She answered nothing, only nodding her head and cuddling nearer to him.

They had come upon the slope and could now see Jonas a good way in front of them. Karin threw her arm around Jan's neck, kissed him again with a smile, and twisted herself gently free from his arm.

"The boy might see us," she said.

Then with a skip she pushed him away and began to run along the road. He ran after her, and they overtook the cattle at full speed, after which they proceeded at an easy jog, warm and breathless, while the cow-bells tinkled, and the little brook down in the dell hurried along purling over stones and roots.

Karin had been on the farm six years, and they had all gone as if they were one, quickly and happily, as time passes when one is young, happy, and cheerful in one's work; and all these years had been like an ardent dream of love, at first remote and unconscious, then nearer, more actual and complete, when Jan himself began to speak and to tell her he cared for her and that sometime they should certainly have a home together, although he was a rich farmer's son and she only the daughter of a poor villager.

The work days passed neither silently nor sullenly. The girls took their spinning-wheels and went into the house to old Gammer, the mistress's mother. Old as she was, she sang to them for days on end of Rosendal who went away for seven long years but returned to his bride, who had remained faithful; or of the shepherdess who sang a song to the king so that he set a gold crown on her head; or of Duke Frodenborg and the maiden Adelin:

"And then upon one bier they laid those youthful forms so fair,
And high-born dames and damsels did curl their flowing hair.

They laid the bodies in one tomb, that knight and lady gay,
And there the twain in peace repose unto the judgment day.

And there from out the lovers' grave did grow a linden tree,
Whose leaves unto the judgment day shall aye unwithered be.

And still it grew the church beside until it reached the spire—
By all the love that's hapless and true-hearted—
And evermore the leaves embraced for good folk to admire.
But oh! meseems that mortal life is weary."

She sang also unhappy love songs, sad little songs:

Gustaf af Geijerstam

"Your love is like an April snow
That tarries but a day,
And I must die when it doth go,
I can no longer stay.

You treat me ever as you choose,
You plan but to deceive.
You do not think what I must lose
When I am left to grieve."

And so Karin learned to sing many songs.

Or old Gammer would relate old sagas, bold and merry stories about how the devil was cheated, or of poor Peter and rich Peter; but first and last she told about the princess who was imprisoned in the mountain and wept night and day because the horrible mountain king wanted to make her his bride; and of the poor younger son whom everybody laughed at because he dared to look so high, but who nevertheless went out into the world and won the princess with half her father's kingdom to boot. These tales she told as the spinning-wheels hummed, and the girls sat thinking wondrous thoughts as they worked.

At Christmas and Midsummer there was dancing and merrymaking with all sorts of fun indoors and out. They danced the bobbing dance and "Two old men came out of the woods" and "Simon" and "The girl she goes a-dancing," and many others which are now done with and forgotten. And then Karin would dance with Jan Nils and be happy from morning to night, and they would always have a great deal to say to each other.

When spring came and the sun enticed the flowers and green leaves to come out on the hedges, they would meet in the open, and on summer evenings he would seek her where she was milking, or they would find each other in any case. And they would talk and caress and play, and she would sing him songs about those who had died for each other and about love. It was the song of Lord Rosendal that she used especially to sing for him:

"When Rosendal set forth upon the stormy sea
He said unto his true-love, 'Be faithful unto me.'

But scarce had he departed when to the maiden's
bower
Another lord came riding and sought to be her
wooer.

'Your love he has departed across the salt sea
foam,
I wot he will be false to you or ever he come
home.'

'I promised well my faith and troth, and even so
did he;

*And God in heaven, were I forsworn, He would
     requite it mo.'*

*The marriage was appointed for three days from
     that tide,*
*And not till then the bridegroom might look
     upon the bride.*

*'Have thanks, my own heart's dearest, that wert
     so true to me,*
*For, till I came, seven thousand miles I sailed
     upon the sea.'*

*The maiden then she slumbered upon her true-
     love's breast,*
*And till they came to Engeland she waked not
     from her rest."*

Then he would weep and she would weep every
time she sang the last lines, and they would swear
a thousand vows to each other and smile through
their tears.

But Mother Berg could not look with cheerful
eyes at the prospect that her Jan Nils should take
a poor girl to wife, so when she thought the affair
had continued long enough to be dangerous, she
said one fine day that Karin must go. Thereupon
Karin went back to her mother, who lived in the
village on the other side of the woods. Her
father had died during the time she had been
working at the Bergs'.

However, Karin did not grieve at this state of things; she was so sure Jan would be true to her. And on summer evenings they always met at the big stone that lay under the high firs midway between Jan's home and hers. He feared to come to her house, for then the news might get out all over the parish and be spread abroad so that his mother would hear of it; that was what he dreaded.

Karin noticed after a while that Jan appeared depressed, and she realized that it was because they were hard with him at home. This hurt her, but she could do nothing else than be doubly tender to him in return. She told him many times not to think of her, but he would always answer that he should be unhappy all his life if he couldn't marry her.

Then came a Sunday. They had cut the new rye and baked on the Saturday night before, and she went alone to church. When she came into the sunlight on the church slope and pressed through the groups that slowly descended the dilapidated stone steps to the road, Karin heard a peasant girl whisper to another that Jan Nils' sweetheart was to come from the neighboring parish with her mother next week to look things over, and that the marriage was as good as settled.

She could not get a word with Nils, for he was busy harnessing the horses. But when he caught

sight of her, he let the horses stand and came up
to her, bidding her meet him at the stone next
morning. Then he left her, and she went home.
But she thought nothing of what she had heard,
and when morning came she did not even feel
anxious.

There was such a fresh scent in the woods, the
birds were twittering briskly, and the dew lay
glittering brilliantly in the sunlight upon grass
and thicket. She passed lightly along the narrow
woodland path, which was so good to walk on,
and a thousand limpid melodies caroled to her
spirit.

But when she arrived at the stone, her heart
grew so hot within her that her knees could hardly
support her. She heard some one weeping, and
when she advanced, she saw it was Jan Nils lying
prone in the grass and sobbing so that his whole
body shook. Without daring to come nearer, she
sat down a little way off, while strange thoughts
began to course through her brain. He must be
very unhappy when he wept so bitterly that he did
not hear her come. "The rumor was true after
all," she thought, "and now he's weeping because
he will come into conflict with his mother on my
account. For he won't give me up—that couldn't
be thought of. We have been happy in each
other so many years and have promised each other
to be faithful—oh no, that couldn't be."

"But it would be a hard fight for him to be disobedient to his mother, just the same," she thought further, "and no good would come to us." She realized this. "There will never be any happiness for him, because he is so weak and never can put through his will. There will always be quarreling and division, and he will become a shuttlecock between all the women in the house; he will suffer when they are bad to me and still not be able to protect me."

She had thought of all this before, though she had never said anything. But now it stood before her as plain as if it were printed how everything would be, as he lay there weeping, and she sat on and couldn't decide to go to him.

Finally she got up, and he caught sight of her. At first he grew red in the face, then he started to weep again.

"I won't have anyone but you," he muttered. "The girl that mother sent was sent against my will. I won't have any one but you."

Karin sat looking straight before her. She now looked up and said in a dry, unnatural voice, "That may be as it will. But I have come to tell you that you're not to trouble about me but obey your mother."

She could speak no more in this strain, for Jan was weeping, and she felt it was so hard to see his distress that she wished only to comfort him, so she kept repeating that everything would be all right again after a little while. Finally he went, and Karin sat on alone looking after him.

But then her heart grew hot again to think that he could have gone away and not have even said a word about trying to turn his mother's mind. Suddenly she felt herself so utterly deserted that she laid down in the grass where he had just lain and wept as if her heart would burst. She did not know how long she lay there. She only knew that he had gone from her and would never come back. When she got up, the sun stood high in the heavens, the dew lay no more on the grass and bushes, the birds were silent, and no more fragrance breathed from the firs. She went about as in a dream for many days, not believing she could live on for long. But time passed, and she was still alive somehow. She turned against her sorrow and taught herself to work without being happy and without singing.

There is no time in one's life so painful and so trying as when one gives up the hope that life will bring something new, when with a heart-stifling certainty one clearly realizes that one must be content with things as they are and not hope for something grand to come. A poor man—if he does not fall into misery and apathy—has no time to lament over a thwarted life or to grieve over a broken heart. When one day demands that he shall sorrow for the evil of another, he must yield to the demand, no matter how much it hurts, but it is seldom his life grants him a respite when he can survey the past and throw bridges across the future. Quietly and silently dies the happiness of his life, and vacancy urges him neither to rebellion nor despair. The habit of privation means much in making a human being submissive, and it is expedient to have no time for thinking of oneself when there is need to hush a sorrowing heart.

Karin learned this during long years, and it became the history of her solitary life.

She did not speak with many people about her sorrow. Her mother said nothing to her about it. She knew that such things must run their course, and that when the time has passed, the suffering ceases of itself. And there was no one else for Karin to talk to. She did not care to confide in the girls of the district. They had only made fun of her and been envious when they thought she would get Jan Nils. So she stood by her mother at home and helped the youngsters with their clothes and such things. Karl Johan was terrible at tearing his trousers. She looked after the barn with its cows and chickens, and it was she who in the spring dug up the field and set out the potatoes. Her mother was getting old too, and could not do as much as she used.

But many a summer morning when Karin had got up earlier than the others and stood alone in the doorway, looking out across the slope with the little fenced terrace for potatoes, and saw the sun gleam above the cottage door and on the woods in front of her, there would run in her mind a strange little song, which she had never understood before but which she now thought was the truest and best of them all, much truer and wiser than the ballads about Duke Frodenborg or Lord Rosendal:

"*And little Karin stood a-grinding at the mill.*
She sang a song at cockcrow while yet the air was
chill
To the oak leaves and linden leaves so green,
oh."

Yes, she was to be at the mill all the days of her life, and she was to have no one else for whom to sing her song. Sometimes she thought it could never in the world be right and that God could not wish it should be so for her.

When several years had passed, her mother fell from the loft one day and injured her back. For twelve years she lay in her bed without being able to do anything for herself; for the first ten years she could not get out under the bare sky, but in the last two she could crawl to the doorstep on warm days in summer, and there she would sit and look out across the slope and the potato field, enjoying the mild sunlight. During all these years Karin had to tend the house and look after her mother alone, as the younger children had left the home to marry or find places in the neighborhood. They were often pinched for food and other necessities, and it was the folk at the Manor Place they had to thank for it that they could go on living in the village without paying rent as long as the mother was sick. Karin had grown paler in hue, and the clothes hung more loosely about her waist and hips. But she never complained, and a bright, gentle smile lay upon her lips, a smile that it did folks good to see.

Jan Nils had been married meanwhile, but it was said that his mother, who had manipulated the affair, had no joy of it. The two women got along ill together, and Jan became weaker and weaker in disposition, letting his wife manage and arrange things as she chose. And Karin wept many times on his account. In these last days he had taken to drink. He died early, and Karin felt almost light at heart when she heard it.

.   .   .   .

One day—it was in August—her mother grew worse than usual. In the dusk of the evening a few days later she died, while Karin sat beside the bed and read aloud to her from the gospel of St. Luke.

That evening Karin sat long in thought. She thought of all the good days when she and Jan Nils used to meet, she thought of all his loving words and of how they had sung and played together. It hurt her like sharp thorns when she remembered the old melodies. And she thanked God that she had been separated from him in time, since his life had later grown so sad.

With that she thought of how it was when she was lying alone in the woods weeping after he had gone away from her. She had never cried so since that day, and she thought that now nothing really bad could happen to her any more. But she remembered wonderfully how everything had been that day. Beside where she lay was a flat stone with red edges. She could see it whenever she chose as soon as she shut her eyes. And she thought of how nearly twenty years had gone since then and that now she was old and could not separate one year from another in her thoughts. She only recalled the day when her mother fell and hurt her back, when her sister and her youngest brother had taken service, and when her eldest brother had married.

She sat with clasped hands and looked at her mother's body, which lay stiff and motionless before her, and the thought came that she had nothing in the house, and that she did not even know in what she would shroud her mother.

She went about all next morning thinking of this, until well on in the forenoon she resolved to go up to the Manor and ask the mistress if she hadn't anything she could give her.

Karin dressed neatly and set out in her black Sunday dress and silk fichu with a gray woolen shawl on her arm. The mistress herself came out into the kitchen to speak to her.

The lady was young and happy, pretty as the day, a person who had not thought much about others, poor or otherwise.

"Ah, is your mother dead at last, Karin?" she said. "Poor old woman, it was a good thing she went. She was ill so long."

The pretty lady's eyes glistened with tears.

"Yes, it was surely well that God took her to Himself," said Karin. She then came to her request about the shroud.

The young lady considered a little, then went up into her room and searched the closets. She could find nothing but an old white tarlatan dress, which she took along and gave to Karin. She meant no disrespect, but she could not repress a slight smile as she brought it. She thought it was such a droll idea that Karin should shroud her old mother in the tarlatan dress.

Karin could never forget that smile. She saw

it, and it hurt her deeply, for she could not understand what there was to laugh at. She kept thinking of it all the time as she ripped the pleats of the skirt to make it suitable for a shroud, and it occurred to her again when everything was ready and she sat with folded hands beside her mother, who lay in the white apparel with hands crossed over her breast.

When her mother was buried, Karin moved over to her brother, who was married and lived in another parish. He had been disabled, and his wife had become blind, so that now Karin had the charge of his numerous children during the years when they were growing up.

Karin remained unmarried, though she had many good offers. But she always thought it was better to be poor as she was than to go even to a rich farmhouse without love in her heart.

A few years later her sister-in-law died, and when the children could look out for themselves, Anders and she moved into a little gray cottage which stood at the edge of a wood, and from which one could look out across the wide monotonous plain.

There they lived for many years on the little that Karin could earn and what good people gave them. During the last years Anders had mostly been confined to his bed.

.   .   .   .

It was late autumn. The noonday sun shone across the plain, lending a glow to the fields where the rye stubble was still standing, to the slope of oaks whose leaves were still dark green, to the glittering birches that gave back a red and yellow sheen, and to the solemn rows of pines and firs which began where the birches ceased and extended in a sharp curve out along the plain.

Wonderful thoughts come to the beholder on such an autumn day when he is out walking alone; it seems as if the sun was doing all this to delude the eye and to gild the fallen beauty of the vanished summer. The air is warm and the sky is blue as in spring, while the boughs of the trees stand out half naked, and every moment the foot is treading withered leaves.

I went in through the fir wood and over a clearing with tall dry stumps and small rank fir-shoots, which were trying to spring up and grow big before they too should be cut down or burned. A moist glow rested on the mossy rocks and lichen-covered tufts. I followed the path, which curved in through the wood and soon reached the edge of the plain. There it lay stretched before me in the blinding sunshine.

A short distance away stood Karin's and Anders's cottage with the high chimney that was set askew on the roof, and the mended panes which glistened like soap-bubbles in the light.

Karin stood in the enclosure busied with putting up some stone-work to support the chimney. We greeted each other cordially, for Karin and I had long been good friends. I then asked for a glass of water and stepped into the cabin.

Poverty was very apparent within, yet things were neat and tasteful. Like all other cabins, this had its fireplace, its floor strewn with juniper; its red corner-cupboard painted with large flowers and bearing the initials of Karin's parents and the date of their marriage, 1797, done in white; a brown folding table, a wooden bench and a bed, where Anders lay asleep.

I had been there many times, and Karin had told me bit by bit all that I have narrated about her life. I now sat down a little while on the bench and asked how things were.

Oh, one day went by pretty much like another for her, God be thanked, but Anders was very poorly. He had to keep to his bed and couldn't so much as go to church; but still read he would, he was as fond of books as ever and would explain them to her.

"Things are hard enough to be sure," she finished, "but God helps us when there seems no remedy by mortal means, and as long as I keep my health, we can make out. I'm only afraid I shall die before him, because he can't get on without me."

Then we began once more, as we had done so often previously, to talk over how Karin's life had passed, and about her love and how Jan had forsaken her. In the meantime Anders had wakened and lay listening to the conversation, nodding his head from time to time.

I looked at Karin. She did not seem embittered. Her face was lined, but her eyes were bright and gentle, and her mouth had a mild and sad expression.

I could not forbear to ask, "Don't you ever think how much better things might have been, Karin?"

"Ah yes," she answered, "ah yes, now and again. But mostly I've not had time. Still I think it wasn't meant that I should marry, for who would there have been for mother and the little ones then? I've had weary times enough in my days, and when I sit here alone I ponder sometimes how it comes that some folk are given such a weight of trouble. But Anders expounds God's word so fine to me, as if he was strong he could proclaim it to us all here; and he has the idea that God has a special purpose for them he lays such crosses on. And that I seem to understand so well."

She was silent a while and looked down at her hands, which she held clasped in her lap.

She then raised her eyes and said quietly, "I

do still think upon how much better it might have been if I had come to be married the way I thought to be. But now I am old I see my days behind me, and so I understand that as he was so he would have stayed. For as the tree falls there it lies, and as love couldn't make a man of him when there was need, he wouldn't have become a man afterwards.—I'm so calm about everything now, for soon it will be done, and when troubles come and we are hungry and cold and ill off for clothes, I think it won't be for long. For it's getting on to spring."—

I rose and said goodbye. Karin followed me to the gate.

"It's a beautiful season this; St. Britta's summer, they call it," said Karin. "It's a blessed beautiful autumn."

"It is so."

She looked around at the changing colors of the birches and at the sun-bathed plain where the harvest had just been mowed, and her eyes glistened as she took my hand.

But when I had entered the wood, I turned, where the path made a bend, to nod to Karin as she stood in the gateway. It was then my turn to remember the old verses of which Karin had told me, and I repeated them many times in my thoughts as I went along:

"And little Karin stood a-grinding at the mill."

VERNER VON HEIDENSTAM

THE SHIELD-MAIDEN

A CLEAN WHITE SHIRT

VERNER VON HEIDENSTAM (1859–) is descended on both sides from families of the Swedish nobility. He was born in Olshammar Manor on Lake Wettern, in a region filled with historical traditions and impressive for its natural beauty. At sixteen he was sent abroad with a tutor, and thus imbibed that love of the Orient and the Latin countries which is seen in his early works. He meant at first to be a painter, and studied under Gérome in Paris, but soon found that literature was the means of expression best suited to him.

Returning to Sweden, he published *Pilgrimage and Wander-Years,* which, in colorful, boldly fantastic verse, conjures up images from the Orient. His first novel, *Endymion,* has an Eastern background, but in the next, *Hans Alienus,* an imaginative allegory in prose interspersed with verse, he leads his hero through the ages and the climes, to let him find at last the meaning of life in his own country, among people of his own race.

From that time on, Heidenstam devoted himself to interpreting the past of his own country. *The Charles Men* is a series of stories revolving round the figure of Charles XII. *St. Birgitta's Pilgrimage* deals with the greatest religious character of medieval Sweden. *The Folkung Tree* is the title of a double novel, the first part, *Folke Filbyter,* taking us back to the dawn of Swedish history, the second, *The Bjälbo Heritage,* describing Sweden's consolidation as a Christian state. Finally Heidenstam gathered the fruit of his ripe historical knowledge in *The Swedes and Their Chieftains,* a series of pictures from the Stone Age down to the nineteenth century.

Heidenstam's prose is lofty, sometimes rising to the rhapsodic, though by no means lacking in humor or drastic detail. His poetry is perhaps even more intimately revealing, and is regarded by Swedish critics as the finest flower of his genius. He is a member of the Swedish Academy and in 1916 received the Nobel prize for literature.

Verner von Heidenstam

THE SHIELD-MAIDEN

From *The Swedes and Their Chieftains*

TORGRIM was the chief landholder in Roslagen. One evening he sat conversing with
his guests. The cleft and lighted sticks of dry
wood that were stuck in the wall gradually
burned out, but the moon shone in through the
opening in the roof, spreading its joyous and
friendly radiance over the table and the high seat.
Great years had dawned for both the Svear and
the Gotar, and the talk was of exploits and adventures, for the guests under the landholder's
thatch had just come back from a foray.

At this moment a thrall came running in and
set a helmet in the midst of the board in front of
Torgrim. It was adorned with four peaks, upon
which it stood like a kettle on its feet. In the
helmet lay a naked new-born girl-baby that struck
out with its arms and kicked and cried.

"You have wide-stretched lands, master," said
the thrall. "Who is to inherit and care for
them? Hitherto you were childless, but this evening is born to you a woman-child. Woe is us
that it is not a son!"

The guests began to laugh, and the helmet was sent along the board so that one and all could look at the child and take hold of its little hands. "Aha, Torgrim," the merry voices murmured, "here you have some one to guide the plough. This is something for you to dress and adorn, and to sit and pamper. But much avail you're not like to get of her in all of her days."

When the helmet had passed from hand to hand down to the foot of the board, which was dark because the moonlight could not reach there, the thrall took it under his arm and went toward the door.

"Master," he said, "it will be wisest that I set the child out in the woods and let it perish."

But thereupon he chanced to bear the little one again through the moonlight so that Torgrim could see her.

"Nay, worthy guests of this house," he exclaimed, springing up, "far otherwise shall ye learn. Since the girl has been handed to me in the helmet which I so often bore in my youth, when I stood in my own ship, I shall now lift down my shield and my ashen spear as well and lay them by her. Wash her in snow, you thrall there, and lay a bit of bear's marrow between her lips so that she will be quiet. Daughter, here under the clear moonlight I name thee, and thou shalt be called Hjälmdis."

The mead-horns were then filled anew, and the glad guests drank the birth-ale in the glittering moonlight.

.   .   .   .

The child's mother was a thrall woman. She died shortly, and Hjälmdis grew up alone with her father. She followed him when he went to the forest with his axe and sat astride before him when he rode to the cheaping-steads in the villages. During the long winter evenings, when she came to him and played with his shaggy beard, he taught her to twist bow-strings and to set on the heads of arrows. She had no pleasure in sewing together dolls out of cloth shreds as other girls did; her greatest joy was to sit on bearskins by the fire and turn over her father's sword, which was a good bit longer than she was herself.

But the dice of fate have strange power over men. Though Torgrim was always good to her, he grew even more and more gloomy with the grief of having no son who should inherit his war weapons and estate, so as to bring glory to the race. He sat and brooded on his melancholy thoughts. The thralls sorrowed with him, and he no longer had any peace at home.

One day he took his axe as usual and went out into the wood, his daughter following him. They came into a thicket of birches which was so dense that her hair was tangled in the leafage. The

[115]

sun shone beauteously both through the birch leaves and her rich brown hair, as she was loosing it from the twigs, so that anyone might have danced for joy. But Torgrim went straight on without looking back. When she called after him, she received no answer; and from that hour he was gone forever.

She continued to roam about as before and bathed herself in snow so as to become strong. One of the merry guests who had sat in the circle when she was carried around in the helmet was called Torwald Heròsson. He was a saga-teller from distant Iceland, and though he himself could not compose, he was mightily learned. One day on his wanderings he came again to the place, sat himself down, and talked long with Hjälmdis of her father and of the shades in the underworld. "I shall seek for him even among the dead," she said to Torwald when he ceased, and with that she hastened out again into the woods.

When she had been gone all day, she picked berries to still the worst of her hunger, but even then she thought not of resting. She went ever farther from the abodes of the living, until at last even the trees were no more alive but stood gray and stunted. No moss made soft resting places on the stones; the earth was covered with sand, and great boulders lay strewn on every side. But now she noticed that she was surrounded by a band of pallid forms, about whom the air was cool as above a spring. "Ye are the dead," she whispered, and began to tremble.

It was now necessary to climb down, ever down between the damp rocks. The lowest steps lay in a wide ring, high as benches, and on them sat the Pale Ones to be examined and judged. Still deeper down thundered a terrible river with hissing foam, and on the opposite side was a throng of shades, head after head, as far as it was possible to distinguish anything in the half twilight. The girl, however, did not feel herself utterly helpless, for beside her went a good woman with a friendly glance that reminded her of the moon's glitter in Torgrim's hall.

"So small a child is not to be judged," said she, pushing Hjälmdis on past the benches and in among the troop of other children. "Look! she is still purple on mouth and fingers with the berries she has just been picking."

The pallor of the children frightened Hjälmdis at first. But there was a glow of innocent happiness that shone from them, so that soon she began to play with them and pat them with her berry-stained fingers. "What is your name?" she asked of a girl whose hand she held. The other answered, "I think my name is Forgotten." And of the others the one who stood nearest answered also, "My name must be Forgotten."

White as chalk, Hela, the grim queen of the underworld, now rode past along the opposite shore on her three-legged horse. "I have sharper eyes than the others," she called across the river, "and I see well that you do not belong here, little child. Whom do you seek? If it is your father, know that he sits with Odin, if he has fallen by the sword or thrown himself from the cliff of his ancestors; and to Valhalla it is hard for women to win. But whether he is with Odin or with me, I hope for one thing: that is, that he too shall soon come to be named Forgotten."

Therewith the daughter of Loki laughed so that the echo rolled through the vaults.

Hjälmdis had covered her head in the garments of the good woman, who still stood beside her, but now she dropped them in terror and fled up the stairs. She bent and leaped, while she felt the cold cloaks and headcloths of those she met sweep across her back. No one hindered her, since she was but a child. Unnoticed she felt her way out to the trees under the open heavens.

The night was not too dark for her to see where she was, but it was full daylight before she came back to the house. The thrall sat on the threshold with a milk-pail and fed the snake which lived under the corner of the house and often used to wriggle as far as the hearth.

When the thrall had listened a while to

Hjälmdis, he said to the snake in a sort of sing-song, "Wise creature, the child has gone to sleep in the woods and dreamed of all the lore which that Icelander spun together yesterday. But who knows? Perhaps it was more than only dreams. Thereof a poor simple thrall such as I dare not speak. And of a truth seems it hard that so good a master as Torgrim should be forgotten for all time."

The Icelander, hearing his words, came forth bare-headed with rapid steps from the hall and answered, "You speak according to your knowledge, good house-thrall. But now through Odin have come to us runes, and they are the wisest and greatest of all his gifts. Compared to them gold and iron are nothing. Empty memorial stones there are many here, but runes shall adorn the stones as leaves the branch, and now even the dead can speak with us. Victory runes, law runes, skaldic runes, family runes, hail to you, for ye have slain forgetfulness!"

He took the thrall with him and under the hanging birch by the water he raised a stone to the memory of Torgrim. After he had cut the runes which he thought fitting, he kissed Hjälmdis on the brow and went his way.

Afterwards she liked to sit of an evening in the grass by the memory-stone, and when she began to understand the power of the runes, she had to weep for joy. This came about when a wayfarer would stand and read aloud: "Hjälmdis raised this stone for her father Torgrim, the worthy landholder. Whoever passes may read his name and remember it."

. . . .

When Hjälmdis was fourteen, she set her father's helmet on her head, took up his shield and spear, and rode to Upsala. On one of the grass-grown ancestral mounds there sat a youth, who looked to be about the same age as she was. He had a hard and defiant expression, and in his play he had got a blow from a drinking-horn, which had left a scar above his nose.

"Good-morrow, shield-maiden," he saluted her. "Have you in turn no friendly word for him who sits on his father's grave-mound and demands his inheritance? My father Olov and his brother Erik were joint kings over the realm of all the Svear."

"Who then is king, if it is not you?" she asked.

"I am Styrbjörn, and me they will not lift on their shields and proclaim," he sighed bitterly. "I have just been driven from the council with stones and blows, because they will not have so young a king."

"Is Erik wise and victorious?" she asked, laying her spear crosswise on her horse's back as she waited. Styrbjörn answered nothing, but hate flushed his forehead, and he leaped up with knotted fists. She then said, "I see that Erik is wise and victorious, and therefore is he the right man to rule over us, but you are proud and fierce. Better it were, therefore, that you should pray him for some of his greatest ships and go on a viking voyage." After this she rode on to the king's abode.

Styrbjörn followed her advice. In the evening, when they were all assembled, he strode into the hall. Erik the Victorious sat on the high seat; brown-hued he was, tall and of great manly beauty. With frank speech he promised Styrbjörn sixty ships fully fitted out. Notwithstanding, Styrbjörn had no thank-word to return, but stood sullenly at a distance.

By the wall farthest away from him stood twelve chosen shield-maidens. Hjälmdis had already been admitted to the band as the twelfth and youngest. Many a grim berserk brightened when he looked at their lovely faces, but the shield-maidens gave no heed to the warriors, talking gladly among themselves instead about their weapons and their steeds, which were stamping outside in the stables.

When without bidding any one farewell Styrbjörn went to the door and came abreast of the glittering line of shield-maidens, he turned to Hjälmdis and said, "Dismal it is for a banished king's son to sit alone out on the stormy waters. Come with me, spear-bearer!"

But forthwith the shield-maidens began to laugh, so that it sounded like a torrent in spring when the ice tinkles together.

"A shield-maiden goes with no one," answered Hjälmdis, unable to check her smile. "Also I had a father. Though he were ten times dead, yet shall he one day come to hear that I have wielded his simple peasant spear with as much honor as if he had had a son. Put on the armor of your ancestors, Styrbjörn, and let not yourself be laughed down by women!"

Styrbjörn then went down to his ships at the river, and in the dawn set out to sea. The sails of the finest ships were covered with red and yellow canopies, as with tranquil dignity they glided forth amid the rushes. When the fleet swung out on the Malar between the leafy islands, where the cattle stood and stared, it was met by a head wind. But thirty pairs of oars were stuck out .from each of the ships and drove them rapidly off toward the distant unknown. Styrbjörn then turned, looked over the shores, and said to his men, "If I do not come back some day as king over that land, I do not wish to live."

. . . .

The young viking now sailed from place to place, winning fortresses and lands, till he re-

ceived the surname of "the Strong." Thus he
came to the island of Wollin in the Baltic, where
the Jomsvikings had their famous stronghold,
Jomsborg.

It appeared to be impregnable, and the sagas
relate that within the walls was a harbor so great
that two hundred dragon-ships could lie there
gunwale to gunwale. Styrbjörn got intelligence
that the chieftain was away, and commanded his
men to row there. Across the harbor entrance
was a stone battlement crowned with a tower.
From the loopholes boiling pitch and stones were
rained upon all who ventured to approach, and
the iron-bound gates were fastened within. With
a ringing war-cry the rowers threw themselves
backwards, and Styrbjörn's ship whizzed forward
through the foam. Crashing as though living
rock were shattered, the timbers gave way, and
the gates flew open, but the ship herself opened
her seams with the blow. The warriors then
laid aside their oars and swam into the fortress.
The wild and haughty Jomsvikings were then compelled to take Styrbjörn the Strong for their chief.

No one was received into the band of the Jomsvikings who was younger than fifteen or older
than fifty. The aspirant had to be hardened in
body, frank of spirit, and brave enough to fight
one against two. For such youths and men it
was a joy to follow a leader such as Styrbjörn.

[123]

He was nearly always out on a raid. As a Joms-viking he might never appear discontented or complain and lament, no matter what might happen; neither, between waves and weapon-play, was there much time for such moods. But the men at the oars heard at night how he tossed on his bed in a torment of sleeplessness. Power and renown, all that a sea-king could desire, he had attained, yet not the one thing of which he dreamed day and night: to stand on his father's mound at Upsala and be hailed as king of the Svear.

Harald Bluetooth of Denmark, who required his help, gave him his daughter in marriage. But Styrbjörn still thought many times of the proud shield-maiden in the hall of Erik the Victorious and became ever more stern of soul. By threats he forced Harald Bluetooth to join him with two hundred ships. Finally not even the great harbor of Jomsborg could hold the combined fleets, and it was with twelve hundred dragon-ships that Styrbjörn sailed up the Baltic toward brighter nights and more thickly wooded islands.

As soon as he had landed his men at the entrance of the Malar, he defiantly burned his vessels. But when Harald Bluetooth saw the flames, he suddenly turned his ships into the wind and fled home to Denmark. Yet Styrbjörn's courage sank not, and he cut his way through the woods until he came to Fyrisvall. "Either shall I soon be sitting in the high seat at Upsala," he muttered, "or in a grave-mound of the earth that should have been mine."

   .   .   .   .

Erik the Victorious, who was an alert and valorous monarch, had already sent out the gathering-summons and got together the whole army of the Svear. For two days the hosts fought on the plain without any yielding on either side.

As night drew on after the second day, Styrbjörn made sacrifice to Thor. In the clouds of smoke appeared for an instant a red-clad and red-bearded man, who looked upon him sorrowfully. "I see that you forebode my death," said Styrbjörn, drooping his head. "Much you have given me, only not that for which I most longed. Such is human fate."

Meanwhile Erik the Victorious went to the great temple in the grove of sacrifice. Outside, it was ornamented with a border like a chain of gold, but within it was dark, and the earth sank down many steps to the images of the gods as if toward the underworld. "After ten years I give myself and my life to you, Odin, if you grant me victory," he whispered softly. As he spoke, there stood before him a one-eyed man with the brim

[125]

of his hat drawn down. "Ye all belong to me," said the apparition, who handed him a spear and vanished.

When the day broke, Erik the Victorious mounted the nearest ridge of sand, followed by the faithful Torgny Lagman, who had stood by his side with good counsel in many a fight. The trumpets blew the onset, and from mounds, ridges, and roads the sand was torn by foot-beat and hoof-beat. "All things are Odin's," cried Erik the Victorious, hurling his spear, and at that signal a rain of arrows leaped from the bows.

As the sand cloud drew near across the plain, Styrbjörn and his vikings thought it was horsemen, and held out their spears to repulse them. But out of the yellow mist rushed bulls and horses, which had been fastened together several in a yoke, the yokes being thickly set with knife-blades, spear-heads and hooks. The bellowing of the bulls was blent with the ring of weapons, and the grass was strewn with bleeding men. Styrbjörn, who feared less to die than that his last faithful warriors should flee in shame, struck his standard deep into the earth and defended it, though he had already sunk to one knee under his wounds. He then saw a glimmering as of torches in the whirlwind of sand. It was the shining troop of the shield-maidens, who rushed forward with upraised spears, and he recognized Hjälmdis by her fluttering hair. He called to her that, if she had followed him, they would now both on the same day win the glory of riding to Odin's hall. She answered that this might well chance as it was, and that there she would perhaps be more gentle toward him. But soon neither could hear the other any longer; and Styrbjörn fell under the arrows of his foemen.

Erik the Victorious was waiting on the sand ridge, holding by the arm his little son, Olov Child-King, as he became in the chronicles. Down among the courtiers stood the Icelander, Torvald Herösson. Hurriedly he snatched a harp and hastened up on the height with head flung back and eyes aglow. He who never before could compose received for this once the enthusiasm which is the fountain of the poet's art. Erik the Victorious slid the broadest ring from his arm to hand him as a reward. But Torvald's glance was far away, and with rich and richer harp tones he sang the one song of his life, a thunderous paean on the battle of Fyrisvall.

The song resounded over the silent plain, where the flocks of ravens had already appeared, and the valkyries led forward their steeds to fetch the pale heroes. Many renowned warriors lay there with a look of proud and happy expectation, and the valkyries, the stern maidens of death, lifted them in their arms with sisterly tenderness and set them before them on their horses. At length they came to the place where the rain of arrows had fallen thickest. They had to pause a moment and wonder, for there lay the twelve shield-maidens, fallen side by side, lovely even in death.

One of the valkyries lifted up Hjälmdis on her steed and sprang off up the bridge of the rainbow. The tremendous thunder of the hoofs awakened Hjälmdis, and when she opened her eyes, she saw the gleam from Freya's hall and the glow from Thor's ruddy stronghold amid the cliffs, whence flames flickered and rumblings echoed. With that she was brought into Odin's hall.

The walls there were of spear-shafts, overhung with golden shields, and from the mail-covered benches rose the feasters to embrace their sons and old comrades in arms from among the newly fallen, and to hear tidings of the earth. But off by himself an old man sat without heeding the others. "I have no one to wait for," he sighed heavily. "My only child was a girl, and that shame smote me so hard that I went forth in silence and cast myself over the precipice."

Hjälmdis shaded her eyes. She now saw that it was Torgrim. Running forward, she wound her arms about his shoulders and sobbed, "Father, so I have found you at last! Here I come to bring back your weapons. Great use have I had of them till I myself sank under the sword blows."

There was a rustling in the old man's breast, and he drew her to him. But in the hall around them it had grown still, for the distant sound of the harp-strings from Fyrisvall could be heard even up here, and all wished to listen. Then the valkyries all bent toward one another, as they stood in the doorway with their raven-winged helmets, and whispered, "Well now may Torgrim, the worthy landholder, rejoice that he had a daughter!"

A Clean White Shirt

From *The Charles Men*

PRIVATE BENGT GETING had got a Cossack's pike through his breast, and his comrades laid him on a heap of twigs in a copse, where Pastor Rabenius gave him the Holy Communion. This was on the icy ground before the walls of Veperik, and a whistling norther tore the dry leafage from the bushes.

"The Lord be with thee!" whispered Rabenius softly and paternally. "Are you prepared now to depart hence after a good day's work?"

Bengt Geting lay with his hands knotted, bleeding to death. The hard eyes stood wide open, and the obstinate and scraggy face was so tanned by sun and frost that the bluish pallor of death shone out only over his lips.

"No," he said.

"That is the first time I have heard a word from your mouth, Bengt Geting."

The dying man knotted his hands all the harder, and chewed with his lips, which opened themselves for the words against his will.

"For once," he said slowly, "even the meanest and raggedest of soldiers may speak out."

He raised himself painfully on his elbow, and ejaculated such a piercing cry of anguish that

[130]

Rabenius did not know whether it came from torment of soul or of body.

He set down the chalice on the ground, and spread a handkerchief over it, so that the leaves which were tumbling about should not fall into the brandy.

"And this," he stammered, pressing his hands to his forehead, "this I, who am a servant of Christ, shall be constrained to witness, morning after morning, evening after evening."

Soldiers crowded forward from all sides between the bushes to see and hear the fallen man, but their captain came in a wrathful mood with sword drawn.

"Tie a cloth over the fellow's mouth!" he shouted. "He has always been the most obstinate man in the battalion. I am no more inhuman than another, but I must do my duty, and I have a mass of new and untrained folk that have come with Lewenhaupt. These have been scared by his wailing, and refuse to go forward. Why don't you obey? I command here."

Rabenius took a step forward. On his curled white peruke he had a whole garland of yellow leaves.

"Captain," he said, "beside the dying the servant of God alone commands, but in glad humility he delivers his authority to the dying man himself. For three years I have seen Bengt Get-

[131]

ing march in the line, but never yet have I seen him speak with any one. Now on the threshold of God's judgment-seat may no one further impose silence upon him."

"With whom should I have spoken?" asked the bleeding trooper bitterly. "My tongue is as if tied and lame. Weeks would go by without my saying a word. No one has ever asked me about anything. It was only the ear that had to be on guard so that I did not fail to obey. 'Go,' they have said, 'go through marsh and snow.' To that there was nothing to answer."

Rabenius knelt and softly took his hands in his.

"But now you shall speak, Bengt Geting. Speak, speak, now that all are gathered about to hear you. You are now the only one of us all who has the right to speak. Is there a wife or perhaps an aged mother at home to whom you want me to send a message?"

"My mother starved me and sent me to the troops, and never since then has a woman had anything else to say to me than the same, 'Get away, Bengt Geting, go, go! What do you want with us?'"

"Have you anything to repent?"

"I repent that as a child I did not jump into the mill-race, and that, when you stood before the regiment on Sunday and admonished us to go patiently on and on, I didn't step forward and strike you down with my musket.—But do you want to know what causes me dread? Have you never heard the wagon-drivers and outposts tell how in the moonlight they have seen their comrades that were shot limp in crowds after the army and hop about on their mangled legs and cry, 'Greetings to mother!'— They call them the Black Battalion. It's into the Black Battalion that I'm to go now. But the worst is that I shall be buried in my ragged coat and my bloody shirt. That's the one thing I can't get out of my mind. A plain trooper doesn't want to be taken home like the dead General Liewen, but I'm thinking of the fallen comrades at Dorfsniki, where the king had a coffin of a couple of boards and a clean white shirt given to each man. Why should they be treated so much better than I? Now in this year of misfortune a man is laid out as he falls. I'm so deeply sunk in misery that the only thing in the world I can be envious of is their clean white shirts."

"My poor friend," answered Rabenius quietly, "in the Black Battalion—if you believe in it now —you will have great company. Gyldenstolpe and Sperling and Lieutenant-Colonel Mörner already lie shot on the field. And do you recall the thousand others? Do you remember the friendly Lieutenant-Colonel Wattrang, who came riding to our regiment and gave an apple to every soldier, and who now lies among the Royal Dragoons, and all our comrades under the meadow at Holofzin? And do you remember my predecessor, Nicholas Uppendich, a mighty proclaimer of the Word, who fell at Kalisch in his priestly array? Grass has grown and snow fallen over his mould, and no one can point out with his foot the sod where he sleeps."

Rabenius bowed yet deeper, and felt the man's forehead and hands.

"In ten or at most fifteen minutes you will have ceased to live. Perhaps these minutes might replace the past years, if you sanctify them rightly. You are no longer one of us. Don't you see that your spiritual guide is lying on his knees by you with head uncovered? Speak now and tell me your last wish; no, your last command. Consider but one thing. The regiment is disorganized on your account, and meanwhile the others go forward with glory, or stand already on the storming ladders. You have frightened the younger fellows with your death-wound and your wailing, and you alone can make it good again. Now they listen only to you, and you alone have it in your power to make them go against the enemy. Consider that your last words will be last forgotten, and perhaps sometime will be repeated for those at home, who sit and roast their potatoes behind the oven."

Bengt Geting lay motionless, and a shadow of perplexity passed over his glance. Then he gently raised his arms as if for an invocation and whispered, "Lord, help me to do even so!"

He gave a sign that now he was able only to whisper, and Rabenius laid his face to his so as to be able to hear his words. Then Rabenius motioned to the soldiers, but his voice trembled so that he could hardly make himself heard. "Now Bengt Geting has spoken," he said. "This is his last wish, that you should take him between you on your muskets and carry him with you in his old place in the line, where he has stubbornly marched day after day and year after year."

The drums now struck up, the music began, and with his cheek on the shoulder of one of the soldiers Bengt Geting was carried forward step by step over the field toward the foe. Around him followed the whole regiment, and ever with bared head Rabenius went behind him, and did not notice that he was already dead.

"I shall see to it," he whispered, "that you get a clean white shirt. You know that the king does not regard himself as more than the humblest soldier, and it is so that he himself wishes some-time to lie."

OSCAR LEVERTIN

MIDDLE-CLASS ROCOCO

OSCAR LEVERTIN (1862–1906) was a member of one of the Jewish families which have to a remarkable degree been conservers of international culture in the Scandinavian countries. He was primarily a critic, and in this capacity ranked as the first of his generation. As professor of literature in Stockholm, and as a regular contributor to periodicals, he did much to stimulate interest in Swedish literature.

Levertin's poetry and fiction have a subtle, exotic quality. They were to some extent a flowering of his literary and historical studies, and therefore are not so readily comprehended by the average reader. He attempted first to write in the realistic style of the 1880's, but through Heidenstam's influence he was enlisted in the new romantic phalanx and became its ablest exponent. His *Legends and Songs* and the poetic cycle *King Solomon and Morolf* were inspired by medieval Christian-Jewish motifs. His *Rococo Stories* are delicate sketches on a background of the eighteenth century, a period which was his especial field.

The novel *Masters of Österås* is a succession of pictures, from an imaginary cathedral town, beginning with its ancient origins and coming down to the present, when the masters at the old cathedral school are withering in the stifling atmosphere of tradition. Levertin paints the old town with so loving a hand, however, that the reader's sympathies are really drawn to the side of the old against the would-be revolutionists. As a picture of a certain phase of Swedish life the book is charming.

Oscar Levertin

Middle-Class Rococo

LETTER from the silk manufacturer's widow, Nora Wolfram, to her sister the dean's wife, Louise Megander.

August 15, 1779.

My dearest Sister!

I should have answered my sister's amiable letter a week ago, had I not been so overwhelmed by both gay and serious matters that pressing occupations did not leave me a moment to myself. But now, God be thanked, all of Anne-Charlotte's arrangements are in order, even to ordering her shoes of the Queen's bootmaker at the Traskport. My sister might imagine that the child is now in the seventh heaven, since the wedding is already fixed for September, and that she thanks God for her happy union with so good and worthy a man as Pastor Hesselius, who has given a hundred proofs of his tenderness and is about to set her future beyond all care; but instead, what does she do? Weeps, sighs, and mopes, desires but to be alone and to plunge into meditations without being willing to confess to her dear mama the cause of her trouble.

[139]

I fear me greatly that young Stenfelt, who is said to have posed as her adorer at the last masquerade, has cooled her affection with his *galanteries,* so that now she goes about with her head full of that kind of love and no longer finds any charm in Pastor Hesselius, who—God forbid!—is no foppish *petit-maître* in stiffened cuffs and lace with a hired horse and lackey, but a prudent man, serious in person and apparel, wondrously good and intelligent, though not given to vanity and display. Hesselius is, God be thanked, a well-provided man, owns a house on Österlånggata and has the king's promise of the next vacant pastorate. All this is nothing, more shame on our degenerate days! My little Anne-Charlotte should be rejoiced at this worthy man's free and magnanimous offer. But so it is with our hardened girls, they naturally give the *pas* to any young cavalier who lisps compliments in French ahead of a true and straightforward man, whose love has to do with the heart and not the money-chest. But as long as I live no dandified ninny such as goes to assemblies and picnics, makes jokes and sweet speeches, sits out his days at drinking clubs and coffee-houses, revels and carouses till he ends in bankruptcy and the debtors' prison, shall be my son-in-law, not if he were so eager that he'd offer to pay for the wedding.

Oscar Levertin

My sweetest Louise, there is much else of which I should write, but I cannot remember it all because I have so much to arrange for the marriage. And the worst is I have had to show my scullery maid the door—she was a hussy, shameful at answering back. And only think, Louise dear, when the groom was out yesterday, he saw her monkey face at the Green Flounder in Beswärsbacken, where she was delivering herself of all kinds of absurdities and impertinences about me, which the groom, who is a good-natured fellow, repeated. Such are the servant folk these days. Truly was not my excellent Hesselius right when he said to-day that the times were evil and full of contumaciousness? If the world lasts to next Olaf's Day we shall have reason to be thankful.

Convey my best wishes for the convalescence of your most estimable husband, and do me the kindness to accept the trifle accompanying this. There is some superfine Hyson tea which I bought of a captain at the Holland Wharf, muscat raisins from Wannerdahl's in the Kyrkobrink, and a couple of flasks of Professor Berg's most recommendable gooseberry wine.

Adieu, my dearest Louise, no more in the present haste from your faithful sister

Nora Wolfram

.   .   .   .

Letter from Anne-Charlotte Wolfram to her friend Ulrique Haldin.

Aug. 17, 1779.

My own little beloved and kind Ulrique!

What deluge of enjoyments is absorbing my precious Ulrique's attention out on her amiable father's delightful estate, since she has completely forgotten her little Anne-Charlotte in the city? I must chide a little, for it was really I who wrote last to you, you horrid child. Anyhow I send you another line by this post, for my pen is my only relief when I am divided from my Ulrique, the tenderest and noblest object of my heart's worship. Oh, of all artists I praise none so highly as he who invented writing. What joy through its means to be able to speak with an absent friend, especially on the delicate occasion when one's heart is full of anxiety and regret!

My sweet Ulrique knows that next month I am to be a bride and stand at the altar with Pastor Hesselius. He is a tender-hearted man of noble and righteous conduct, but his seriousness, his age and ailments, and his strictly pious nature take away from me, who am young and giddy, all means of reciprocating his tenderness. *Ma chere confidante* knows furthermore that the picture of another now engages my heart. Think, the unknown black domino at the last masquerade was

[142]

none other than Major Stenfelt's son Gustaf,
newly returned from Paris. Oh, what a handsome agreeable man! The moment he opens his
mouth one expects to hear a thousand pleasant
turns of exquisite wit. Also he is in favor at
court and associates only with men of quality; but
mama, who is horribly strict, has forbidden him
to visit us, because she has heard that he is supposed to be a reckless youth, who will shortly
bring his old father to ruin, and no fitting society
for a young girl who in less than no time is to
be a staid parson's wife. But I trust not the
world's evil rumors. Is there, Ulrique dear, any
crime so mean as backbiting and slander?

En secret, though, I have had some communi-
cation with the charming cavalier. Last week he
was so gracious as to send me a delightful present,
consisting of a tortoise-shell snuff-box and a jar
of *pommade de Paris,* sovereign for the hair, and
yesterday evening he passed me in the corridor
when I came back from a promenade in the city.
Do you know what he said to me? *"Mon Dieu,
mademoiselle,* how fortunate I am to have met
you at last alone! Ah, you are too lovely!"
Whereupon I answered *en souriant,* "I have never
heard any one say such a thing before."—"Indeed! Then I felicitate myself on being the first
who has said it to you."—*"Badinage,* my kind sir,
badinage. Though, God be praised, I have no

deformity."—"Oh, *la belle modestie!* I swear that you are ravishing, and that I am consumedly in love with you. I shall be the happiest of mortals if you vouchsafe to call me your chosen knight."

Just as I was about to answer this, he had to vanish, because some one was coming, but before he went he slipped a billet-doux into my reticule. When I came in, I was all red and white at once, and my head went round. "What is the matter with you?" asked my ever-tender mama. I had to answer that I must have been in a draught and got a touch of lumbago, so that I had to go to bed. Then you can imagine how *mère* came to me with camphor and elder-tea, Trawenfelt's ague salve, and the whole family pharmacopoeia. There was nothing for it but to keep up a good appearance and take all the horrid medicine. The little sick-lamp was lighted, and there I lay under the bolsters and pillows and perspired. But hardly had *ma chere mère* gone to bed when who but I threw off the covers, took the letter from my pocket and read. Here's what was in it:

"My little Fair One!

"Since fate is unwilling to grant me the happiness of reaching you in peace and propriety, I am forced to seize my pen in order to let you know that you are my soul's goddess, and that I am de·

voured with longing to meet you once more. Let me hear soon after all this waiting that you too have a sensitive heart that will not let me go about pale and sad, the counterfeit of a continual sigh. My little enchantress, consider that time passes, and let us be glad while we are young. Soon you will be privileged to go to the bridal chair, and then it will be too late to think of love. Little nymph, be not cold to me, but let me soon bend the knee before you and orally protest with a thousand oaths that unto pallid death I love you."

My own Ulrique will understand into what unrest this letter threw me. How disturbed was my soul by the beautiful persuasiveness in these lines! But at the same time I trembled with the thought that Anne-Charlotte should diverge from the path of prudence, should cause a break, perhaps with tears of repentance quit her home, and fill with grief the heart of a mother who had surrounded me with unstinted love and solicitude ever since the tender years of a happy childhood. But, on the other side, what rapture to open one's heart to that charming and amiable youth, what an ideal existence to enjoy with him the pleasures of a life devoted to happiness! For why else should we live except to enjoy happy and pleasing emotions? Yet has the affianced bride of Pastor Hesselius any choice of her own?

Alas! my Ulrique, what a hard and icy thing is an old man's love. To share it is oneself to cross the threshold of age. As I write these lines, my heart is disturbed more and more. Tears mingle with the ink, and a sickness wastes my bosom, against which no remedy can help. My sweetest Ulrique, what shall your unhappy friend do? Virtue and Love struggle for her heart. Advise me and let me soon receive some precious lines from your hand.

Your little, most devoted
Anne-Charlotte

qui toute sa vie t'aime!

.   .   .   .

Letter from Lieutenant Gustaf Stenfelt to his friend, Freiherr Rutger von Düben.

Aug. 20, 1779.

Mon cher ami!

A thousand thanks for my brother's kind invitation to picturesque Elfdala. Most surely it would be a pleasure to emigrate thither from the wearisome heat of the city, the more because my previous knowledge of the exquisite refinement in my friend's way of life assures me of the most agreeable combination of all the pleasures of country life. The wine cellar of the Dübens has won a deserved celebrity in both ancient and modern Sweden, and I fancy that the daughters

of the region under my brother's mild sceptre
have laid aside somewhat of their former Northern hardness in order to listen more favorably
to the solicitations of love. One might then
make good cheer, drink champagne, cosset one's
sweetheart, etc.! So when, despite all these
enjoyments, I send my regrets, my gracious
brother may know that I am once more bound
to the city by those ties of *qalanterie* and *amour*,
which my impressionable nature could never
withstand.

"*Mon Dieu,* smitten again with the tender passion!" I hear my beloved Düben exclaim. Yes,
mon ami, ever defenceless against the assault of
Venus. "And who is your goddess this time?"
A charming little *bourgeoise!* She first enflamed
my heart at the last masquerade. I was standing as a spectator of that endless rout of ridiculous scarecrows, meditating over the illusions
that self love enjoys under a mask. A little
puritan fancies that in the minuet he takes the
hand of a countess, and a chit from the suburbs
with hair *a la François* and jacket *a la Suedois*
imagines she is sitting knee to knee with a baron.
Everything at a masquerade is badinage and
repartee. Yes, these *fêtes* at the Pavilion are
really charming. Under the protection of our
incomparable King Gustaf, Lady Pleasure deigns
to visit in person our sullen and phlegmatic land.

In the midst of these reflections I suddenly caught sight of a beauty in a sky-blue domino, who surprised my glance with the full delight of a Juno. She was escorted by a little shepherdess in pink with a basket of straw and all the rustic accompaniments. I approached my domino, ventured a compliment—which was no-wise ill received—and after a few moments of badinage *a trois,* my domino and I went forth into the dance.

The whole evening afterwards I was the inseparable cavalier of the rogue in sky-blue, whose eyes shone mischievously through her mask, while her laughter rang like fresh music, and in the *anglaise* I pressed my arm tenderly about her waist. My brother knows that ladies, otherwise most bashful, will permit an embrace under the masque.

At midnight, when she took her departure, she gave me her shoulder-rosette as a souvenir of our *soirée* and bade me accompany her to her carriage with the little shepherdess. In vain I begged her in the tenderest manner to reveal her incognito or at least to appoint a rendezvous. But she was inflexible. Brother Düben may conceive my chagrin. Whereupon my charming sky-blue domino vanished without giving a hint of her name or her abode.

I paraded about the town for a week's time like a mad fellow in the hope of recovering a trace of the fair one, when a few days ago a lucky chance led my steps to the Djurgårdsbrunn. Whom should I see there but my *belle inconnue* with an elderly matron in a gigantic *roberonde*. Each of them drank her glass of the waters to cure the vapours and strengthen the nerves. I at once requested the good doctor, Archiater Hallman, by whose assistance I had myself benefited last winter in a quite different complaint, to present me. My dear friend may imagine my surprise when I heard that my domino of the masquerade was Anne-Charlotte, daughter of the rich silk merchant's widow Wolfram. She is betrothed to an original in the form of a parson named Hesselius, rich as Croesus, but miserly as a Jew and old as Methuselah. I made a deep reverence, expressed my enchantment at meeting once more my lady of the masquerade, and ventured at last to offer a cup of coffee or a glass of *persicot*. But Dame Wolfram—a plague on the old ape!—met me with a none too courteous refusal. It was impossible to persuade her even to take a few moments' relaxation in a grove in order to enjoy the beauties of nature. She turned her back on me and when I spoke of paying a call, answered that Mr. Stenfelt would not find any pleasure in her meagre home. But Anne-Charlotte simpered and smiled quite tenderly upon me. She resembled the goddess

Flora, clad as she was in flowered muslin with a tea-rose at the base of her throat, and she seemed not disinclined to receive the attention which your humble servant showed her.

At that instant I drew my mental plan of campaign, and when I got home I at once despatched my lackey, the rascal Claes, with a trifling present to my little fair one—one can always turn the heads of these small city maidens with Paris fashions. And a few days later, when my wily Claes spied that the old dragon had betaken herself off for an hour of gossip to appease the worthy curiosity of some neighboring dame, I presented myself and succeeded in having a tête-a-tête with *ma belle* Anne-Charlotte. I handed her a billet-doux of the naïve and tender sort, and soon, my brother, you shall see me sail with a fair wind past love's Cape of Good Hope. On with the voyage as fast as may be!

My dear friend now understands without further evasion why I must sacrifice the pleasure of sharing with him the rural solitude of Elfdala. My friend knows the lines written by one of the choicest pens of France, or shall I give him my own poor attempt to turn them into our crude Northern speech?

> *Use the moment ere it pass,*
> *Weave the flax that Venus lends you.*

[150]

Flax availeth naught, alas!
When the cold of winter ends you.
Weaving time is quickly o'er
And we weave no more, no more.

Adieu, my dear Düben! I enfold myself in
your friendship and remain
>> your faithful friend and servant
>>> Gustaf Stenfelt.

* * * * * *

Letter from Anne-Charlotte Wolfram to Ulrique
Haldin.

Sept. 2, 1779.

My charming Ulrique!

Let me thank you, my darling little Ulrique,
for your sweet letter, which I loved beyond everything, and I can never be grateful enough for
your faithful and generous sympathy. But alas!
all you write about youth and love, and all your
advice to poor Anne-Charlotte about breaking
her pledge and suffering all kinds of ennui rather
than marry Hesselius is no longer *a propos.*
On the contrary your Anne-Charlotte begs her
little friend most urgently to tear completely
from her memory the imprudent letters she sent
you these last weeks and to forget the adventure
of the masquerade, together with every thought
that a person who calls himself Gustaf Stenfelt
ever crossed your friend's path. That youth is

[151]

unworthy of being a subject of conversation between me and my Ulrique, and my heart hopes to have forgotten him as completely as the snow that fell last winter. Let this be sufficient, for I can write no more, and I know that neither will my Ulrique insist on being further enlightened on the subject.

Let me tell her instead that on Wednesday next I am to wed Pastor Hesselius. Wonder no more at this. A man full of honor and sincerity, though he may be old, is nevertheless a far better stay in life than these fawning and flighty Stockholm cavaliers, whose faith and vows are like the cobwebs that the slightest puff of wind tears asunder. Time, too, has its balm of patience, so that one may adapt oneself to everything, and a steadfast man's home is a happy refuge where one may peacefully cultivate kindly feelings, undisturbed by the deceit and wickedness of the world.

Soon, then, my precious Ulrique, your Anne-Charlotte will be no longer a pretty, wayward girl, but a married woman, the staid wife of an old, worthy, and esteemed clergyman. She will think no more of vanity and silliness but devote all her attention to her husband, her home and household duties, and not entertain her Ulrique with conversation about sentimental attachments and *billets-doux,* but talk about servants and "What do you pay for butter, Ulrique?" and "How much is milk?"

Perhaps, moreover, my little friend also, before she can imagine it, will go the same way to—as I pray the Lord—a most pleasantly suitable alliance. I wager that the son of the rich firm in Dantzig will be the happy man, and that my Ulrique, a sweet and charming little merchant's wife, will send as a Christmas present to her Anne-Charlotte a case of Dantzig cordial, Brunswick beer, and other delicacies. And if in those days, when many a lustrum has gone by, we should meet again, when we have both become quite old, wrinkled and sensible, we may smile together as we chat of our girlish memories and of a masquerade at the Pavilion, when I wore a sky-blue domino, and you were the daintiest of shepherdesses, and my Ulrique will take it upon her very gently to rally her old Anne-Charlotte about the unknown black domino for whom she cherished a little while such a tender passion.

When one is *triste,* one should console oneself and not burden others. I hope you have not gathered from the sense of my words that I am in despair; I only feel a little out of spirits. I should write much more to my Ulrique but for the bridal preparations, so I close with embracing

[153]

her in my thoughts. I pour a thousand tender sighs into your bosom and am with deepest affection

faithfully yours till death
Anne-Charlotte.

. . . .

Letter from Gustaf Stenfelt to Rutger von Düben.

Sept. 6, 1779.

My dearest Brother!

What a wild and incalculable venture is love! 'Twas but a week ago that I was approaching Cythera with the glad hope of seeing my wishes crowned with success, and to-day I sit and write to my dear friend, disconsolate as a Pantaloon. It was but Sunday last that I went expressly to St. Clara's to amuse myself with that original, Hesselius, who very devoutly expounded his text on "the ungodly, whose ways should be shunned;" and while he was exhorting in the sweat of his brow, I smiled to myself, humming a couplet from the last parody at the Humlegård:

The man ordained to win the cuckold's high degree
May shortly wear two horns as high again as he.

Thus did I hum, and to-day this same ridiculous personage with his liver-colored surtout and his droll bag-wig is to marry the object of my affection, the charming Anne-Charlotte, and may taste without encroachment those first delights of love which beckoned as the reward of my devotion. Ah, my dear friend, vouchsafe me a tear of sympathy!

But I must with better logic unfold for my brother the course of affairs and the miserable conclusion of my negotiations with *la petite* Wolfram. After my former letter all had gone ahead smoothly, and my little sweeting and I, in spite of Mother Wolfram's Argus eyes, had met several times and dallied right sportively together. Finally, after much hemming and hawing, I had persuaded her to take a clandestine carriage trip with Brother Düben's humble and happy servant. This excursion was to have taken place on Thursday, when the old dragon was occupied in another direction, and all Wednesday evening I stayed at home and enjoyed my *far niente* in the prospective enjoyment of what was to come, devising all manner of compliments and *finesses* to whisper in my fair one's ear during the ride. I was just reaching the climax of my happiness, for my brother well knows from his own experience how delightful it is to be one of a pair in a snug *vis-a-vis* coach.

But while I was philosophizing on my sofa like a not unworthy disciple of the blessed Epicurus, who should come in to disturb my amorous fancy but our brother, that devil's fool of a Liliecreutz? He pirouetted in as if he had on a lace hood, stuck out his enormous buckles *d'Artois,* and said as solemnly as a *maître de cérémonie* in the royal presence:

"Arise, O happy mortal! *La petite* Slottsberg awaits you below."

La petite Slottsberg?

Yes, the absurd Liliecreutz, who some evenings ago in the wings had seen me show this priestess of Terpsichore a somewhat extraordinary attention—I was praising her incomparable *pas de rigaudon* in Alceste—had prepared me the surprise of engaging her for supper with me at Lilieholm in company with himself and his goddess, Madame Augusti.

"Go to the devil!" exclaimed I, and firmly declined. But Liliecreutz was inflexible—in the end I had to go along to Lilieholm, but with a dark foreboding of ill. Soon, however, I was put into good humor by several bottles of Hermitage, little Slottsberg had a thousand allurements, and before long we were lost in intimate conversation. But think, *mon cher ami,* for that tender moment my evil fate had been saving a thunderbolt! Just as I was arranging the little darling's somewhat disordered *coiffure,* in came by mistake a company of ladies and gentlemen who were gathering in our room for a middle-class picnic, and my brother may conceive of my desperation when I recognized among them my Anne-Charlotte! The intruders hastened out, but I blushed and paled alternately over the fatal accident. Without an adieu, and continually cursing my grudged favor to the little Slottsberg, I hastened off, divining that I had spent in vain my efforts for the, at that instant, doubly desirable Anne-Charlotte.

Quite correct. Next day I go with my carriage to the place appointed for our rendezvous. No Anne Charlotte appears. I write her a humble and flattering letter. My epistle is returned with the seal unbroken. Finally I send Claes, who has made acquaintance with the family's *femme de chambre,* to explore the situation. He relates that there were scenes of fainting, weeping, and despair. The poor little fool had made a general confession of her sins to her mother, was soundly scolded and admonished; whereupon her fiancé, the ancient Abraham, was sent for, who with great unction declaimed to the little wretch some pages on biblical femininity. The wedding was appointed for to-day, and at this very moment, alas! *mon cher ami,* all is over. Hymen has snatched from me my charming lady of the sky-blue domino. I have already heard the night watchman cry eleven, and in the par-

[157]

sonage of St. Clara's church a sportive cupid has drawn the curtain of my goddess's tent. Sighing and with mournful voice I exclaim, "Adieu, adieu, my Anne-Charlotte! Adieu, O baskets, the vintage has been gathered!"

But you, my Pylades, leave your shady Tusculum to embrace a friend who seeks consolation in the bosom of friendship for the mockeries of inconstant love. Your Selinda has already been asking after you, as she trips in black shoes with white heels at Maia Lisa's coffee-house. Haste to the city! May our names resound in unison through the alcoves over midnight supper-tables, and let us moisten with the gracious juice of Bacchus our much too melancholy parchments!

O my pattern of Friendship, hasten hither to embrace

its faithful worshipper
Gustaf Stenfelt

SELMA LAGERLÖF

THE LEGEND OF THE CHRISTMAS ROSE

SELMA LAGERLÖF (1858–) in her autobiographical book *Mårbacka,* has described the influences that stimulated her first literary effort. The hospitable Lagerlöf home was not only a social centre for the "quality" in Värmland, but a refuge for the decrepit cavaliers that the region seemed to abound in. It was their tales, heard as a child, that became transformed and lifted up in her imagination and grew into *The Saga of Gösta Berling,* a book consisting of a series of episodes bound together by the character of the charming, shiftless hero.

A very different background is that of *Jerusalem,* which tells of a religious revival that swept over a parish in Dalecarlia. In the struggle between spiritual longing and the honorable ambitions bound up with inherited land, the soul of the Northern peasant has perhaps been more intimately revealed than in any other Swedish book.

In *The Wonderful Adventures of Nils* Miss Lagerlöf described Sweden as seen by a little boy who was changed into an elf and rode on the back of a goose. Written primarily for school use, the book has had a phenomenally wide distribution, not least in the United States, where it has done a great deal to. stimulate interest in Sweden. The novel *Liljecrona's Home* is a return to the scenes of *Gösta Berling. The Emperor of Portugallia* is a story of Värmland peasants, and is considered by many her most finished book. Miss Lagerlöf excels in the legend, where she can give free play to her imagination and find full expression for the spiritual fervor that moves her.

Selma Lagerlöf was the first Swedish author to receive the Nobel prize for literature, and is the only woman member of the Swedish Academy. Her works have been translated into almost all European languages.

Selma Lagerlöf

The Legend of the Christmas Rose

ROBBER MOTHER, who lived in the robbers' cave in Göinge Forest, went down to the village one day on a begging tour. Father Robber himself was an outlawed man, and dared not leave the forest; he could only plunder wayfarers who ventured within the borders of the wood. But in those days travellers were not very plentiful in northern Skåne, and if the husband had had a few weeks of bad luck, the wife would take to the road. Her five children in their ragged buckskin tunics and birch-bark shoes —each child with a bag on his back as long as himself—always accompanied her. When Robber Mother stepped inside the door of a cottage, nobody dared refuse her anything she demanded —for she was not above coming back in the night and setting fire to a house where she had not been well received. Robber Mother and her brats were worse than a pack of wolves, and many a man felt tempted to run a spear through them. But everyone knew, of course, that the husband was back in the forest, and that he would take revenge, were anything to happen to his wife or his children.

Now that Robber Mother went from place to place begging, she appeared one day at Övid, which was then a monastery. She rang the bell and asked for food. The watchman opened a small wicket in the gate and handed her out six round loaves of bread, one for herself and one for each of the five children. While the mother stood quietly at the gate, the youngsters were running about. And now one of them came and pulled at her skirt, which meant that he had found something which she should come and see, and she went at once.

The monastery was enclosed by a high, strong wall, and the youngster had discovered a narrow back gate that stood ajar. Robber Mother pushed the gate wide-open and walked in, as was her custom, without asking leave.

Övid Monastery was under the priorship of Abbot Hans, who was a collector of herbs. Just inside the cloister wall he had planted a little herb garden, and it was into this the woman had forced her way.

Robber Mother was so astonished at first that she paused for a moment and only looked. It was high summer, and the Abbot's garden was so full of bright flowers that her eyes were fairly dazzled by all the reds, blues, and yellows. But a smile of satisfaction overspread her features, as she walked down the narrow path between the many flower-beds.

A friar was at work in the garden, pulling up weeds. It was he who had left the gate half-open, that he might throw the couch grass and pigweed on the rubbish heap outside. When he saw Robber Mother in the garden and all her youngsters, he ran over to her and ordered her out. The beggar woman walked right on, now glancing at the stiff white lilies that spread before her feet, now at the climbing ivy that covered the cloister wall—and took no notice of the friar. He, thinking that she had not understood him, was about to take her by the arm and turn her round toward the gate when she gave him a look that made him draw back. She had been walking quite bent under the weight of her beggar's pack, but now she drew herself up to her full height, and said:

"I am Robber Mother of Göinge Forest, so touch me if you dare!"

It was obvious that she was as sure of being left in peace as if she had announced that she was the Queen of Denmark. All the same the friar dared to disturb her, though now that he knew who she was he tried to reason with her.

"You must know, Robber Mother, that this is a monastery, and that no woman is allowed within these walls. If you do not go away, the monks will be angry at me for leaving the gate open, and perhaps they may drive me out of the cloister and the garden."

But such prayers were wasted on Robber Mother. She continued her stroll among the flower-beds, looking at the hyssop with its magenta flowers, and at the honeysuckles with their rich clusters of deep orange.

The friar then saw nothing for it but to run to the cloister and call for help. He came back directly with two stalwart monks. Robber Mother realized that now they meant business! She planted her feet firmly in the path and began to shout in a strident voice all the awful things she would do to the monastery if she were not allowed to remain in the garden as long as she wished. The monks did not appear to be alarmed by her threats; they thought only of getting her out.

Of a sudden Robber Mother, with a wild shriek, threw herself upon the monks, clawing and biting at them. And so did all her children. The men soon found that she was too much for them, and went back for reinforcements.

They were running through the passage leading into the cloister, when they met Abbot Hans, hurrying out to see who was raising all this racket in the garden. They had to tell him that Robber Mother of Göinge Forest was in the garden, that they had not been able to drive her out and must call for assistance.

Abbot Hans rebuked the men for resorting to force and forbade their calling for help. He sent the two monks back to their work, and although he himself was a frail old man, he took with him only the friar.

When he came out, Robber Mother was still walking about among the flower-beds, and he could not help regarding her with admiration and wonder. He was quite certain that she had never seen an herb garden before, yet she sauntered leisurely between the many beds, each of which had its own species of rare plant, and looked at them as if they were old acquaintances; at some she smiled, at others she shook her head.

Now the Abbot loved his garden as much as he could love anything that was earthly and perishable. Savage and terrible as the intruder looked, he could not help liking her for having fought with three monks for the privilege of viewing his garden in peace. He went up to her and asked her meekly whether she was pleased with the garden.

Robber Mother turned upon Abbot Hans defiantly, expecting to be trapped and overpowered; but when she saw his white hair and frail, bent form, she answered quietly:

[165]

"I thought at first that I had never seen a more beautiful garden, but now I see that it can't be compared with the one I know."

Abbot Hans had expected quite a different answer. So, when Robber Mother declared she had seen a garden more beautiful than his, it brought a faint flush to his wizened cheek. The friar, who was standing close by, began to admonish the woman.

"This is Abbot Hans," he said, "who has collected from far and near, with the utmost care and diligence, the herbs you see in his garden. We all know there is not a finer garden to be found in all Skåneland, and it is not for you who live in the wild forest the whole year round to pass judgment on his work."

"I've no wish to set myself up as a judge of either him or you," said Robber Mother. "I am only saying that if you could see the garden I'm thinking of, you'd uproot all the flowers planted here and cast them out as weeds."

The Abbot's assistant was hardly less proud of the flowers than the Abbot himself, and he said with a scornful laugh:

"It must be a grand garden you have made for yourself among the pines of Göinge Forest! I'll wager my soul's salvation that you have never been inside the walls of an herb garden before."

[166]

Robber Mother went crimson with wrath to think that her word was doubted. "It may be true," she said, "that until to-day I was never inside the walls of an herb garden. But you monks, who are holy men, must know that every year on Christmas Eve the Göinge Forest is transformed into a pleasure garden, to celebrate the birth night of our Lord. We who live in the forest have witnessed this miracle every year. And in that garden I have seen flowers so lovely that I did not dare so much as to put out a hand to pluck them."

The friar wanted to retort, but Abbot Hans motioned to him to keep silent. For, from his early childhood, the Abbot had heard tell how on every Christmas Eve the forest clothed itself in festal verdure. He had always longed to see it, but had never had the pleasure. And now he begged Robber Mother fervently to let him come up to the robbers' cave on Christmas Eve. If she would only send one of her children to show him the way, he would ride thither alone, and he would never betray her or hers. On the contrary, he would reward them to the full extent of his power.

Robber Mother refused at first, for she was thinking of Robber Father and the harm that might befall him were she to permit Abbot Hans to visit their cave; but her desire to prove to the monk that the garden she knew was more beautiful than his prevailed, and she finally assented.

"But you cannot take with you more than one person, and you are not to waylay us or trap us, on your word as a holy man."

Abbot Hans gave his word, and Robber Mother went her way. The Abbot then commanded the friar not to reveal to a living soul that which had just been arranged. He was afraid that his monks, if they heard of it, would never allow a man so advanced in years to ride up to the robbers' cave.

Nor did the Abbot himself intend to speak of his project to any one. But it so happened that Archbishop Absalon of Lund came one day to Övid and stayed over night. While Abbot Hans was showing the Bishop his garden, he got to thinking of Robber Mother's visit, and the friar, who was at work in the garden, heard the Abbot tell the Bishop about Robber Father, who for many years had been an outlaw in the forest, and ask him for a letter of ransom for the man, that he might again lead an honest life in common with others. "As things are now," said the Abbot, "his children are growing up to be a worse menace than the Father himself, and you

Selma Lagerlöf

will soon have a whole band of robbers to deal
with up in the forest."

Archbishop Absalon replied that he could not
think of letting the wicked robber run loose on
the countryside among honest folk; it was best
for all that he stayed in his forest.

Then Abbot Hans waxed zealous, and told the
bishop about Göinge Forest, how every year at
Christmastide it arrayed itself in summer bloom
around the robbers' cave. "If these outlaws are
not too wicked to have revealed to them the glory
of God, surely they cannot be too bad for the
grace of mortals."

The Archbishop knew how to answer the Abbot. "This much I can promise you, Abbot
Hans," he said with a smile, "any day that you
send me a blossom from the Christmas garden
at Göinge Forest, I will give you letters of ransom for all the robbers you may choose to plead
for."

The friar understood that Archbishop Absalon
no more believed this story of Robber Mother's
than he himself did. But Abbot Hans had no
such thought; he thanked the Archbishop for his
kind promise, and said that he would surely send
him the flower.

. . . .

It was Christmas Eve, and Abbot Hans was on

his way to Göinge Forest. Before him ran one of Robber Mother's wild youngsters, and behind him rode the friar who had talked with Robber Mother in the herb garden.

Abbot Hans had looked forward to this journey with longing, and was very happy now that it had come about. With the friar, however, it was quite a different matter. He loved Abbot Hans devotedly and would have been loath to let another attend and guard him; but he did not think they would see any Christmas garden. To his mind, the whole thing was a snare, cunningly laid by Robber Mother, to get Abbot Hans into the clutches of her husband.

As the Abbot rode northward toward the forest, he saw everywhere preparations for the celebration of Christmas. On every farm fires were burning in the bath-house to warm it for the afternoon bathing. Great quantities of bread and meat were being carried from the larders to the houses, and from the byres came the men with big sheaves of straw to be strewn over the floors. At each little church along the way the priest, with the help of his sexton, was decorating his sanctuary. And when he came to the road leading to Bossjö Cloister he saw the poor of the parish coming with armfuls of bread and with long candles which they had received at the cloister gate.

The sight of all these Christmas preparations made the Abbot the more eager to reach the forest; for he was thinking of the festival in store for him, which was so much greater than any that others would be permitted to enjoy.

But the friar fretted and complained, as he saw how at every lowly cabin they were preparing to celebrate Christmas. He became more and more apprehensive of danger, and begged and implored Abbot Hans to turn back, and not throw himself into the hands of the robber.

Abbot Hans rode on, paying no heed to the friar's lamentations. The open country was at last behind him, and he rode into a wild and desolate region, where the road was only a rocky, burr-grown path, with neither bridge nor plank to help them over brook and river. The farther they rode, the colder it grew, and after a while they came upon snow-covered ground.

It was a long and hazardous ride. They climbed steep, slippery by-paths, crossed marshes and swamps, and pushed their way through windfalls and brambles. Just as daylight was waning, the robber boy led them across a woodland meadow, skirted by tall fir trees and denuded leaf trees. Just beyond the meadow rose a mountain wall, in which there was a door made of thick pine boards.

Abbot Hans, understanding that they had arrived, dismounted. As the child opened the heavy door for him, he found himself looking into a poor mountain grotto with only bare stone walls. Robber Mother was sitting by a log fire that burned in the middle of the floor. Along the walls were beds of spruce-fir and moss, and on one of the beds lay Robber Father, asleep.

"Come in, you out there!" Robber Mother shouted without rising. "And fetch the horses in with you, so they won't freeze to death in the cold night air."

Abbot Hans bravely walked into the cave, the friar following. Here were wretchedness and poverty! Nothing had been done to celebrate Christmas. Robber Mother had neither brewed nor baked. Nor had she washed or scoured. The children sprawled on the bare floor around a kettle, from which they were eating. The only fare provided them was a thin water-gruel.

Robber Mother now said in a tone as haughty and dictatorial as that of any well-to-do peasant woman:

"Sit down by the fire and warm yourself, Abbot Hans. If you've any food with you, eat; for the food we prepare in the forest I don't think you'd care to taste. And if you feel tired after your long ride, you can lie down on one of these beds, and rest. There's no fear of your oversleeping, for I'm sitting here by the fire, keeping watch.

I'll wake you in time to see what you've come here to see."

Abbot Hans opened his food bag, but he was too fatigued to eat, and as soon as he had stretched out on the bed, he fell asleep.

The friar had also been given a bed to rest on. But he thought he had better keep an eye on Father Robber, lest he should jump up and try to bind Abbot Hans. However, he too was so exhausted that after a little he dropped into a doze.

When he awoke, Abbot Hans was sitting by the fire, talking with Robber Mother. The outlaw, a tall, thin man, with a sluggish and gloomy appearance, also sat by the fire. He had his back turned toward the Abbot as if he were not listening to the conversation.

Abbot Hans was telling Robber Mother about all the Christmas preparations he had seen on the journey, and reminding her of jolly feasts and Christmas games in which she had participated in her youth, when she lived at peace with mankind.

"I am sorry for your children," he said, "who can never run on the village street in fantastic array, or tumble about in the Christmas straw."

Robber Mother at first made short, gruff replies; but after a little she became rather subdued, and listened intently. Suddenly Robber

Father turned round and shook his clenched fist in the Abbot's face.

"You miserable monk!" he cried. "Did you come here to lure away my wife and children? Don't you know that I'm an outlawed man, and cannot leave the forest?"

Abbot Hans, unafraid, looked him straight in the eyes. "I propose to obtain a letter of ransom for you from Archbishop Absalon," he said.

Whereupon the outlaw and his wife burst out laughing. They knew well enough the kind of mercy a forest robber could expect from Bishop Absalon!

"Oh," said Robber Father, "if I get a letter of ransom from Absalon, I'll promise never again to steal so much as a goose."

The friar was indignant at their daring to laugh at Abbot Hans. Otherwise he was well pleased. Never had he seen the Abbot sitting more tranquil and meek with his own monks at Övid than he now sat with these robber folk.

Of a sudden, Robber Mother arose. "You sit here talking, Abbot Hans," she said, "so that we are forgetting to look at the forest. I can hear, even in this cave, that the Christmas bells are ringing."

And now they all jumped up and ran out. It was still black night in the forest and raw winter weather. They saw nothing, but they heard a distant chime, borne hither on a light south wind.

"How can this bell-ringing ever awaken the sleeping forest?" Abbot Hans wondered. For now, as he stood outside in the dark of winter, it seemed far less likely to him that a summer garden could bloom here than it had seemed before.

The chimes had pealed but a few seconds, when a wave of light broke upon the forest; it was gone in a moment, and then suddenly returned. Now it came floating through the dark trees like a luminous mist, and the night was merged in a faint daybreak.

Abbot Hans noted that the snow had disappeared from the ground, as if some one had removed a carpet, and that the earth was turning green. The ferns shot up through the soil, their fronds curling like a bishop's staff; the heather growing on the hill and the bog-myrtle rooted in the marsh quickly put on fresh green. The moss-tufts expanded and rose, and the spring flowers came out with swelling buds, which already had a touch of color.

Abbot Hans' heart beat fast at the first signs of the awakening of the forest. "Shall I, old man that I am, behold so great a miracle?" he mused, the tears springing to his eyes.

Then it grew so hazy that he feared the night darkness would again prevail; but immediately there came a new rush of light, which brought with it the murmur of brooks and the roar of water-falls. And now the trees put out their leaves so rapidly it looked as if millions of green butterflies had flown up and settled on the branches. It was not only trees and plants that had awakened, but grossbeaks hopped from branch to branch and woodpeckers hammered on the boughs till the splinters flew about them. A flock of starlings on the wing alighted in a spruce top to rest, and every time the birds moved, the bright red tips of their feathers glittered like precious jewels.

It darkened again for a moment, and again came a new light-wave. A warm, fresh south wind came up and scattered over the forest meadow all the little seeds brought from southern lands by birds and ships and winds. These seeds took root and sprouted the moment they touched the earth.

The next warm wave ripened the blueberries and whortleberries. Cranes and wild geese came shrieking their calls; bulfinches began building their nests, and squirrels played in the trees.

Everything went so swiftly now that Abbot Hans had no time to meditate on the wonder of the miracle that was taking place. He could only use his eyes and ears.

The wave of light that now came rolling in brought the scent of newly plowed fields, and from far, far away were heard the voices of milk-maids coaxing their cows, and the tinkle of sheep bells. Pine trees and spruce trees were so thickly laden with small red cones they shone like crimson mantles. The berries on the juniper changed their color every second, and wood-flowers covered the ground till it was all white, blue, and yellow.

Abbot Hans bent down, broke off a wild-strawberry blossom, and as he straightened his body, the berry ripened in his hand. The mother fox came out of her lair with a big litter of black-legged young. She went over to Robber Mother and scratched at her skirt. Robber Mother leant down to her and praised her babies. The horned owl, who had just started out on his nightly hunt, blinded by the light, flew back to his ravine to perch until dark. The cock cuckoo crowed, and the hen cuckoo, with an egg in her bill, stole up into the nest of another bird.

Robber Mother's children sent up twittering cries of delight as they ate their fill of berries from the bushes, where they hung large as pine cones. One of the children played with a litter of baby hares; another raced with some young crows that had ventured down from the nest before their wings were quite ready for flying; a third picked up an adder from the ground and wound it round his neck and arm.

[177]

Robber Father stood out in the marsh eating cloudberries. When he looked up he saw a big black bear at his side. He broke off a willow twig and switched the bear on the nose.

"You keep to your own ground," he said; "this is my turf." The huge bear then turned and lumbered off in another direction.

And all the while new waves of light and warmth kept coming. The chatter of ducks could be heard from the wood-pond. Golden pollen from rye fields filled the air; and now came butterflies so big they looked like flying lilies. The beehive in a hollow oak was so full of honey, it oozed out and dripped down the stem. All the plants which had come up from seeds blown hither from foreign lands suddenly burst into bloom. The most gorgeous roses clambered up the side of the mountain in a race with the blackberry vines, and down in the meadow bloomed flowers large as a human face.

Abbot Hans thought of the flower he was to pluck for Archbishop Absalon, but each flower that came out was more beautiful than the last, and he wanted to pick for the Bishop the most beautiful flower in the garden.

Wave upon wave of light rolled in, until the sky became so dazzlingly bright that it fairly glittered. All the life and beauty and joy of summer smiled on Abbot Hans. He felt that the earth could hold no greater bliss than that which welled about him.

"I do not know what new glories another wave may bring," he said.

But there came more and more light; and now it seemed to Abbot Hans that it brought with it something from an infinite distance. He felt himself being enwrapped, as it were, by an atmosphere superterrestrial, and, trembling with awe, he awaited the approaching glories of Heaven.

There was a hush, a stillness in the forest. The birds were silent, the young foxes played no more, and the flowers stopped growing. The glory now drawing nigh was such as to make the heart stand still and the soul long to rise to the Eternal. From far, far away came faint strains of harp music and celestial song.

Abbot Hans folded his hands and went down upon his knees. His face shone with bliss. Never had he dreamed that in this life he was to taste the joys of Heaven and hear the angels sing Christmas carols!

But close by stood the friar who had come with the Abbot, and in his mind dark thoughts arose. "This cannot be a true miracle," he thought, "since it is revealed to criminals. It can never have come from God, but must have been sent hither by Satan. The powers of evil are bewitching us and compelling us to see that which has no existence."

Angel harps and angel voices sounded in the distance; but the friar believed that the spirits of Hell were approaching. "They would charm and seduce us," he sighed, "and we shall be bound and sold into perdition."

The angel hosts were now so near that Abbot Hans could see their shining forms through the trees. The friar saw them too, but he thought that behind all this wondrous beauty lay something malevolent. To him, it was the Devil who worked these wonders on the night of our Saviour's birth. He thought it was done only in order to delude poor human beings the more effectually and lay a snare for them.

All this time the birds had been circling round the head of Abbot Hans, and had let him take them in his hands. But the birds and animals were afraid of the friar; no bird perched on his shoulder, no snake played at his feet. There was a little forest dove who, seeing the angels draw near, took courage and flew down to the friar's shoulder and laid her head against his cheek. The friar, thinking the Adversary himself had come right upon him, to tempt and corrupt him, struck at the dove and cried in a loud voice, that reverberated through the whole forest:

[180]

"Get thee back to Hell, whence thou art come!"

Just then the angels were so near that the motion of their great wings fanned the face of Abbot Hans, and he bowed his head to the earth in reverent salutation. But the moment the friar uttered those words the singing stopped, and the holy visitors turned and fled. At the same time, the light and the warmth departed in unspeakable terror of the darkness and cold in a human heart. Black night descended upon the earth; the frost came, the plants shrivelled, the animals ran to cover, the roar of the rapids was hushed, the leaves fell off the trees with a rustling noise that sounded like a shower of rain.

Abbot Hans felt his heart—which had just been so full of bliss—contract with insufferable agony.

"I can never get over this," he thought, "that the angels of Heaven had been so near and were driven away; that they wanted to sing Christmas carols for me, and were put to flight!" He remembered the flower he had promised Bishop Absalon, and in the last moment he fumbled among the leaves and moss for a blossom. But he could feel the ground freezing beneath his fingers and the snow that came gliding over the earth. His heart gave him still further trouble; he tried to rise, and fell prostrate on the ground.

When the robber folk and the friar had groped

their way, in utter darkness, back to the cave, they missed Abbot Hans. They snatched brands from the fire and went out to search for him. . . . And they found him lying dead upon a blanket of snow.

The friar wept and wailed—for he knew that he had killed Abbot Hans by dashing from his lips the cup of happiness which he had been thirsting to drain to its last drop.

When Abbot Hans had been carried back to Övid the monks who took charge of his body noticed that the right hand was locked tightly around something which must have been grasped at the moment of death. And when they finally got the hand open they found that that which had been held in so firm a grip was a pair of white root-bulbs, which had been pulled up from the moss.

The friar who had accompanied Abbot Hans to the forest took the bulbs and planted them in the Abbot's garden. He nursed and guarded them the whole year, hoping to see a flower come up from them. He waited in vain through the spring, the summer, and the autumn; and when winter set in and all the leaves and flowers were dead, he ceased caring for them.

But when Christmas Eve came again it brought Abbot Hans so vividly before his mind that he went out into the garden to think of him. When he came to the spot where he had planted the bare root-bulbs, he saw that from them had sprung flourishing green stalks which bore beautiful flowers, with silvery white petals.

He called out all the monks at Övid, and when they beheld the plant that bloomed on Christmas Eve, when all the other plants were dead, they knew that this flower had indeed been plucked by Abbot Hans in the Christmas Garden at Göinge Forest.

The friar then asked for permission to take a few flowers to Archbishop Absalon. When he appeared before the Archbishop and gave him the flowers, he said:

"Abbot Hans sends you these; they are the flowers he promised to pluck for you in the Christmas Garden of Göinge Forest."

And when Archbishop Absalon saw the flowers which had sprung from the earth in darkest winter, and heard the message, he went pale as if he had met a ghost. He sat silent for a long moment, whereupon he said:

"Abbot Hans has faithfully kept his word, and I shall keep mine." He ordered a letter of ransom to be drawn up for the robber who had been outlawed and compelled to live in the forest from the days of his youth. He entrusted the letter to the friar, who left at once for the forest.

When the friar stepped into the robbers' cave on Christmas Day, Robber Father came toward him with axe uplifted.

"I'd like to hack you monks to pieces, many as you are!" he said. "It must be your fault that the forest was not dressed last night in Christmas bloom."

"The fault is mine alone," the friar replied, "and I am ready to die for it; but first I· must deliver a message from Abbot Hans." He drew forth the Archbishop's letter and told the outlaw that he was now a free man.

"Hereafter," he said, "you and your children shall play in the Christmas straw and celebrate your Christmas among men, as Abbot Hans wished to have you."

The robber stood there pale and speechless, but Robber Mother answered in his name:

"Abbot Hans has kept his promise, and Robber Father will keep his."

When the robber and his family left their cave, the friar moved into it; and there he lived all alone, in the solitude of the forest, in penance and prayer.

But Göinge Forest never again celebrated the natal hour of our Saviour, and of all its glory there remains to-day only the flower which Abbot Hans plucked. It has been named the Christmas

Rose. And every year at Yuletide it sends up from the mold its green stalks and white blossoms, as if it could never forget that it once grew in the great Christmas Garden.

PER HALLSTRÖM

A FLORENTINE FANTASY

PER HALLSTRÖM (1886–) has won distinction especially in the realm of the short story, which he has developed along simple, classic lines. He began his career as a scientist, and in his youth spent a few years in the United States as a chemist. From this period date some of the experiences that he used for his first collection of short stories, *Stray Birds,* dealing with more or less derelict human beings, and written in a realistic manner with a decidedly satiric bent in the humor. Hallström was one of the authors who felt the liberating effect of the romantic revival in the beginning of the 1890's, and his next volume of stories, *Purple,* showed even by its title that he had gone over to a more colorful, exotic style. He had by no means abandoned Swedish subjects, however, and his novel *An Old Tale* gives an exquisite picture of life in Sweden in the thirties of the nineteenth century. In *Thanatos* Hallström has collected a number of stories from different times and places, all variations on the theme of death, a subject that always fascinates him.

Hallström conceives of the short story as a condensed drama. He has also written plays, some of which have had considerable stage success. Among them *Bianco Capello* and *A Venetian Comedy* show Shakespearean influence. In the years since the beginning of the war he has written little of a creative nature, but has devoted himself to literary criticism and to translating Shakespeare. He is a member of the Swedish Academy and chairman of its committee for the Nobel awards.

Per Hallström

LEONZINO DA BELLOSGUARDO wandered around idly all the day, and at night on the terrace opposite his garden slept a light and tranquil sleep without dreams. Formerly he had been wont to work, carrying on his father's business of money-changer as the latter had decreed at his death. He sent Florentine gold to Venice and Bruges to put with it other gold, which in turn he coined; but when he found that the only object in this was to increase the wealth and cares which he already had, he gave it up. Instead, at great expense, he had a fountain built on the eminence where his villa stood. He watched the water rise in gleaming jets, then fall into the basin and run back into the well, whence his white oxen, slowly tramping around, forced it up to start again on the same journey. He rejoiced at the rainbow glitter as the drops were resolved into mist and at the delicate tinkle of water on water, so that he could think away long hours in front of it.

He had also gone to war against the enemies of his native city for honor's sake; but when he

[189]

realized that the chief quality of honor consisted in finding oneself stronger than one or another opponent, he became likewise weary of this, set his armor at dice against a comrade's dog, lost it, and went home. He did not even care to boast about the scar of a wound he had received on the cheek, but let his curling hair hang over his ears to hide it; and when this became also the fashion for those who had no wound, he smiled, but stayed as he was.

To pass the time he then addicted himself to love and after the manner of the day worshipped two famous beauties. In one of them, Monna Giulia—whom he had never spoken to and hardly seen except from a distance—he adored the complete perfection of his own ideal and the inventiveness of his own emotions, which found the most choice and beautiful words to celebrate her; and he held aloft the flame of his love to the clear sight and wonder of all, like a wax taper in a procession. With the other, Monna Monetta—whom also he had never rightly seen, because it was in the dusk that he had won her heart, and it was dark in the chamber where he met her —he tasted the kisses of sensual pleasure and enjoyed in the gray of morning the deep twitter of the lark which forced him to leave her. But when his best friend, Giacomo Calandra—in a moment of that enthusiasm kindled by friendship in all souls which know how to prize and play upon the golden strings of Plato—having just returned home from a journey, confided to him that he had enjoyed the favor of Monna Giulia, and read him a fine sestina which he had composed to his dawning adoration of Monna Monetta, Leonzino smiled and pressed his hand three times—in farewell to his two mistresses and to the friend himself.

After this Leonzino went about entirely alone, without the desire of occupying himself with anything.

One day he stood in the garden of his friend Gentile Buonacorsi, watching the latter direct his short, dark, and active peasants in the digging of a well, where two hillocks clad with great cypress trees intersected one another. As he beheld the rich brown earth turned up by spades and picks, it occurred to him from the bits of stone which were cast out that a small building had formerly stood there; an old heathen tomb, or a wall with a niche around a spring, which had been adorned with the statue of one of the early saints. He wondered what it was that made the soil so lustrous and soft: whether it was the water which had been spilled there, amid laughter, from the laden shoulders of girls; or whether it was tears or the ashes of the dead. He spoke with Gentile of this and evolved many beautiful and strange thoughts, as he followed out the line of similar possibilities. Thereupon a workman's pick, its violence partly arrested by the earth, struck against something hard, which rang sharply even at this light impact; something hollow, therefore deep down. Leonzino broke off his talk, and smilingly, but with a touch of curiosity, noted Gentile's eager instruction to the men that, without injuring it, they should fetch up the object—possibly a heavy mass of precious bronze or even something with coins in it. He stood there quietly until, with great difficulty, the mysterious thing had been dragged to the surface. It had the shape of a large urn, and when the earth had been scraped off by brown, worn fingers, it gleamed white—it was therefore only marble. Gentile had the urn placed at his feet, cautiously removed the lime and mouldered leaves that filled the neck, and felt about in it with a stick.

"There is nothing heavy in it," he said, "no coins, only something in the nature of light ashes." Therewith he turned away, disappointed.

" 'Tis the dust of cremated heathens, like enough," said the eldest of the peasants; "and such may bring misfortune. Let us break the whole to bits and strew the ashes to the wind!"

He had already raised his pick; but Leonzino, who fancied he could discern something like the contour of a human body under the earth, felt a sudden, inexplicable twinge of pity and solicitude, and sprang forward to check him.

"Have it at least cleaned off so that we can see what it looks like," he said to Gentile. "It seems to have figures carved on it, and there is beading around the rim."

Gentile felt inside it again with his stick. "It's nothing," he replied. "There are images of idols on them all." He thought it safest to have nothing to do with such things but to let the workmen do as their prudence dictated.

"Come, give the thing to me," commanded Leonzino with a continuous tremor of inexplicable solicitude. "Give it to me. I will give you in return whatever you want that is mine."

When his friend had agreed, he straightway caused water to be brought in a bucket. He then himself washed and cleaned the urn—while the others were digging at their well—until the marble, white and glittering with the moisture, sent out a radiant gleam like a pearl freed from its shell.

The mere labor had diverted him, and now that it was done he stepped back to look at the urn, in order to grasp in its entirety what he had only seen bit by bit. It was truly like a pearl, bright and delicate, despite its large and firm shape; its swelling breadth below the neck was lightly held aloft by the base, like a giant pearl poised on a wave, and the two handles reached up toward the decorated rim like slender lifted arms. There was something buoyant, as of a burden sportively sustained, in the whole. Around its form danced three women, young, with tranquil, serious countenance and flowing attire, which was swept back in rhythmic folds by their motion, not by the wind; their hair, too, fluttered backwards. There was in all this movement only the breeze of their own dancing, otherwise not a breath of air. A dead sky, a strange rigidity, was in the white curvature of the marble, as the supple outlines sank into and lost themselves in it. The faces of the girls, bent lightly back, were dull as if with the fumes of wine.

Leonzino had never seen or dreamt of anything of the kind. Walking around it again and again, he gazed at his treasure and was happier than he had ever felt before. He would have to have it up at Bellosguardo directly and there gaze and gaze at it his whole life long, he thought.

He despatched an order to his people to loose the white oxen that labored at the fountain, set on their best purple-painted yoke, and harness them to the finest wagon to fetch home his urn; and while he waited he busied himself with removing the smallest dimming traces of its age-long repose in the earth. The team arrived, he had the urn loaded upon it, and himself followed along beside to watch over it.

At the gate of Gentile's garden, where he caught a glimpse of the city and thought of all the people he would meet, he broke off long, bright branches of the fresh-leaved poplars and black cypress boughs, which he twined together into garlands for the horns of his oxen as they brought his trove back to the light from its realm of the dead. People stood still to look at him and laughed wonderingly, but he paid no heed to them.

The road passed between walls with bluish leaves of grape-vines on the edge beneath the trembling blue of the heavens. The oxen dragged their hoofs deliberately out of the moist earth and stood still in the brooklets to rest, slowly turning their garlanded heads. Whenever they halted, Leonzino stood by them patiently, enchanted with his white urn and the play of the warm sunlight over the dancing girls. As he came higher up, he saw the bell-towers of Florence between the cypresses and peaks behind. Yet higher, and the plain was open; Arno burned in the sun with the bright city around it, enclasped in blue hills to which the olive foliage gave a glimmer of silver and the humid air a pearly radiance as they receded into the distance.

Leonzino had never seen his city thus and had

never loved it as now. There was a bloom like the transitory beauty of flowers upon it, and when he thought of the churches that had taken long generations to build—one gable, one doorway at a time with their lacy ornamentation—which had ripened their color in sun and wind, then faded before the next were completed—they seemed to him like groves and thickets of giant trees, whose destiny it was to shoot up, spread, and die above the roots of their fellows in eternal change and evanescence. But for the men who moved about—laboring, quarreling, hoping—among these blossoming ruins he felt a compassionate love; and it seemed to him that he was departing from them forever with his strange white treasure, which had in it release from all things, freedom from all things.

He was now near his home and saw to the right Mont' Oliveto with the circle of slender cypresses around its rim and other cypresses in the middle, which gently bowed their black crests together beneath the murmur of the breeze. It was like the very throne of death; he knew that in the meadow-grass grew pale yellow irises, the tops of whose flowers shaded into an earthen black. As he passed on and on around the slope, the city seemed far away between the stone-like trunks and harsh whispering of the trees. But his way led still higher. There stood his white villa gleaming in the sunlight between the dark vines. There he was at home, in through that gateway; and he saw with fresh delight how charmingly his garden would smile with flowers and grass to greet the newcomer.

He had the urn set on a marble ledge under a blackish-green live oak so dense that no rain could press through its rustling foliage. He then lingered alone beside it, caressing it with his looks and his hands, while he longed to penetrate into its meaning, to hear the music of the maidens' dance, to feel the stone breathe against his breast. When he knew himself to be unseen, he kissed the delicate backward-leaning heads of the dancers, and, as if in pity of their chilly state, twisted blood-red climbing roses about them. It was wondrously beautiful to see the marble glimmer tawny-white between the purple shadows; it seemed as if the fragrance of the roses caused the intoxication in which the dance floated forward.

Leonzino dreamed long in this idle occupation; he was happy but tremulous with desire to come yet closer to the being whom the urn concealed in its nobly tranquil form, in the stony repose across which the petrified flutter of the reliefs was passing; he yearned to commune with the spirit hidden beneath the white dust of these ashes. He therefore took up a great glowing rose, kissed it, and let it fall into the urn.

But the rose was borne up again within a pearl-white mist. The mist billowed around it like smoke from a pyre upon which great drops of rain have fallen; billowed in time with the dance of the three maidens, folded itself together like a great white flower at evening, and took form. It was a young and slender female figure, poising with naked feet on the beading around the neck of the urn. In the breast glowed the rose in the place of the heart, which was covered by the white folds of a chiton; the arms were held up towards the temples, like those of a child that has not yet fully awakened from sleep. The hair fell on both sides over the beautiful contour of the head in smoothly waving lines across the ears, being held together in a soft knot above the neck. The forehead was wondrously calm, the mouth calm and happy, and the closed eyes seemed to have been kissed into repose amid the whirl of the dance. The chin, with the delicate line of the cheeks, was raised, while the head leaned lightly back. As the fingers of a slender hand glow transparent red before the flame they shelter from the wind, so the limbs of this figure trembled with the red perfume of the rose heart, taking the hue of life, but somewhat paler. The eyes opened in a deep, dark glance, the hands fell and were clasped over the bosom, the lips moved, and there was audible a voice with a soft ring like the drip of water on water, the sigh of fresh poplar leaves, and the chill rustle of cypresses and live oaks.

"I was far, far hence," she said; "but your warm rose has summoned me hither. What is the wish of him who has twined life and beauty around my tomb?"

Leonzino stretched out both his arms toward her. "You, you," he answered dizzily, while he felt himself shiver in a sort of numb delight, "your love! You are what I have always longed for. Be your name what it may, happiness or death; your love it is I desire, nothing else."

She smiled sadly. "That you cannot have," she answered, "because I am dead; far from here I repose in eternal sleep. But since you have drawn my shadow from the world of shades where soft, gentle winds bore it about, a leaf among leaves, since you have brought its form into the light of day and caused it to tremble with the red perfume of the past, speak to me before the petals of the rose have withered and shrunken; speak to me, and I will answer you!"

"Who are you, who are you? I would know your inmost being."

Her glance became dreamy and remote, and

she answered softly, so that each tone sank slowly and died away in the rise of the next: "I had once a name as others have, which said of me what I was not. Now I am earth in the earth, light in the light. The voice that you hear is not my own but an echo of the dead winds of all time; of the dead voices of all time. I lived——" She became silent in a dream even more remote, and only her lips moved unconsciously.

"And you were happy?"

She found voice again and seemed to listen wonderingly to her own words: "Yes, I think so; it was called being happy. I died young. I hoped and looked forward, and what I looked forward to never came, because when it came it was already past and whispered behind my ear. Then, too, I often dreamed back, when the twilight fell, deep green and limpid, as it will soon do again, and the magnolia petals sank like dead white butterflies in the dusk. All my days seemed precious to me then; all was fair."

"And did you never act, did you never truly *live?*"

"Act? Ah, yes, often, much. Something impelled me, now hither, now thither; I called it my will. There were many voices within me, but one of them was the strongest and overmastered the other as the great wave, swelling, stifles the small; but whether this voice was mine more than the others, how shall I tell? I knew love, I knew hate, and I ruled over many. Love and hate grew into deeds, but they glided out of my hands like bursting bubbles, and with their bursting I no longer understood them. Men believed that they possessed me, and I thought myself happy in this, was kindled with desire and hope, and smiled at memory, while the twilight fell over the red poppies. In the end I had only the desire to rest in this ancient urn beneath my feet, which I had by me in the sunlight of my garden, gazing upon it till my thoughts grew numb and I slumbered in the shadow of the arcade, lulled to sleep by the ripple of running water. Once I fell asleep in grievous pain. I awoke and wrestled with the pain, and it vanished in my bosom and I with it. Then they laid my young rigid body on a pyre, and it too was embraced and lifted on the red arms of the flames until it vanished; but the white dust that remained was bestowed to rest as I had commanded. Then even this was nothing to me, even this longed-for fate was past me in the very coming. But I had a dream. It seemed to me that yonder three maidens offered me their hands to draw me into their dance. I took them and stood as they did with fluttering hair and garments blown backwards, but I knew not whether I moved and circled about, or whether I was of stone as they were."

During these words, Leonzino's glance had taken on the same dreamy depth that was in hers. "These maidens," he said, "what are they, what is the meaning of their dance? Why do you wish to repose within their circle?"

"Because they encompass all things. Invisible they dance around us all our life, inaudible their footsteps float; their garments fan coldly about your hands, their fluttering hair grazes past your cheek. They are the Hours, they dance the dance of Time. I often used to lie still a long time watching their motion with half-closed eyes, but when I looked at them full, they stood still. And I would ponder: Time, time, what is it? Does it sink behind us or fly away, when it has breathed coldly on our mouths? We travel on a ship; what is it that bears us on? The sails are swelled, the wave roars beneath us and subsides—now a new wave rises; it gives forth the same sound. Time is the wind which sighs over our head; but the ship, does it move on in the same way? Does it not stand quite still, while we believe that we go on only because the foam glides past? Do we live, do we die, or is all an illusion which we dream amid the sighing around our hair? The present is destroyed by fear—by anxiety over what may

come—or by hope; but hope that strains ahead
is itself unrestful. Only the past is completely
lovely and great and tranquil in its sadness. Look
at the maidens there on the marble, and you will
perceive the rhythm of their steps, but their feet
do not move, their garments do not fall, their
hair is ever the same—they are the hours of the
past, the restlessness that has become fixed in
noble tranquillity."

Leonzino shivered slightly as in a morning
dream, when the hour of dawn would send forth
a chilly caress, pure and scentless, from the tepid
summer night, almost awakening him, so that his
trembling eyes nearly opened with the paling
gleam of the stars.

"And do you now have that noble tranquillity,
and are you content with it? Do you lack nothing, regret nothing?"

She looked at him, smiling a gentle and pallid
smile.

He stood leaning slightly forward in a posture
of beseeching tenderness, his hands outstretched,
his glance lifted; his attitude that of a youth who
sees gliding from his clasp a happiness which has
never been his, which he knows he has never been
worthy to possess, a life he has wished to live,
a sorrow with which he fain would have struggled.
On his silken robe of pomegranate red the light
glowed warmly, so that the very shadows in its

folds were luminous, and his bronze complexion gleamed like amber under his long curled locks.

She answered, "You have given me again the shadow of life and with it the shadow of desire, the shadow of unrest. When death comes to me again, as it soon will, it will give me the shadow of pain—I feel it already in my flower heart.

"Yes, there is a something I lack, something I regret. When I see you there so beautiful, I can almost remember how it was to love, to feel one's being melt into something other than itself, to be mysteriously enfolded in something. That only could give me fulness of joy. I did not gather enough, for I was weary and blind, and there was much that my love could not attain to. Now at times I dream of the things I could not make mine: of every sun that bled to death without the caress of my glance, of every life that I passed dumbly by, every song I did not sing. And, feeling myself beggared, I am chill with the emptiness of my being. Far warmer might I have made the bed about me, far wider might I have stretched my arms and my glance. I might have been far greater. Only so can one gather happiness from the past, only so can one attain to the fairest repose.

"The rose's perfume will soon be over; it's heart already beats more softly. Speak, what would you more?"

Per Hallström

Leonzino stretched out his arms in agony and cried with a mighty voice, "You, you, I would have your love! Your words chill me, but your beauty glows and kindles. I have never before known what beauty was. You I would have in my embrace."

Her look became mournfully gentle but shone more brightly than before, her breast heaved, her hands closed more tightly about the rose as if to guard the last ember of its flame.

"But me you have, you have me now in your love. You clasp the form which the moment gave you while it was fair, you have twined roses about the fixity of the ever changeful in the ever beautiful. You have me already. Look yonder!"

As she spoke, she drew a circle before her with her white hand, and Leonzino turned and looked.

There lay Florence in the warm golden light which the day bestows just before it dies; Florence, lovelier than ever before, more flower-like than ever before. A trellis of thin clouds was across the sun, so that its rays were stretched like wide, trembling, resonant strings from the blue top of a mountain down over the valley, and between the dusky shimmer of the shadows gleamed the slender towers and smiling habitations of men. The hills wore sharply shining crests like billows ranged one above another with the night behind them; and on the fairest, the lofty ridge of Fiesole, the clear outlines of cypresses stood like black flames in the conflagration. All this was framed in the silver gray of the olives on the slope beneath and in the dark expanse of the live oak, which raised its vaulted roof above with metallic gleams on its hard, smooth leaves.

"Do you see," her voice grew ever softer in its dying cadence, "do you see? There lies my city, lovely as I was, living as I was, dreaming now, as the play of the shadows passes onward. Around it moves the dance of the Hours—do you not feel its breath? do you not see how the tree-tops are softly bending?—but it still lives on. It has the eternity of beauty. Cherish it, live its life, and you will not miss me. Sometime you will sleep as tranquilly as I within the circling dance of the white maidens, not one fold of whose fluttering garments ever subsides, nor do their tresses tremble in the breath of what is to come."

There was a beat as of a failing wing, a sigh in the air. When Leonzino turned to her, she was gone, and there remained only the pearl-white mist, melting transparently in the beginning of the afterglow. The rose lay on his own breast, clasped between his hands.

He kept hold of it and gazed upon it: the petals had fallen outward and grown limp, the two

largest giving it the form of a heart. It had perfume still, most faint but even more delicate and
caressing than before. Ever oftener and longer,
too, his glances dwelt on the city, now growing
darker in the fleeting twilight which shimmered
like depths of limpid green water, while the night
rolled in from the blue-black heights to westward.

"Dangers threaten it," he thought, "dangers
threaten all that lives. The present is an unceas-
ing strife in which I would take part in order that
I may also have my share in the lovely legend
of the past. What is it that keeps my city so
radiantly youthful in the sunlight, if it be not the
adoration of her many lovers? What is it es-
tablishes her, if not the stout hearts which must
be worn like flames upright in the breast? Only
that can make a man worthy to await the dance
of the Hours in beauty around his ashes."

He was still sitting there with the rose in his
hands, when night came with the moon, and the
scene below him became an indistinct ocean of
cold radiance and grandeur and dusky-black
shadow, through which the silver Arno glided
toward the sea.

PELLE MOLIN

MEN'S MEN

PELLE MOLIN (1864–96) was a young author whose career was cut short by an untimely death. His fame rests upon a single volume of short stories and sketches, collected after his death by Gustaf af Geijerstam and published, with a sympathetic preface, under the title *The Romance of Ådalen (Ådalens poesi)*. In spite of the slenderness of his production, Molin holds an enduring place in the estimation of the critics and the heart of the general reader.

Pelle Molin was the son of a peasant in the far north of Sweden, and he himself believed that he had a strain of either Gypsy or Lapp blood on his mother's side. He went to Stockholm to study art, but could not adapt himself to city life, and soon returned to his native valley, where, having broken with his family, he lived for four years alone in a cabin. Afterwards he crossed the border to Norway, and tried to maintain himself by writing newspaper accounts of the great winter fisheries and all the adventures connected with them.

There is a primeval savagery in everything Pelle Molin has written. He describes fighting and rough courtship as in *Men's Men,* or the struggle for supremacy between man and the king of the forest, as in *Bear-Solomon (En ringdans medan mor väntar).* He charmed his contemporaries by his revelation of primitive life in a region then new to literature, and by the humor and poetic feeling that softened the wildness.

Pelle Molin

MEN'S MEN

TWO red mountain hamlets stood opposite one another, each on its high bank, while down between them, with thunderous tumult of rapids and falls, the mighty black river flowed on its way to the sea.

Between the villages the river widened in a tranquil stretch, but above and below the current was white and foaming.

It is at the Boundary Rock that this story begins.

When the stream ran high, the Boundary Rock was nowhere near the surface of the water; but when it was low, the Rock would sometimes stick its black polished head out of the deep. Like all strong obstructions in a current it made a backwater below it.

In that region it was called the Bull. If neither the south wind brought the heavy hissing of the lower fall or the mountain wind the rush of the upper cataract, the rock would bellow on quiet and windless nights as the water went over it. From that it got its name.

Now, as everyone knows, a salmon likes to

rest in such places when he is tired of the current, and there he is easy to catch.

The peasants of the southern side had nets there, because the Boundary Rock defined their water rights; the northerners looked at them enviously and put out nets on their side, but caught nothing worth speaking of.

The head peasant of the southern side was called Zakris and got half of all that was taken. The head on the north was called Kerstop, and he assumed to himself the half of all the northerners' vexation. Every time he went down to his empty nets he pondered on effective devices to make the salmon go into the northern channel.

Late one summer night he rowed out in the half-light with a queer contraption in his boat. Now the Boundary Rock was so shaped that the upper edge was high and narrow. Below on the southern side was an indentation, and in it Kerstop set a water-wheel, made it fast, saw that it moved, and rowed back into the shadow of the bank.

Next day he stood behind a barn and watched the southerners draw their nets. Not a fish! "Haha!" says Kerstop. Next day the same: never a fin. "Well, well!" says Kerstop. He heard the fishermen summoning the Prince of Darkness. The third day he had his own nets out but waited to watch the others draw first.

Still nothing. "Why, confound the luck!" says Kerstop. He listened to the chorus of curses. Only when he had seen the last blue cotton blouse vanish behind the top of the bank did he row out and take from his own nets a pile of silvery salmon.

Up at Kerstop's place his son Olle sat pressing his little nose against the kitchen window and looking to the south. All his childish fancies went thither to the enchanted land on the other side of the gorge. Mornings, when his father's place was still in shadow, the southern mountains stood out in strong violet light, and the cabins with their quaint four-sided roofs burned purple. On midsummer evenings, when the sun declined, the farm just opposite was the last that kept the light. The sun glowed and sparkled. The windows glinted and shone like stars, and the light dwelt on the linen sleeves of the women who passed between their quarters and the summer houses with wooden dishes in their hands.

On such evenings father would come back with salmon on his shoulders and smile all over his big face so that Olle grew warm. Later in the summer father would not smile, he had got so used to catching salmon. In autumn he came home one evening with many colors on his face. Then father swore, and father and mother talked a great deal up in the attic room after they had gone to bed—more in one night than they had talked before in a year and a day. Olle heard it, almost all, but remembered only that the salmon were afraid of the wheel that moved with the water, and that the man who lived just opposite had brought many people with him and argued with father, so that father was sick afterwards.

From that time father went fishing no more, not even so much as to fetch his nets. He only fetched them when the snow fell about Martinmas—but when he came up through the gorge that trip his gait was slow, for revengeful thoughts are a heavy burden.

Olle inherited the home from his father; he was the only son. His father's position as the foremost man north of the river he did not inherit before he had sowed his wild oats, and that took many years' time. Big he was as the biggest of them, and he it was—none other—who, blue-eyed and blond-haired, had driven a hungry bear from a torn cow with a handspike. That happened up at the dairy on Tanflo Heights and is God's truth.

Nature in the mountains here is grand and hard, the air transparent and brittle. If the sun is high, everything stands out so distinct that from leagues away one can count all the teeth on the ragged combs of the mountains; but on summer nights and mist-heavy days of autumn the grandeur may melt, grow warm, and then there is no country that grips and holds one's devotion like the mountains. Olle was tall as a river bank, his hair bright as the foam of the rapids, and a hard man to stop he was when he began to feel his strength. But neither could any one kindle another with the fresh fire of the heart as he could when he chose.

Wooing in this region is done as follows: a young fellow will visit his sweetheart on Saturday night and lie side by side with her fully dressed. So long as any one can remember, it has been so; father and mother, grandsire and grandmother, down into the past. There is no disgrace for him who knocks or for her who opens. The endless toil of the day leaves no time to run about and talk fine like gentlefolk; a peasant would soon be tired out with that sort of thing. Night conduces to intimacy. Lad and lass have everything to themselves, as they wish and ought to have, since wooing is not a matter for the public.

In this parish, north-of-the-river and south-of-the-river are two different regions. A lad seldom crosses the river for a sweetheart.

But Olle had his own ideas. One evening in late summer he went to the ferry cove, pushed out his boat, rowed across, climbed carefully up the steep bank to Zakris's place and rapped at

Imbär's window. That time he had to turn
back. A week later the same, but she went to
the window to see who it was. She didn't let
him in. The third time Olle had a pair of pincers and pulled out the window nails—at that she
opened the window and spoke sharply.

"It's a rough way you've got," said she.
"Aren't you ashamed of anything? You're a
fighter, you chew snuff, drink brandy, mislead girls
and—and—you can go away from here. Keep
north of the river!"

Next year at the same time, though, Imbär
was his. How it came about is too long to tell
here. He now came across every week, but what
he didn't know was that gossip crossed too.

One autumn evening he knocked.

Soft steps passed through the big cottage, the
kitchen door opened, the steps grew more cau-
tious as they reached the entry, but the outer door
swung in. The first thing he felt was not a kiss
but a burning blow in the face, and with that Zakris came out in his shirt. Zakris struck again,
so that Olle took a step backward. For a brief
moment he thought of Imbär, but the next his
eyes went red, and that night old Zakris was
thrashed within an inch of his life.

"You hated father," said Olle as he struck.
"You've hated me." And he struck again.
"Coward you were, you old booby, when you

destroyed father's nets. Will you admit it?"—
Smash!—"You were a cur when you called in a
crowd and shortened his life with your blows.
Here's interest for your money!"—Bang!—
"Here's rent for your farm!"—Biff!—"Bring
along your hirelings and kinsfolk!"—Slam!

But with that he thought of Imbär and that
now they would be further apart than ever—and
so he let the old man be and went off.

For long and long he did not cross again.

Neither did Imbär go to a dance. Olle saw
no more of Zakris and took to going about alone;
every one got out of his way. He tried to write
Imbär a letter, but couldn't bring himself to ask
any one to take it over. He felt an inward fire
which made him toss the harrow as if it were a
stick, or he would have a sinking at the heart and
would urge his horses with the plow so that they
almost ran.

One Saturday evening in late autumn he
brought in his steaming pair earlier than usual—
they had been hounded back and forth all day on
a new piece of land. Olle went into the house,
ate precisely nothing, and sat staring across the
river. With that he struck his fist on the table
and called for warm water. The old woman,
who had the same respect for him as for his father Kerstop, hastened to fetch it.

A while later she sat at the window with tears

in her eyes and a choke in her throat. Olle, new-shaven and in his best, went past the outhouses and vanished behind the big barn. The old woman sat waiting. A moment later she saw him rowing back and forth in his skiff, but she well knew it was not fishing for grayling that he had most in mind. Only when the darkness was thick as a wall did she go sighing to the fireplace and put on the coffee-pot.

The day after Olle did not leave his bed—he was dishevelled, shame-faced, and silent.

Out in the district there was much talk of that night's doings. Olle had been chastised, that was sure. He had been outnumbered. But it was an open secret that he had won no little honor in his overthrow. That went without saying. To defy such a hard-handed fellow as Zakris, to row up and down the river in his Sunday clothes and indicate where his thoughts and his journey were directed, and then to go straight to the place where everybody knew he meant to go! On the near side of the river they said it was Zakris and his men. On the other side they said that all the folk in the village had had sticks and cudgels with them when they went to Zakris in the evening and drank coffee with brandy in it. It was truth that Olle had been so packed in the crowd of his assailants that he had to beat his way out. Truth it was too that such many-colored, swollen heads and sore limbs had never been known at one time in Häxmo village.

The old woman once came out with some of the talk before her son, but she never did it again.

For many days Olle was not himself—it was as if he were sorry for something. His mother was bursting with the wish to talk to her son; but no, it seemed he had no ears for her, and she kept still.

Up in the clothes closet she saw one day that the best things were gone from Olle's hanger. Further on the hangers were thinned, and on thorough inspection she came upon a half-packed chest. She went there day after day, sat by the chest, and looked at it. With every garment her son packed, his mother laid in fervent prayers for his welfare, no matter where he should go; but she had little hope as things now were that happy days would return to the old place. As she wept there one evening when the chest was full, she heard the clatter of steps on the loose floor-boards and hastened to dry her tears. She would have run away, but a trembling came upon her, and her legs sank under her.

"Is it to America?" she stammered. Embarrassed at being caught in the act, Olle was standing still and gazing at her.

"No, so far it won't be. But—but look after the place for me, mother. I shall be long away, but home I'll come whatever happens. And now I'd like to say goodbye to you, mother; tomorrow I shall be off."

That evening he went about restlessly putting everything to rights. He patted every horse, talked to the pigs, called the chickens and gave them their corn; looked at everything as if it were for the last time.

It then occurred to him that the boat was not drawn up for the winter. That thought transfixed him to the spot. He began to burn inside, and without thinking what he did, went down the path through the valley. The boat was there, afloat and pretty. He was impelled to row— and, however it happened, he was over the river and stood before the house where Imbär lived.

That evening he and old Zakris met again. When the old man opened the door and saw who it was, he tried to abuse him but was so hoarse that hardly a syllable could be heard. Neither did Olle say anything: he is supposed to have simply shoved the old man aside and gone in. "I just want to say a couple of words to Imbär," he said.

The old man quickly caught up a poker and tried to bar him out. "If it's for your life, you shan't come in!"

That was their last tug of war. "I'm not going to hit you," Olle hissed to the old man, as he gripped him around the waist. Zakris dropped the poker and blocked him with clenched fists. Olle bent his head, lifted him as lightly as if he had been a mitten and carried him up and down with the idea of throwing him out in the yard, barring the door, and going in to the girl; but it was cold, and the old man was half naked. No one said a word. Zakris was too proud to cry for help. In the dark entry the old man's shirt rustled up to his armpits as he struggled to slide out of the other's grasp; his limbs cracked. He panted heavily, and now and then gave a bump against the wall when his foot struck out. The dog began to bark outside.

But now Olle was mad with pain. He felt the other's teeth biting deep into his shoulder. That made him furious. There was no longer any thought of sparing. He lifted Zakris again from the floor and fastened him in an iron grip. "You devil—you'll bite, will you?" Had it not been for Imbär and his mother, Olle would have been a murderer that night. But he grasped the old man so that he groaned, carried him about the entry for a good while, and finally brought him into the kitchen. There Zakris made a desperate effort so that his skin wrinkled where Olle held him. He got his knee against Olle's body. —"Oho! that's what you're after. It's a hell of a rascal you are, old fellow. But now I'm going to put you to bed." With that Zakris lay in the baking-trough, where the dough yielded and made room for him. "Lie there now!" hissed Olle, holding him down with one hand while he smeared him over with dough. "You shall have covers, you—and you shall have a footwarmer— your feet have got cold—and you shall have the covers over your head—and so at last you can have a good sleep."

With that he ran off.

Every one had gone to bed when Olle came home. He was not pleased with his last stroke. God knows why, but it hurt him that there always had to be violence in the course of his wooing.

He waked the stable-man, they harnessed up quietly, and in the dark of night drove off at full speed down to the highroad.

. . . .

Two summers' suns had parched the bluffs of the valley, and two winters' cold made bridges between the villages before Olle came home. After that came several quiet years, in which nothing happened that need concern us. Olle had been in some sort of school in the south. He went about sedately almost like an aristocrat; he even carried a cane on Sundays. In the town meeting he took the first place and voice, and soon had a large share in its proceedings. He brought in new voters who followed his leadership; new matters were put in motion, of which no one would have thought a few years back; and, however opposition might raise its angry head, he went on calmly and as a rule carried his point.

In the meetings and committees Olle and Zakris met. But they had met before that in the churchyard soon after Olle had come home. Do you know what happened in the churchyard just before service, when the peasants stood in a clump talking about the harvest?

Why Olle came forward, straight up to Zakris, as he stood in a circle of south-of-the-river men, stretched out his hand, and said with a wonderfully quiet and controlled voice, "Let what's past be as if it had never been, Zakris. I've been away and learned better conduct. I must beg your forgiveness. If I've been rough, you have too—and if two honest fellows strike hands together after they've struck each other's ears, they're both the better for it. That's what I think."

"You may kiss my ear," answered Zakris. As a matter of fact he said something else, but not of a sort that can be set in a printed book.

With that they separated.

After the encounter Zakris was against everything that Olle wanted, but was opposed in a quiet and conciliating manner. And when Zakris had a single good thing to say, Olle chimed in heartily at once and knew how to do it in such a way that the man got more credit than his idea.

Zakris was softened at heart, but outwardly never showed it by a hair. Olle might at any time have forced old Zakris from the few offices of honor in the mountain district, but declined everything, and always nominated the old man.

Of Imbär never a word was said. Neither did Olle row to the wooing in his skiff, but it was believed that letters passed between them.

Then came the big doings.

In the autumn the old Riksdag representative died, and a new one was to be chosen. As things were, no other district of the electorate could compete with this in good candidates. The greatest part were behind our two enemies. Zakris did his best to bark down his adversary; it's even supposed that he was the originator of the foul poster against his rival which was nailed up one night in many conspicuous places. In it the departed Kerstop was called a poacher and a thief, and Olle a housebreaker and disturber of the peace who ought not to be at large.

To this Olle answered in the local paper by resigning his candidacy. Not only that, he nominated Zakris Månsson. Not only that, he pointed out clearly and plainly a life of unusual achievement, a respect higher than any one else could claim, a spirit of integrity which few possessed, and all this was Zakris Månsson! And not only that, he had ballots printed—an unheard-of thing in the region—had his men go about distributing them, and on all the ballots in the finest letters stood the name of the old man.

In the middle of all this came winter unexpected. It was time for it to come, but the old saying was: no snow before election.

Zakris was sitting down by the cove, reading Olle's resignation in the paper and swearing at the river. Over he had come, but back he couldn't get.

The ice floated so close together that there was no hope of putting in an oar between the cakes. There had been an attempt to see whether the stream was better a couple of hundred yards further down, but only one lad had crossed alive, and he had blasphemed when the current brought him headlong into the Bull.

Olle was a little way off sawing wood. Sometimes he glanced out at the river, sometimes over at the old man. Finally he left the sawhorse and went over to speak to the ferryman, who likewise wished to cross over to his cottage.

It was then that the great event occurred.

"Ah," said Zakris, "You're keeping on at your wood."

"Y-yes."

"Hmhm."

Then there was a pause.

"Why won't you—why have you put this in the paper?"

"That appears in the explanation."

"Explanation—explanation?"

"Yes, the reason I give for my decision."

"Oh, hmhm."

Another pause.

"It's remarkable how the river runs. I've never seen the like. It doesn't look like I should get home to-day."

"You won't need to go if you'll spend the night with me."

"Are you crazy, man? That surely can't be—in this life."

"You are welcome—and no need for thanks. If you want to be square, you'll be forced to believe that."

"Hm, yes—mmm."

Zakris Månsson laid a pile of snuff behind his molar teeth and looked dubiously across the river. The ice was coming in a closer pack. The edges bumped more than ever. The green hissing blocks were polished rounder. The water flowed black between, but it was never visible. If the pieces swung so that there was a wider open space, a new skim would freeze between them. If this ice was forced together by fresh masses coming down later, it rose in angular shapes that stood straight up and glittered green.

Directly opposite stood Imbär, looking toward her father.

"You're a good rower, you Olle, as far as I know," said Zakris.

"You think so?"

"Any one who goes across the river after a freshet must be that. But it isn't always—to be sure—"

"Not always what?"

"It isn't always—autumn dusk and bright water—; it's—it's so that the river can stop a man sometimes too. Try it now! The lass is looking at you. I shan't stir a finger if you want to lie by her to-night. I'll look on as if it was none of my business."

"You're not thinking much what you say, Zakris. That girl I've given blows for, that girl I've taken blows for, and I'll strike again if you'd like to know it. He that comes between us comes between my two hands, and I'll never let him go with breath in his body."

"Between—between? For me, there's nothing between you but the river, and that's fine. You're good at rowing; row now! She's waiting."

"That's just what I'm going to do. Just that.

[227]

She's worth it and more too. But afterwards, if I don't—don't—. It's damned ugly."

"Hmhm, hmhm. I don't want to tempt you. It's right you should know that. But if you want to be a son-in-law in Häxmo, now's a good time— for the master is away."

Zakris had a look of I won't say what.

"All right," burst from Olle, and his eyes sparkled. "I'll row over, I'll row over this day. Straight off! But"—and he shook his fist in the old man's face—"if I get safe over, and you go back on your word, I'll—I will—I don't know what."

With that he ran down to the ferryman's boat, after he had knocked down the owner who wanted to stop him. He rowed out of the cove where the boat lay. The water hissed under the keel. With his first stroke he examined the oars, with his second the withes of the oar-bands; it was good gear.

The men on the shore shouted. He did not heed, continued not to heed. It was all Imbär and happiness with her.

Along the shore the ice was frozen to the land for a stretch of ten yards. He tried to wedge through between it and the floe; for some yards he succeeded, but then his boat jammed. A few moments later he went on again, but bearing away from the shore. He progressed slowly, watching all the time. Now he had to point straight upstream, now straight across to clear the biggest blocks. An oar would slip, and he would dip it as in a dream, without seeing that he had no water to row in.

Dusk fell. He did not notice it before he was hemmed in on all sides, a good way out. He had been in the ferry passage when he started, now it was above him. He could hear the rapids near him roaring shrilly. Imbär ran along the southern shore, the old man on the northern. He saw clearly how Zakris slipped on the rocks, ran and slipped. They waved their arms like drunken folk, and he heard shouts as from a great distance. Then he could not hear them at all.

Olle jumped out of the boat and pulled it along with him over the ice. Mountain skiffs are light. Away he went for dear life. When the boat's bow came to an open space, he stooped down and with all his strength set it across on the next ice, ran over it with three hops, jumped out and pulled again. Just here the river made a bend and grew narrower. The ice was packed so that the blocks could not be separated. Around the point the river began to slope toward the rapids, the deadly suck of the rapids.

On the shore at that instant the ferryman cried to old Zakris, "How's that for murder?" Zakris's eyes were wide, but ears he had none just then. Why was Olle standing still and looking around? He shouted. Didn't Olle realize that in a few minutes it would be too late? He screamed, but what he screamed he didn't know. "Now he's leaving the boat with an oar in his hand that he pushes against the ice. Now he's beginning to run—he'll never do it."

Zakris ran along the shore, falling and rising, falling and rising. He had to keep his eyes fixed on the man out there whom he had wished to see dead a little while ago, but who was now—he couldn't deny that this was the most detestable fellow and the bravest that he had ever known.

But on ran Olle—stood still—went around and looked—pushed with the oar—took hold of it and jumped—ran straight toward the rapids—turned up toward the ferry—went down sometimes and half disappeared—stood the next moment as straight and tall as a pine. Everything went green before his eyes. The ice glittered with phosphorescent light; there was a hissing from the rapids and the hissing was green, however crazy that might sound. Now the shores pressed closer together. The clashing of the ice-floe grew to a roar. Blocks shot up and were shattered; they ground and cracked, trembled and displaced one another. Fragments of ice romped like wild beasts, tussled, struck each other down, rode one another ruttishly, till from the shore it sounded as if some one stood there shooting into that hissing hell of green.

He who ran out there never forgot that day: how the ice stuck out where he was to set his foot; how a crack opened its black squinting eye where he had to climb; how the jagged green blocks, loosened from the jumble, swung into the suck of the rapids and vanished; how the blood streamed red and warm over his hands from the bite of the ice when he fell; and when the slender black boat swung into the whirlpool and went down, down till, half capsizing, it vanished in the upper falls— the sensation as he looked was one he remembered all his life but could never find words for.

The great log barrier of the lumber company stuck out of the dusk at the head of the rapids. It seemed to float like a mastless ship, and against its shoulder there was a snapping, crackling and hissing, as great discs of ice turned sidewise, broke, passed into the white foam, and were seen no more.

All this the man saw as he ran for his life.

Imbär was not far from him. He could have spoken with her from where he was. But he had something before him that made him run and jump forward and back like mad: the water. He knew that part of the river well. Just so far one could row along the shore. Here was the black swirl of a tentative little eddy, and down below—there was no use thinking of that! There stood Imbär waiting. Between her and him black rocks stuck out of the ink—by good fortune, this was no water to drown in. He ran upstream a few steps more. Imbär kept parallel with him on the bank. He heard her cry out to him—and with that he took a start and jumped as far as ever he could.

The thin ice-crust tore his face as he came up; his hands had been ragged before. He would have had to break the ice with his whole arm for every stroke he swam, so he lay deep and panted. Imbär stood above him so high and fair, and he was so far below that he could surely never get up to her. That he had held to a stone and waited he remembered afterwards; that he might have swum further, he believed; but that Imbär stood up to her shoulders in water long before he reached her was absolutely certain.

So these two wet mortals stood, feeling themselves warm while their clothes were freezing to ice . . . and on the opposite shore Zakris yelled and swung his cap in exultation when he saw them so oblivious of everything in their happiness.

HJALMAR SÖDERBERG

MARGOT

THE BURNING CITY

ARCHIMEDES' POINT

HJALMAR SÖDERBERG (1869–) is a native of Stockholm. In his youth he tried journalism in the small city of Karlstad, but tired of "serving caviare to the Bœotians" and returned to the capital. Söderberg is akin to the realists of the 1880's, and his autobiographical novel, *Martin Birck's Early Days,* the story of a young man who is unable to find his place in the world, has its prototype in J. P. Jacobsen's *Niels Lyhne.* The first part of the book, picturing Martin's childhood and his home, has a quiet, sober charm and possesses lasting value; but the latter part, describing the life of a young man who gives up the fight before it is begun, suffers from being read in the light of the present more practical day.

Before publishing *Martin Birck,* Söderberg had already, in 1898, brought out a collection called *Storiettes* which showed that he had even then carried to perfection the literary form that is peculiarly his, the very short story, usually told in the first person, and based on some trifling incident close at hand. In this form he is unsurpassed.

In the novel *Dr. Glas,* Söderberg takes up the question of whether it is ever allowable to kill. The purpose of the book is to show that ethical ideas which have grown up with the human race need not be final. In the drama *Gertrud,* which has had great success on the stage, he treats love from a fatalistic point of view, showing that so-called free love is just as much subject to the law of change as love within marriage. Love is also the subject of his novel *The Serious Play.* The World War is dealt with in the drama, *The Hour of Fate,* which appeared in 1922.

Hjalmar Söderberg

MARGOT

To Oscar Levertin

I HAD known Paul Herbst over a year before
I learned accidentally that he had been married and that his wife had been dead long since.

We used to meet at one place or another with
common friends, and it sometimes happened, too,
that we looked each other up to talk away an
hour over a game of chess and a glass of wine,
especially if it was getting on to the twilight
of a long and gloomy day, when solitude began
to feel oppressive. I was twenty or thereabouts,
and he was a good bit over thirty; which is probably why he so seldom spoke to me of himself and
his life.

One evening my glance fell on a woman's portrait in the recess with the porcelain stove, a
faded portrait behind a glass. I had presumably
seen it many times before without its having
tempted my curiosity or my even noticing it at all.
This time it occurred to me to ask who it was.

Herbst looked up, a bit surprised.

"That is my wife," he answered.

[235]

My astonishment made me embarrassed. There was a moment's silence.

"I never knew you were married . . . Or that you . . ."

Herbst smiled meditatively in his sofa corner, while he gathered together the chess-men and laid them in a drawer, each in its place according to a regular scheme.

"Yes, I believe I was married."

"You believe!"

"It's so long ago. I've almost forgotten."

His eyes stared into the dusk with a blind and empty look.

"If I didn't know that I have a worn ring with her initials in a drawer somewhere, and a church certificate and some other trifles, I might sometimes believe the whole thing was a dream—a bright and happy dream, whose contours break up and fade in my memory inch by inch, a shade more with every passing year."

"A good many have passed since then," he continued. "I was twenty, and she was eighteen. After two years she died."

And he added, while he slowly stirred the fire, "Her name was Margot."

I could not take my eyes from the portrait, which surveyed me with a faded and stiffened smile. But behind the smile I caught a glimpse in the half light of a sad and winsome girl's face, almost a child's, framed in long curls after the style of the time, with a wonderfully blue and bright glance.

Some days later I was in company with Herbst on the way home from a party.

He lived on the outskirts of Östermalm, and we went out there along Strandvägen. That was in the days when new and old flourished together on the street, two or three modern houses in the midst of gray dilapidation, outhouses and old wharf sheds.

It was a cool night in the early part of October. The moon was up; a cold, moist wind was blowing. The big buildings on Blasieholm formed a dark mass, whose broken and irregular edge seemed to be catching at the wisps of cloud that drove forward against a deep blue background. The still, heavy water of Nybro Inlet mirrored a broad glittering moon-path in oily rings, and along the wharves the lumber sloops raised a thin and motionless forest of masts and tackle. In the upper air was haste and tumult; the clouds hunted each other from west to east, till over the woods of Djurgården they congested into a low black wall. It was as if heaven were breaking camp for a journey, for a flight.

It was late, and Herbst seemed weary.

"Let's hurry up a bit," he said. "Moonlight isn't healthy. One doesn't sleep well after it."

[237]

"Perhaps . . . But it's beautiful just the same."

"I suppose so. Sunlight's more beautiful."

We went on a stretch in silence. The city slept around us. A policeman's rapid step rang on the pavement, iron heels against the stone; a shrill laugh came from an alley, a heavy carriage rumbled past somewhere in the distance.

Herbst picked up his thread of thought anew:

"The sun, you see, is healthier and above all more up-to-date. It celebrates the new, the fresh, the present, what we must admire so as not to be out of things—even if it seems tiresome sometimes. Toward the old, the past, it is pitiless; it calls an old ruin straight out an old ruin. —The moon, on the other hand, the moon is a reactionary. It reveres the dynasties of banished beauty. It makes us think of the beauty that enchanted us in our first youth, which we laugh at now or have forgotten; of voices that are silenced; of caresses under which we trembled long ago."

His voice shook a little.

"—And of the dead whom we loved."

He was very pale, and his look had a sickly gleam. I had never seen him like that. I felt that I was walking beside a strange man whom I had never known and never seen by daylight. Was he drunk? His features had new lines, and his voice sounded with a new tone. I don't know why, but at that moment it occurred to me that he was a passionate worshipper of music. I recalled that I had heard him play the violin one evening when I stood outside his closed door, and when I had rung, the violin ceased, but no one opened. Perhaps music was to him like a fair but depraved mistress, for whom he fevered in darkness and solitude, but for whom he blushed in daytime, in the sunlight.

We had come into the newly-planted avenues. All was silent and bare; not a human being was visible. The sparse, thin skeletons of the trees threw long shadows in the moonlight.

Neither of us spoke for a long while.

Finally Herbst took my arm: "Let us turn off! I have something to show you over there. It's nothing remarkable, only an old house."

We turned to the left into a dark side street. The houses stood sleeping in low irregular lines, and far away a lamp flared in the wind with a reddish light.

The street ascended sharply. Herbst stood still before a high-paled fence.

"Here is where we used to live," he said.

It was an old dilapidated two-story house with a pointed gable and a high, steeply-inclined tile roof—probably an old citizen's residence of the last century—shaded by five or six tall lindens and a gigantic chestnut. The moonlight burned white on the wavy glass of the gable windows. On the gray masonry the net of linden branches was outlined like the broken web of a monster spider, and from the round attic window with broken glass in its ragged frame stared the darkness.

The gate stood open, hanging on one hinge. We went into the yard.

The house appeared desolate, abandoned, dead.

"Yes," repeated Herbst, "it was here; here we used to live. Through that door there she entered in her bridal dress one evening, when the stars were burning in the tree-tops. And through the same door they carried her out one winter day. They carried her out in a black chest and drove off with her in a grotesque wagon ridiculously gotten up, carried her off somewhere, God knows where. I doubt if I know where the grave is. I have never been there since."

We sat down on a green bench which ran around one of the old tree trunks. We sat there a long while in silence. Paul Herbst was tracing flourishes in the sand and now and then spearing a withered leaf with his stick.

"You see that left gable window up there," he went on. "There she sat when I came home and

when I went away. There we both sat together
as evening drew on. When the sunlight fell in
aslant, it painted the shadow pattern of the
chestnut's leaves on the bright wall-paper and
brought out a warm glow from her red mahogany
sewing board. There we would sit in the bright
May evenings with the window open. And in
the dusk of December afternoons I used to un-
fasten her hair and let it run between my fingers
. . . while the city down below there was sunk in
wintry darkness . . . in silence and dream.

"She was a good child, Margot. I remember
a New Year's Eve, our last. We had gone to
church together, she had wanted to. It was
packed and fearfully warm. Margot went to
sleep with her head on my shoulder. Suddenly
the preacher broke out with a thunder; she awoke
and was frightened at having been asleep. He
was her spiritual adviser, and we had our pew
right under the pulpit; she was positive that he
had seen her. She thought he looked at her so
sternly and coldly. She was depressed all the
evening afterwards. She was afraid she had
been too happy, she whispered to me; what if
God had grown angry and would do her some
harm?

"She was a guileless, conscientious little being.
She knew little of the world's evil, and my own

knowledge was much the same—at that time.
. . . Toward spring she got brain fever and died.
In three days it was over."

There was a rustling in the trees. Herbst sat
in silence and traced in the sand.

I sat and stared at the moon's reflection in the
left gable window. There one might have had
some notion of happiness once. A peaceful nook,
protected, remote.

"Who lives here now?" I asked so as to say
something.

"Some artisans' families, I believe. The house
has run down."

And he continued with a smile, "That must be
their wash hanging out there. It reminds me of
a story from the time when we lived here. Before us the house had belonged to an apothecary
who had come to grief, I don't know how, and
gone bankrupt. More than once I saw him out
on the street looking in through the palings. One
night—it was bright moonlight as now, and I
was standing at the window with Margot—one
night I saw him steal into the yard. The tears
came into Margot's eyes when she recognized
him. Our laundry was hanging out. He looked
cautiously round; it was dark in our window, and
he didn't see us. When he thought he was un-
observed, he hurriedly tore down all the clothes
from the line and threw them higgledy piggledy

on the ground. He acted as if he was on the rampage. The man obviously had a screw loose; he couldn't stand seeing strangers' clothes hanging to dry in the same yard where in the old days his own shirts and drawers had dangled in the moonlight."

A cloud slipped over the moon. Herbst rose. "Well, let's go! I'm freezing."

He had won back his calm. When he was out on the street he lighted a cigarette and after a while resumed:

"So happiness passes from one to another. It's no good shutting your hands on it with a convulsive grip; no matter what you do, some day you'll be standing with your hands full of empty air. The only thing to do is to take everything with the same imperturbable equanimity as a well-conducted gambler when he loses the last thing he owns. . . . What if existence afterwards should be like a worn and faded coat which one would gladly give away to a beggar; it's all one has anyhow. So one can only refrain from exposing his poverty too openly, one must keep close to the houses on the shady side of the street; and when one sees the stream of humanity billow forward on the opposite sidewalk, one may console himself with the knowledge that in time they will all come over to the shadow side—one by one, sooner or later."

[243]

"That's a fine consolation, 'A solace for a tiger heart.' "

"Yes, it leaves much to be desired, I grant . . . but there is no other. Furthermore there is a certain interest in seeing one after another of one's friends and acquaintances slip into the freemasonry of the shadow side. One sees it on them when they have passed the line—in their walk, their carriage, the lines around the mouth, and the corners of the eyes. After that nothing matters. The end will be the same, whatever happens: one will be carried out of his house by six fellows dressed in black, who smell of brandy and have white cotton gloves, and one will be buried in the ground amid reading and mumbling of incantations."

We went along the street in silence; only our steps echoed between the rows of houses. A company of night revellers took a clamorous farewell at a street corner. A door with a rattling chain was pushed open and shut with a bang. Herbst turned up his coat collar and bade me a hurried good-night.

"I shall wake up with a headache to-morrow," he said. "I can't stand moonlight."

THE BURNING CITY

THROUGH the two windows with their bright lattice-figured curtains the level sunlight of the winter morning falls in two slanting oblong quadrilaterals on the soft green carpet, and in the warm sunny spaces a little boy skips and dances. He knows but little of the world as yet. He knows he is little and is going to be big, but he does not know either that he has been born or that he will die. He knows he is four and will soon be five, but he does not know what is meant by "a year"; he still measures time only into yesterday, to-day, and to-morrow.

"Papa," he suddenly exclaims to his father, who has just finished breakfast and lighted his first cigar of the day—he being a person to measure time with cigars—"papa, I dreamed so many things last night! I dreamed about the whole room! I dreamed about the chairs and the green carpet and the mirror and the clock and the stove and the shutters and the cupboards."

With that he skips forward to the stove, where the fire flames and crackles, and turns a somersault. He considers the stove and the place in front of it as the most important and dignified things in the room.

His father nods and laughs at him over the corner of his paper, and the boy laughs back, laughs away uncontrollably. He is at the age when laughter is still only an utterance of joy, not of appreciation for the ridiculous. When he stood at the window some days ago and laughed at the moon, it was not because he found the moon funny, but because it gave him joy with its round bright face.

When he has had his laugh out, he clambers up on a chair and points to one of the pictures on the wall.

"—And I dreamed most of all about that picture," he says.

The picture is a photograph of an old Dutch painting, *A Burning City*.

"Well, and what was it you dreamed?" his father asks.

"I don't know."

"Come, think!"

"Oh yes, I dreamed it was burning and that I patted a doggie."

"But generally you are afraid of doggies."

"Yes, but on pictures I can pat them nicely."

Then he laughs and skips and dances.

At last he comes up to his father and says, "Papa dear, take down the picture. I want papa to show me the picture again the way he did yesterday."

The picture is a new arrival in the room; it came the day before. With the other pictures around the walls the little boy has acquainted himself long ago: Uncle Strindberg and Uncle Schopaur (i.e. Schopenhauer) and Uncle Napoleon and ugly old Goethe and grandmother when she was young. But the Burning City is new, and is furthermore in itself a much more amusing picture than the others. The father humors the little boy, takes the picture down from the wall, and they enjoy it together. Over a broad estuary that winds toward the sea and is filled with sloops and rowboats runs an arched bridge with a fortified tower. On the left shore lies the burning city: rows of narrow houses with pointed gables, high roofs, churches, and towers; a throng of people running hither and thither, a sea of fire and flames, clouds of smoke, ladders raised against walls, horses running away with shaking loads, docks crowded with barrels and sacks and all manner of rubbish; on the river a mass of people in a rowboat that is almost ready to capsize, while across the bridge people are running for dear life, and away off in the foreground stand two dogs sniffing at each other. But far in the background, where the estuary widens toward the sea, a much-too-small moon sits on the horizon in a mist of pale clouds, peeping wanly and sadly at all this misery.

"Papa," inquires the little boy, "why is the city burning?"

"Somebody was careless with fire," says the father.

"*Who* was it that was careless?"

"Ah, one can't be sure of that so long afterwards."

"How long afterwards?"

"It is many hundred years since that city was burned," says the father.

This is a bit puzzling to the little boy, as the father clearly realizes, but he had to answer something. The boy sits quiet a moment and ponders. New thoughts and impressions about things stir in his brain and mingle with the old. He points with his little finger on the glass over the burning city and says:

"Yes, but it was burning yesterday, and now to-day it's burning too."

The father ventures on an explanation of the difference between pictures and reality. "That is not a real city," he says, "that is only a picture. The real city was burned up long, long ago. It is gone. The people that run about there waving their arms are dead and don't exist any more. The houses have been burned up, the towers have fallen. The bridge is gone too."

"Have the towers burned down or tumbled down?" asks the boy.

"They have both burned and tumbled down."

"Are the steamboats dead too?"

"The boats too have been gone long ago," replied the father. "But those are not steam-boats, they are sailing vessels. There were no steamboats in those days."

The little boy sticks out his lower lip with a dissatisfied expression.

"But I *see* that they're steamboats," he says. "Papa, what's that steamboat's name?"

He has a mind of his own, has the boy. The father is tired of the labor of instruction and holds his peace. The boy points with his finger to the old Dutch merchantmen and prattles to himself: "That steamer's name is Bragë, and, that one's is Hillersea, and that is the Princess Ingeborg."

"Papa," he cries all of a sudden, "is the moon gone too?"

"No, the moon still exists. It is the one thing of all there that still exists. It is the same moon you laughed at the other day in the nursery win-dow."

Again the little boy sits still and ponders. Then comes yet another question:

"Papa, is it *very* long ago this city was burned? Is it as long ago as when we went away on the Princess Ingeborg?"

"It is much, much longer ago," answers the father. "When that city burned, neither you nor I nor mamma nor grandma was here."

The boy's face becomes very serious all at once. He looks positively troubled. He sits quiet a long while pondering. But it seems as if things would not work out for him.

"Tell me, papa," he finally asks, "where was I when that city was burned? Was it when I was at Grenna with mamma?"

"No, old fellow," replies the father, "when that city burned you didn't yet exist."

The boy sticks out his under lip again with an attitude as much as to say: no, I can't agree to such a thing as that. He then repeats with emphasis:

"Yes, but where was I then?"

His father answers, "You didn't exist at all."

The boy looks at his father with round eyes. Suddenly all the little face brightens, the boy tears himself away from his father, and begins to skip and dance again in the sunny spots on the green carpet, crying at the top of his lungs:

"Oho yes, I did just the same. I was somewhere, I was somewhere!"

He thought his father was only joking with him. Such an idea was clearly too ridiculous! The maids used sometimes to talk nonsense to him in jest, and he thought his father had done the same.

So he skips and dances in the sunlight.

I ONCE knew a little street arab.

He was the same age as I and lived in the same square. But he was superior to me in everything, not only in experience and courage but also in accomplishments; for with the aid of a piece of red chalk or charcoal he could fill the walls of the street with words and symbols whose meaning I did not understand. When I was going out and was alone and unprotected, I used first to stick my nose out of the gate and glance down the street to assure myself that the little rowdy was not in the neighborhood. For he was stronger than I and could never endure with equanimity the appearance of my clothes, which were cleaner and in better condition than his.

But one day it happened that I was given a sled by my father. It was covered with a piece of red-flowered felt, the runners were of sharp steel, which shone in the sun, and it had also a little bell in front. When I first came down into the gateway with this sled, and the scent of new-fallen snow pricked my nose so that I sneezed, I was suddenly possessed by such a mad delight that I completely forgot my usual caution and rushed out of the gate without looking to left or to right, skipping and dancing like a jumping-jack, while I gave vent to wild war-cries.

Just beyond our gate the street began to slope. I at once sat myself astride the sled and let it slide down the incline, but the slope was not steep, and it went but slowly, so that now and then I had to help with my feet. An icy wind swept through the street, my ears began to freeze, and my joy had already begun to chill, great as it had been but a moment before. As the cold wind crept in under my clothes, such reflections as these began to steal into my soul: I'm not having nearly such a good time as I had just now when I came down through the gateway with my sled.

While I was thinking this within myself, I suddenly caught sight of the little rowdy as he stood at his gate with hands in his trousers' pockets. He was dirty, scrofulous, and hideous to look at, and his appearance filled my heart with fear and trembling, for he really was a dreadful little mucker.

I saw no chance of getting away. I sat still on my sled without stirring a limb, like a rabbit before a boa-constrictor, waiting till the little rowdy should come out of his gate and thrash me.

But, lo and behold! my guardian angel was watching over me. The little rowdy did not come out of his gate; he stood where he was with his hands in his pockets and, looking at me with indifference rather than hate, spoke only the following words:

"Give yourself a shove from behind, kid, and you'll go faster!"

Thereupon he took a piece of charcoal from his pocket, scratched a monosyllabic word on the wall, and vanished in at the gate.

But I continued down the slope, scrambling with my feet to keep going, for the track was not very steep. Suddenly, however, it struck me that there might be some truth in the little rowdy's words. If I sit on my sled, thought I, and some one comes behind and gives me a push on the back, I shall slide on a bit. So if I push myself on the back now, it will naturally have the same effect as if some one else did it. It was so simple: how stupid I was not to have thought of that before! I looked around cautiously to assure myself that the rowdy was not near, for I did not want him to see that I was following his advice. After that I began to thump myself on the back as hard as I could.

But as the sled did not stir from its place, I thumped my back till I was red and hot, and two serving-maids stood still and laughed at me; but the sled never moved.

Then I grew vexed and cross, took my sled by the rope and ran home with it, wishing I had an elder brother who could thrash the little rowdy for me.

At the dinner table I related my adventure to my father and asked him to explain how it was that one could not go forward on a sled by thumping oneself on the back. My father neither laughed at me nor said I was stupid, as most fathers would have done, but tried to give me a logical explanation of the phenomenon. He tangled himself up so badly in contradictions, however, that in the end I got the impression that he did not understand much more of the matter than I did. I then doubted whether I should ever find the explanation to this riddle and asked my worthy father if at least he would not thrash the little rowdy. But he answered that he had not time.

Hours fly, and years pass.

The little rowdy grew up to be a big rough. I myself went to school and came to learn a great deal; but I never got any satisfactory explanation of how it is that one can not push himself forward on a sled by hitting himself on the back. It sometimes happens still that I lie awake at night puzzling over the question. And if some day I have a son and he asks me about it, I am fully resolved to laugh at him and tell him he is stupid.

BO BERGMAN

THE SIGN

Bo Bergman (1869–) is first and foremost a lyrist, but has also written masterly short stories. It seems inevitable to compare him with Hjalmar Söderberg. They are both natives of Stockholm, contemporaries, and friends from their youth up. In his prose Bo Bergman has cultivated the same form that Söderberg has brought to perfection, and while in no sense imitations, his stories are of the same school and written in the same spirit. In his philosophy of life he reveals the same pessimism and disillusionment that characterize his friend. His first collection of poems he called *Marionettes* to signify that we are all helpless playthings in the hands of fate. The same mood is prevalent in his first book of short stories, *The Dream and Other Stories*.

Bo Bergman's field is, however, less circumscribed than that of Söderberg, for he occasionally leaves the city to write of simple, primitive types, of people who till the soil. In his later books he glorifies work as the salvation of humanity. This note is struck both in his last prose volume, *My Friend the Baron and Other Stories*, and in his last collection of verse which he calls *Eyes of Life*.

Grace and delicacy are characteristics of Bo Bergman's verse, which is extremely popular among his countrymen. He is a member of the Swedish Academy.

Bo Bergman

The Sign

IN the large corner room which faced the lake
on one side and the paper factory on the other
two men sat talking. The engineer was riding
hobby horse on his chair and had laid his hands and
chin on the back. He looked like an old watch-
dog with his nose between his paws. His visitor,
the district medical officer, sat curled up in the
sofa corner. He was a small nervous man, plum-
yellow in complexion, of Walloon blood, near
sixty, a widower of many years' standing, who
was respected equally for his professional skill
and for his sharp tongue and kind heart. The
factory hands could tell stories of both phases.

The window on the lake was open; twilight had
already set in, but the August air was heavy and
misty, and no moon was visible. The men were
talking of local matters. Gradually, however,
the conversation slid over on another tack, and
stories came in—youthful memories, travels, re-
semblances and contrasts, one thing leading to
another. Both doctor and engineer had lived
an energetic, practical life. They were two able
men, who had got what they had honestly won,

and could adapt themselves to circumstances without unnecessary brooding and without other scruples than those of a man of honor. The engineer told of his student years at Zurich, and the doctor of his Samaritan trips through the district. He made faces as he spoke and chewed at his cigar. His countenance twitched as if there was a whole system of wires under the skin.

Suddenly he gave a start.

"Ha! it's nothing," he said with a laugh. "It's only the bell again."

"What bell?" The engineer raised his chin.

"My office bell."

"Do you believe in signs?"

"Deuce, no. But I can't get away from it. As soon as I sit down, it rattles away at my ears. It's my doctor's conscience, you see. I fear I shall take it with me till doomsday."

The little man went to the window. He had spoken the last words straight out into the air, half to himself. He remained standing; cigar smoke and twilight together flowed around his form. Down at the factory the great turbines suddenly stopped; the drone of the waterfall and the evening cry of the swallows were the only sounds. Workmen came along the road. They made salutations toward the window. And far off on the other side of the lake the night express rushed southward like a row of leaping lights in the mist.

The engineer had again rested his head on the back of the chair. He dozed with one eye while with the other he peeped at his friend. He did not venture to disturb the doctor. Although he could not see his glance, he divined where it had rested; it was somewhere near the deanery to the right behind the grove of birches.

"I feel like telling you something," said the doctor. He had rolled himself up in the sofa corner again like a hedgehog. "You were talking about signs. They're ambiguous phenomena, because they may depend on so many different causes. Some we can trace fairly easily; others we can't as yet. Those we can't recognize we call supernatural. I have never perceived signs myself, but others have perceived them concerning me. The same thing has occurred with many doctors presumably, especially with country doctors. Long distances, long waiting. Long waiting, heightened anxiety. Heightened anxiety, increased likelihood of hallucination. What one longs for unusually or fears unusually never comes soon enough—in the former case because one rejoices at it, and in the latter because at least it brings one certainty. And the imagination so anticipates the doctor's arrival that it becomes a sound

[259]

or a vision. He becomes his own harbinger. Wheels rumble, bells tinkle, stairs creak, the latch rattles. . . . I can assure you I've driven up to many a farm in majestic impersonality, the while my poor sinful human self jogged in the snowdrifts behind a horse's tail a half mile from its destination. Look out, old man! You don't know whom you have with you this evening, whether it's I or only my wraith."

"I'll drink with the two of you then."

"But I must get to my story. It's long ago now. It happened some years after my marriage. As you know I didn't live at the works in those days but close to the Salem church with the dean's family as my nearest and only neighbors. I can't go in that direction without a secret twinge. 'There's no prettier spot in the world,' I thought, as we stood arm in arm, my wife and I, looking out over the lake and the fields. On the point was the church, white as chalk with its black shingle hat rising out of the green. The halo of the evening sky was mirrored in the bay. And in autumn the corn-shocks marched in long battalions down to the shore, where the mist lay and spread like powder smoke.

"Our house—it's gone now—was hidden in a leafy grove. My trap used to stop outside the gate, and from there it was only a few steps up to the porch. It is always the porch I see when

Bo Bergman

I see my wife. She fitted so well with the vines;
her thick brown hair with all the yellow and red
leaves around it made me wish more than once
I could handle a paintbrush and not just a knife.
A little, good-humored, eager child she was, with
a pair of large, frank, ingenuous eyes—as long
as she was well. Oh, you remember her, to be
sure. She was gay and sociable, and she had to
sit alone a great deal. I reproached myself
about it now and then, but the thing couldn't be
avoided. I had my calls, which often took whole
days and more. In the long winter evenings
when I was away she had only the dean's family
to depend on, and that wasn't enough for a young
wife with her temperament. She grew thin and
nervous, and there were days when I became anxious. But she passed it all off; I had my job, as
I've already said, and a man's a man. He
doesn't live on love alone. When I came home
I was tired, naturally, and had the worry of my
work. The community was in a wretched state
as to its medical attendance when I started in;
my predecessor had been quite incapacitated in his
last years, and I had to work for his sins. Ah
well, I was young and strong, and that was all
right.

"But of peace there was none. Sick calls
rained in on me. It's from that time that I've
had the office bell in my ears. I imagine my wife

never hated anything so violently as that clanging cowbell, and if she could have had her will she'd certainly have cut the cord and let the patients or the messengers stay out. She was cruel and unreasonable, for she was in love.

" 'It's as if you were married to all the district but me,' she used to say. 'I have no hold on you. I could wish I was sick myself, good and sick, so you'd have to stay home.'

"The next instant she'd apologize for her poor stupid words with an excessive burst of tears. A week later she'd be rushing about among the poor and sick of the neighborhood, so that her wish was close to fulfillment, and she was ready to take to her bed. She could never do anything in moderation; she had to do everything to the limit.

"She was that way in her love, and the same too in her household affairs. Her home ran like clockwork. She made it a point of honor to have everything in its place, to see that everything was done punctually, nothing lacking, to keep marriage from becoming an old story with dusty corners, languid steps, and wilted flowers. With us the flowers were always fresh and the table-cloth always clean. I had but to step into all that as if it were a matter of course—for to me it was a matter of course, I didn't notice how much love was behind it. We men never notice such things before it is too late. We are so farsighted. We don't see what is near to us. We don't remember the week-day to keep it holy, which is the only thing that counts. It seems as if we needed distance, either of time or space, to give us open eyes and responsive hearts.

" 'I don't understand how you manage,' I said one day, laughing. It was the devil's own weather, I had lost my way in the woods and snow, and had come home a couple of hours later than schedule. I was afraid my wife would be anxious, but she met me as calmly as if I'd arrived on the stroke of the clock. On the table was dinner, just brought in. The dishes were steaming.

" 'How do you mean?'

" 'It seems as if some invisible fairy informed you when I was coming.'

" 'Maybe.'

"Her voice was serious, and her eyes met mine with a peculiar expression. We said no more about it that time, but a while afterwards the subject suddenly popped up again.

" 'Who tells me?' she said. 'You do. You yourself.'

" 'I?'

"Yes, really, dear. I always hear you an hour or so before you are here. You bang the gate and scrape off the snow or the sand on the steps. It's been so the whole time since we've been married. I haven't cared to tell you about it; it amused me to wait and see if you'd notice anything at last. It's taken nearly two years, sir.'

"With that she kissed me passionately. But I must have cut an odd figure, for suddenly she burst out laughing. She laughed long and infectiously, as a child would over a successful trick. I for my part didn't dare say just how astonished I was. I had never concerned myself with the phenomenon of hallucination, yet now I was face to face with it, and in the person of my own wife into the bargain.

" 'Did you ever notice anything—similar before—before our marriage, I mean?'

" 'No.'

" 'Do you know if it runs in your family?'

" 'I've never heard it did. But, darling, you don't need to look as if you'd fallen from the skies for such a thing. I've never wondered about it. It's seemed so altogether natural to me. How is it remarkable that two persons who love each other as—as I love you—that they should communicate with each other without standing exactly face to face?'

"Well, I let it go at that. I did ask a couple of colleagues, but they had nothing to contribute, and as my wife's health grew better and better, I gradually lost my uneasiness. I continued to play the spirit for myself, and an uncommonly attentive spirit it was, a regular old faithful. He almost never missed.

"Then came a bad time in my work. An epidemic broke out in the district, and I had a lot to put up with. The country hospital was overcrowded. For a month no one could think of any decent rest; when I looked at the nurses, I saw they were as white as their aprons, and they worked like heroes. We had got a reinforcement of our staff from Stockholm, and among the new arrivals was a tall blonde girl with an absolute madonna face. She toiled like a slave and seemed to have inexhaustible strength. But everything she did went quietly and easily and at the same time efficiently; she belonged to the few under whose hand work becomes a melody. It was medicine just to follow her motions. She flitted through the room, and when she leaned over a bed to arrange a pillow or support a head, she was to me a veritable incarnation of womanhood and motherhood.

"We used to talk together sometimes when I had finished my night rounds. It was in the beginning of July, and the perfume of the jasmine lay in the garden like a white narcotic. The Sisters sat with their work on the benches which went around the great chestnut tree, and the town doctor and I smoked our night cigars while we rested.

" 'Sister Gertrude sits there like a Botticelli,' said my colleague facetiously.

" 'Who is that?' she asked.

"I was astonished at her simple, steadfast joy, which her professional duties never disturbed. When I compared her with my wife it was like comparing a little restless, ardent child with a deep and silent woman, the victim of life with the mother of life. I was worn out with my work, and that no doubt contributed to making me feel grateful for the repose which the sight of her gave me. At the end came the perilous hour when we imagined we had always known each other.

"One day a patient died on the operating table. It was a little boy of five or six years old. She —Sister Gertrude—had stood and taken his pulse. When it suddenly stopped under her finger, she looked first at the child and then at me. There was a mother's sorrow in the look.

"I then realized that I cared for her.

"But no love-story developed. I succeeded pretty soon in mastering my impulses—at least so far that I did not let her have any suspicion of them. Inside, the feeling was still there. But the work together kept me from moping, and as I had nothing to reproach myself with, I took no great notice, either, of the change that my wife was going through. She merely seemed a bit more silent than usual. However, it became evident at last that she was brooding on something or other. She would sit a long time gazing at me, and when I surprised her look, would immediately turn away. It was as if she sought the answer to a question—or rather as if she had already found the answer and was trying not to credit it. Her manner alternated between vexed reproach over mere trifles and a sickly meekness, which troubled me more than anything else. If I asked how she was, I always got the same toneless 'all right' for answer. She withdrew herself. An invisible and impenetrable wall rose between us. I naturally thought that our having no children was perhaps the cause of the trouble. But when I proposed that we adopt one, she was beside herself.

" 'I won't have anything that I have no share in,' she said. 'No stranger is to come into my home. Neither visible nor invisible,' she added.

"I suggested that she go abroad with me. She shook her head. Shouldn't she like to go alone then? What would that help?—she was lonely enough anyhow. She couldn't do anything from that time on. Looking after the house, which had hitherto been her pride and joy, became suddenly an infliction. The dust collected, and the flowers withered, and everything was left where it was. I might now have to wait for one thing or another without any reasonable excuse. It was obvious that something fundamental was lacking, that a nerve was cut, but that it was I who had cut it I could not get myself to believe. She couldn't know anything of my fleeting inclination toward another. No one but myself knew anything. And besides, the whole thing was over—like a melody that had made the blood sing a few short hours and had hardly left so much as an echo. There was no possibility that she could have the least suspicion.

"But one night I heard her get up and go out into the hall. I wondered why she didn't come back and began to fear something was wrong. She was sitting huddled together on the couch in her long white night-dress like a little frightened and deserted child. But she showed no surprise when I came.

" 'What's the matter with you,' I asked. 'Are you ill?'

"She didn't answer.

" 'You can at least give me a word of explanation. Is there something that worries you?"

" 'Why do you ask? You know very well what it is. You aren't mine any more.'

" 'Nonsense!'

" 'I don't hear you any more.'

" 'Don't hear?'

" 'You don't come, before you come. That's

all over. Why is it? I am the same. It must be you that have changed. Your thought isn't with me. It's been a month now since you came in the first time without my knowing. . . .'

"In a twinkling I saw the day of the operation when the boy died. It had been a month ago. But I said aloud:

" 'You're ill, dear. We mustn't let things go on this way. I'll talk with a specialist.'

"My wife only smiled. I can't forget how she smiled. There was no bitterness in it, but neither was there any doubt that she knew. She didn't die right away. And yet she never really lived afterwards. Now she's gone, and the home is gone; it's only I that's left to traipse around patching and plastering folks. But we're only quacksalvers, the whole lot of us. Those we'd give our life to help are incurable."

The little doctor crept off the sofa and began to pace up and down. The engineer stretched out his hand to him, but he did not take it. In the gray autumn night he wandered about in the room like a little fierce and unhappy goblin. And silence fell between the two men.

ALBERT ENGSTRÖM

CHARLES XII, HERCULES, AND GUSTAV MATTSON

In ALBERT ENGSTRÖM (1869–) humor has found its official recognition in Sweden, for he is one of the Eighteen Immortals of the Swedish Academy together with Selma Lagerlöf, Heidenstam, Hallström, Bo Bergman, and other writers whose fame rests on more serious work. But Engström also is in his own way an interpreter of folk psychology. He is both cartoonist and writer, and has contributed a long series of drawings and stories to the humorous paper *Strix* which he founded in 1897 and which he has since edited.

Engström's favorite types are the small skippers, pilots, and fishermen in the Swedish skerries, and of late this field has afforded an endless series of incidents that turn on the fine art of smuggling spirits. Vagabonds, derelicts, and all who are at variance with the commonly accepted standards appeal to him, and he will often discover a fund of mellow wisdom or caustic wit where least expected. He directs his sharpest irony against sham and hypocritical officialdom.

The son of a Småland station master, Engström has often written stories about the very simple and primitive crofters whom he knew in his childhood. Other tales deal with his university days at Upsala, or with his experiences as one of the impecunious art students in Göteborg. His love of the primitive has led him to Lappland, where he has found much material for pen and pencil. He has also visited Iceland and more recently Bolshevik Russia.

Albert Engström

CHARLES XII, HERCULES, AND GUSTAV MATTSON

I AM invited to take grog with Captain Söderbom aboard his vessel, the brig Alma of
Långsund. It is midsummer, and nearly all his
sailors are off, for he has not wished to refuse
them a dance with the native girls on the new
dance floor, especially as at the same time he
can say a word to a couple of his owners, who
live here. Also there are an ugly lot of fat
fellows from Norrhällan about, besides which
he has to go up to the store once in a while, and
furthermore he does what he likes so far as
that goes. He has brought in money enough for
all those land rats!

So there are many valid reasons why he has
put in here to swing at his moorings.

Old Söderbom is a skipper of the old school,
a short cubic figure, ice-gray hair and beard, sea-
eyed and self-assured. He has been sailing the
seven seas ever since he was no taller than a
marlinspike, and he thinks of the Baltic as a soup
tureen.

His mate, Matts Andersson, is of the same age,

from the same region, and much the same in appearance. The captain and he are a pair of Siamese twins. They have grown up together, taken their examinations together, and lived together all their lives, but they wrangle continuously—except on duty, of course. Andersson never got a boat of his own, and now he would feel out of his element if he stood as commander on his own deck. He is red-haired, with long red tufts in his ears and nostrils, on his nose and over his eyes. Both of them have gold rings in their ear lobes to keep off the rheumatism.

The man who introduced me to both these old fellows is Skipper Mattson of the yacht Albrektina, a man also well on in years. He is a blond giant with long unkempt beard, steady gray eyes, and a mouth full of snuff. He has been a terrible fighter in his day, and nobody in the whole fleet can tell such lies. On the starboard side of his yacht stand the letters A L B R E K T I N A, but on the port they read A N I T K E R B L A, because writing should go forward just the same as the boat does. Shiver his timbers! Mattson has been a comrade of mine on small yachts for many years back, and in that capacity is invited with me as guest of the Alma's captain.

So we four are sitting in the commodious and hospitable cabin—it is almost like a parlor with mirrors, sofas, and chairs. On one wall hangs a picture in a plain mahogany frame under an uneven glass. It represents a ship and was painted by Söderbom when he was a common seaman.

On the space in front of the foremast is written:

> Shipps Name
> Hedvik from
> Netherlands
> bound for Lon
> Don cargo
> oranges and
> figs
> year 1867.

Opposite this naïvely touching masterpiece hangs in a stylishly gilded frame a portrait of Charles XII. It is an execrable woodcut clipped from the Swedish Weekly a generation ago.

Captain Söderbom is well provided, and our tongues are quickly loosed. Mattson enjoys tasting something else than brandy for once. The smoke of the good Bremen cigars reminds him of North Germany, where he sailed as a boy. The whisky calls up pictures of London and Leith. He is in the tippler's paradise. We talk of everything between heaven and earth, of cargoes and sailing, and the steady alteration of humanity for the worse. In the old days there were real people, damned if there weren't. Now there's hardly a seaman left. Nothing but those steamboat scabs that smell of oil and look like niggers. "In the old days things were clean on a ship—like here," says Söderbom, "but now every sloop looks like a coalbin. Soon there won't be a man in Roslagen that can reeve a bight or splice a kevel—not to speak of anything else. And if a man gives a man one in the wind so that he doubles up, he turns around and jaws —what time of day is that? I've tasted the cat so the blood squirted; but now, blast it, you're not supposed to lift your foot to a slacker. No, it's all up with seamanship in Sweden, that's what it is. Skoal to you anyway, Engström!"

"Look there, captain, what's that scarecrow you've got on the wall?" inquired Mattson. "Some relative, eh? But he has a seven-story collar, so it's no relative he'll be."

He was pointing to Charles XII's portrait.

"Don't you recognize the portrait of Charles XII? That's pretty poor for you. Yes, I have his portrait because I like strength. And Charles XII was the last strong man we've had in Sweden."

"Hey go easy there!" said the mate. "Hercules was a bit heftier than him still."

"You're always butting in and chewing the

[276]

rag about your Hercules—he wasn't Swedish at all. How often will I have to tell you that?"

"Wasn't Swedish, you say? Deil take me but you're wrong. Hercules was as much Swedish as I am. Just listen here. Come, Engström, wasn't Hercules a Swede?"

"Oh, he may have been, but I'm not quite sure."

"Yes," said Mattson, "Charles XII was strong as the devil himself, that I've heard. He fought with ten men at once; but for all that he was a babe in arms compared to Gustav Mattson of Södervik."

"Look here now, Engström," said Captain Soderbom, "is there such a shot-thrower or sledge-slinger or wrestler nowadays as Charles XII? The hell there is! I've hung up his portrait just as an example for all that come down in the cabin; and in all harbors, here or abroad, when skippers come down and we begin to argue about strength, I point over to Charles XII with the certainty that they'll all know who *he* is. But that dodgasted Hercules, what sort of chestnut-worm was he? Why listen, Andersson, he couldn't lift a feather. I've heard you squealing about Hercules so long, now you can put that in your pipe. No, Charles XII—let me tell you, Engström—was a fellow that could go to it. And yet he lived on nothing but mouldy bread

and warmed himself at red-hot cannon balls and
slept on the bare ground at fifty below; and when
he got up late of a morning, he was spry as a
cockroach and began to slash around the first
thing so as to get a little warmth in his body.

"And then for you to come along with your
Hercules! Hercules—what the mischief of a
mamselle was he? You're all on the wrong tack,
Andersson. To come here and squeal and bel-
low about a lubber that never hauled in a sheet!
Hercules! Why—"

"Wait a bit, captain," said Mattson. "Both
Charles XII and this Hercules were infants in
swaddling clothes compared to Gustav Mattson
of Södervik just the same. *He* was Swedish,
Judas priest and ring the alarm! For I knew
him—"

"Listen here, Engström! Shut up, Mattson!"

"Skoal, Engström! Will you tell me this:
what does he know about Charles XII? Not a
bean he knows, if he doesn't say he was the strongest lad that ever wore pants. Out with it now!"

"Yes, Charles XII was an uncommonly vigorous chap, but he was a little chap—"

"Little chap! LITTLE! Good Lord and
the devil deliver us! Has this thing gone to
school and doesn't know any better than that?
Why, Engström, he was big as a house, and his
sword there was no one else could lift, it says in

the books. He was little? Like hell he was! How little was he then? How—"

"Listen, captain," Mattson interrupted, "this Gustav Mattson I was telling of—"

"Go hang yourself with your Gustav Mattson!" yelled the captain emptying his glass. "How little does Engström think Charles XII was? Was he the size of a thumbnail? Or the size of Andersson's nose? or Mattson's jaw? A man that's read books like you have ought to be able to tell us that."

"Yes, but we mustn't quarrel, for it's a question about good old Sweden. Promise me, captain, not to get furious if I tell how Charles XII really looked."

"All right."

"But anyway, captain," said Mattson, "he was a flea compared—"

"Keep still, I say! Engström, how big was Charles XII?"

"He wasn't as big as Hercules, I'll take my oath," said Andersson. "For Hercules—"

"Be quiet, mate! Deil's in it but I'll have command of my own people on board my own boat. How was it, Engström?"

"Why, he was a little fellow with reddish hair, about five feet tall and not at all a wrestler or an athlete. But he was remarkably vigorous when there was need. He was a staunch chap

who could do more than most men of his size.
Go and see his clothes in the Nordiska Museum
when you come to Stockholm. You couldn't get
them on with a shoe-horn, captain. Furthermore
I can say that my father-in-law was there and
made a portrait of him when they last opened his
coffin in the Riddarholmskyrka. It's from his
account that I have what I know of the size of
the king."

"Well, that beats the devil," said the captain.

"Yes, but Hercules then?" inquired the mate.
"Was your father-in-law there when they opened
his coffin?"

"No, he was too late for that opening."

"That's a pity, that is," said the mate and took
a mighty pull at his glass. "Is this true then?
It's claimed that Hercules was the very worst
hand for a fight—"

"Poof!" said Mattson, "what a souse he'd
have had if he'd scrapped with Gustav Mattson of
Södervik! For he was Sweden's strongest man,
and that I'll stick to. He came over on the
same boat I did to Kvarken. That'll be forty
years since now and—"

"Whew!" interrupted Captain Söderbom,
"that was the deuce and all, that about Charles
XII. Is it really true what you said, Engström?
That he was little and slight and red-haired? I'll
take down the portrait then, that I will."

"You mustn't do that, captain. For if a fellow's little and slight and red-haired, and still is true blue, does things that others can't do after him, and does them better than the big lummoxes, he's pluckier and better worth admiring just because he's small in size. But now I should like to hear what big things this Gustav Mattson of Södervik has done. Will you let Skipper Mattson tell you how it went?"

"Yes, let him shoot. But Charles XII and Hercules can go to Jericho. Andersson can say what he likes."

"Let's see," began Mattson, "let's see. Where shall I start? I'll start with a skoal. Well, I was sailing on the Rosenklippe, that old brig, you know, that was sold here a while back. We were up in North Kvarken one day lying on the starboard tack before a light breeze north by northeast. There were a whole lot of sloops there, mostly yachts from Roslagen. Right then came the hell of a tearer from the east northeast. Everything was white all at once, and it wasn't a gale, it was a hurricane. Engström, who is a seaman, can understand we got the mischief on our starboard quarter."

"Yes, but what's that got to do with the strongest man in Sweden?"

"Don't break in. I'll tell how it all was. We shipped a sea on the starboard quarter, and with that both the royal sheets went, and the sheets whipped off the royals, and the whole caboodle was carried to Davy Jones. The sheets held on the fore-to'gallant sail, but when we tried to lower, there was a slack in the sail, and the canvas went the same as the other. And—"

"Avast there, Mattson," broke in Captain Söderbom, "that's all fine enough, but keep to your course. It was about Gustav Mattson—"

"Captain," said Mattson, "if I'm to tell this story, I've got to—breath o' my body!—tell the whole thing. Skoal! When we had lowered the main-to'gallant sail, the lee sheet and halliards broke so that it sounded like a cannon shot, and the cordage whipped apart the yard of the main-topsail. All right! The staysail veered, and the sheet and sail blew up on the foremast spars, and when the flying jib was lowered, the blocks tore the inner jib. The topmast held—"

"See here, Mattson, don't cough up so much nautical stuff, for that doesn't interest Engström. This Gustav Mattson—"

"Hold your gaff—and skoal! If I'm to tell this, it's got to be all or nothing. We hauled the stu'nsail up to the gaff. All that was done in a twinkling. But afterwards we had to put her under as little sail as possible so as to keep all clear and not make too much leeway. So we hauled—"

"Keep on the job, Mattson! Deil's in the man!"

"So we hauled in the stu'nsail and made all fast. We lowered the rags of the main topsail and made fast. There she lay under mainsail, foretopsail, foresail, jib and foreto'gallantsail. We let the mainsail alone, for it had held—"

"He's hell for a sermon," said the mate.

"Skoal! But we lay a little too deep and had to steer a' westerly course so as to fall off to the sou'west, and then we got the wind abeam and sailed like in raspberry juice into the northern inlet of Ratan harbor. Is there anyone who's been in Ratan? Deil be thanked for that! Engström's been there. Well, then he knows how it is. We were the first that came in before the storm, but afterwards a whole mass of others came in. A lot of them looked like hoboes, so they had to lay to, repair and patch. The storm held, so one day a bunch of us roughnecks made it up to have a dance and jamboree for the girls of the place. Brandy we had, and what we didn't have we got. There were seven or eight of us boys who fixed it all up and hired a kitchen and room of an old woman. We could all of us play the accordion, but it wasn't all of us that wanted to dance, and so those that didn't want to dance could sit and play poker or tarock or what the devil else there was—"

"Yes, but Gustav Mattson, the fellow that was so strong——"

"If you won't let me tell it the way I choose, you can go up to Ratan yourselves and ask about it. But with that a whole gang of Norrlanders came in, lumberyard men of course, and wanted to get into it and dance. 'Come in and welcome,' says we, for the girls could of course take their chances among the new lot. 'You're welcome to dance,' says we, 'but we have so little brandy that it hardly does for us. But dance you may as much as you like—the music we'll stand treat for,' says we. Then the Norrlanders got ugly because they couldn't have any spirits, and right there a Norrlander tripped a boy from Vaddö, just south of here. But that he shouldn't have done, for that was none other than Gustav Mattson. He has the same name as me, but I won't just assert that it was me. He was of about the same strength as me.

"All right. Gustav Mattson went out to us where we were sitting playing poker and told how things were and asked if we shouldn't begin chucking out. But I was sitting in good luck with the game and answered, 'No-o, Gustav Mattson, plenty of time for that. We'll wait a moment.' Then he went in and began to dance again. But right as he was dancing, there was some one that opened a window and fired in a bucket full of

[284]

grease and slop and such through the window, and it struck Gustav Mattson and the girl he was dancing with, and the floor was flooded, and it smelt like the devil.

"Then Gustav Mattson went into the room again and told how it was and asked if we shouldn't begin chucking out.

"No, I sat in good luck and was near to win back what I'd laid out for brandy. Then says Gustav Mattson, 'I must tell you, Gustav, that I'm nasty. I'm so nasty that sometimes when I wake o' mornings after I've been full, I have my pockets crammed with laces and socks. And my claspknife is always wet. I'm going to chuck them out now myself.'

"With that he went into the kitchen and began to chuck out the Norrlanders. He chucked them out of windows and doors just as it came, without opening the windows or doors, so that he ruined more rixdollars' worth of door-jambs and window-frames than panes of glass.

"And when the Norrlanders were chucked out, it was only their noses that hit the dirt, for nothing else could come down before Mattson was out in the yard and began to waltz with them again. He had grabbed them as they sat on the chairs or leaned against the walls or were dancing.

"Of course they tried to defend themselves,

but after a moment or two there was no blade left on their knives and no lid on their snuff-boxes. And where Gustav Mattson came, he swung his arms like this and like that, and there was a passage behind him, a passage so wide you could have driven a carriage and pair after him.

"Out in the yard there was an old dried-up well. There he threw down sixteen of them, for there wasn't room for more. And both Captain Söderbom and Andersson and Engström may reckon there must have been one hell of a mix-up at the bottom of that well.

"But it's so that when a fellow begins to scrap and is successful and carries all before him, he gets more and more in the swing of it. I know that myself from Hamburg and Lübeck and Genoa, when I was in my best form. And Gustav Mattson was in the swing—there was no limit any more. He began to run and get big stones, which he threw into the kitchen and into the hall. It wasn't one, it was hundreds, that I'll swear as true as I hope to get to heaven and not to Old Nick when I die. And I swear by the same token that none of the stones he threw in were so small it didn't take three or four full-sized Norrlanders to roll them out; I say roll, for to pick them up was clean impossible. The Ratan folks kept rolling at the stones for six days before they could even begin to get anything to rights in the rooms.

"One stone they couldn't get any further than to the garden outside. There it lies still, and on it in gold letters stand engraved these exact words: GUSTAV MATTSON. That's my name, though it wasn't me and though I was along. But it's something of an honor to have been there on such an occasion. Now I ask of Captain Söderbom and Andersson and Engström: Could Charles XII or that Hercules fellow have cleaned out the Norrlander saw-mill hands like that? I just ask them. Come right out with it! I've been in a shindy where I haven't touched my feet to the ground for a quarter of an hour, we were so close, so I know from experience. And Engström knows that they've built the new dance floor at Grisselhamn with so much space between the planks so that the blood can run off as fast as possible; that he knows, for Engström has been in it too. But how much has Charles XII been in? Not a smell! That I'll swear to. If he had known how it goes in Roslagen or in Norrland, he'd have come here on leave of absence and not kept on playing down in Russia and Turkey —that is if he'd really wanted a scrap."

"Well, but Mattson," I asked, "what was Mattson doing all this time while Gustav Mattson was cleaning up the row?"

"I told Engström a while since, and both Captain Söderbom and mate Andersson are my witnesses besides, that I said I was sitting in good luck at poker. If I had come in, there hadn't needed to be any scrap. Skoal!"

LUDVIG NORDSTRÖM

THE AWAKENING

LUDVIG NORDSTRÖM (1882–) has won popularity by his stories of the far north in Sweden. It is the same region, Ångermanland, of which Pelle Molin was the literary discoverer, but where Molin sees it in a romantic light, Nordström is almost too heavily realistic. His knowledge of the fishermen in the northern skerries is based on personal observation, for he has himself hauled nets and rowed in the fisheries. The imaginary fishing-harbor Tvärhamn is the scene of the stories in *Fishermen,* which describe a life of adventure, of danger, and primitive joys. The village Öbacka, also an imaginary place, is the background of the collection *Burghers,* from which the story in the present volume is taken. To these two places Nordström often returns in later stories, and it is there he is at his best, in his sympathetic presentation of the types he knows thoroughly.

In recent years Nordström has undertaken the ambitious task of writing the economic history of Sweden in novel form. The series is entitled *The History of Petter Svensk,* and several volumes have already appeared.

Ludvig Nordström

THE AWAKENING

I

IN Öbacka as in other small coast cities there
are many sailor families, and among these was
the Nordhammers.

There was only one son in the house; his name
was Erik, and he was seventeen.

This autumn he had come home from a three
months' sail on a brig, where he had served as
common sailor, and he was now returning to the
gymnasium.

He was not the only one among his associates
who had spent the summer so on board a vessel, yet there was a slight difference between him
and the others. They had been greatly changed,
in that they swaggered in their gait, chewed tobacco, and wore safety-straps over their caps, besides which they often said "Goddam!" He, on
the contrary, was like his former self, except that
he was more brown and slender and broad across
the shoulders, as well as somewhat more silent.
The others told tales of what they had seen and
experienced in foreign harbors, but Erik Nord-

hammer found that, to put it baldly, he had seen very little.

But when from the school window he saw all the boats out in the roadstead and thought of what it was like to go bare-armed and bare-headed in the wind, to feel the storm on one's face, taste the salt water, put forth all one's strength; what it was to behold the sun sink in the sea, to watch a strange land slowly rise and take on definite form, to see the smoke above great cities, hear foreign speech, observe new customs; then he forgot to breathe for so long that afterwards he had to sigh. And in the evening he would walk all alone on the shore beyond the city, doing nothing else, just roaming about. In these days he was quick with a blow, and as he was strong, he struck hard and made enemies. And in school things went from bad to worse, but this gave him no concern, for it seemed to him as if he were asleep.

II

The weather grew colder and colder; soon it would be winter. But before that came the market fair, when the town re-echoed with drums and shots and shrill brass music.

Erik Nordhammer sauntered about the fair grounds as he had previously done along the shore, but he no longer cared to join in pinning together old peasant women or throwing snuff in the eyes of farmer boys.

His mood grew darker and darker, and sometimes when he was alone he clenched his fists, spread out his arms, uttered a sharp "Ah!" and hurried off he knew not where.

Evening had now come again. There was drumming, howling, and music from all the tents, and clowns in costume were skipping and dancing in the illumination of Bengal lights, when Erik pushed his way into the throng.

A green, cold radiance fell on everything, so that human beings looked repulsive. He turned aside for nobody, and on any one who murmured he fixed his dark glance in a way which rendered further argument unnecessary.

The current of the crowd brought him to a shooting gallery, and there he stood still. He was ground slowly forward to the barrier, and now he could see something. Three girls were standing inside; two of them joked and laughed, and men clapped them on the shoulder, but the third had black eyes and kept herself aloof.

Erik Nordhammer stood with his hands in his coat pockets and gazed at her continuously, until finally she noticed him. When she saw that he was looking at her, without any change of expression she took a gun and came forward to him.

He looked her straight in the eyes and said at last, "I want to talk to you."

She looked at him a while and then said, "Go around back of the tent."

He did as directed, and it was not long before she arrived.

"Are you Swedish?" he asked.

"Yes," she replied. "What do you want of me?"

"I want you to take a walk with me," he said.

"Why?" she inquired.

"Because I want you to," he answered fiercely, but added, "and because I like you. Will you come?"

"Yes," she said.

"Come then!" he bade, and they went off.

"Where are we going?" she asked.

"I don't know," he said. "Just come along and don't talk; I only want you beside me."

"Are you sane or crazy?" she asked him then.

"Sane," he said, "but pretty near crazy. But you needn't be afraid."

So they walked along a good while; she took some caramels from her pocket and ate. They got beyond the city, and the thin crescent of the moon shone in the dusk above them.

"What's your name?" he asked suddenly.

"Laura," she told him.

"Oh!" he said. "Mine's Nordhammer. My father's a sea captain, he lives in the town here."

"Are you a sailor?" she said.

"No."

"What are you then?"

"I'm a gymnasiast."

"Really!" she said. "Why don't you go into a circus then?"

"I'm a gymnasiast, not a gymnast."

"Oh!" she said, not understanding.

"Sit down there!" he said, pointing to a stone. She sat down, and he sat on another stone.

"You have fine eyes, Laura," he said.

"And yours are just as fine," she returned. "You're a handsome fellow. Are you strong?"

"Yes," he said.

With that she got up and came to him. She sat beside him, laid her arms around his neck, and kissed him. He sat with his hands in his pockets and let her kiss.

When she stopped, he said, "More, Laura! That's like a cold bandage on my forehead."

Later he said, "Come down to the shore. You sit on a low stone, and I'll lie with my head in your lap."

"But it's so cold," she objected.

"Take my coat, it's warm!" he said, and flung it off.

"Tell me where you're from now," he said.

"I don't know," she replied; "I've never known who my father or mother was."

"Are you all alone?" he asked.

"Yes."

He said nothing, just looked out across the ocean, which was a flood of moonlight.

Finally he went on, "Well, I'm alone too."

"You have your father and mother, though," she objected.

"Stepmother," he revised. "My mother is dead."

"Does she beat you?" she asked.

He smiled at that. "No."

"But I've no one to talk to," he continued. "They don't understand what I say."

"That depends on what you say, doesn't it?"

"No," he answered bluntly.

But after a while he said, "I don't know what I want. I won't go to school any more."

"Are you at school still? Are you a schoolboy, you big fellow?"

When he heard this, he sprang up.

"You say big fellow?" he demanded fiercely. "Do you think I look like a big fellow? Tell me, tell me."

"Why, of course."

"Do you think I'm active?"

"Why, of course."

"Look at this!" he said, and taking a run he did several cartwheels and handsprings on the sand.

At that she began to laugh. "You foolish fellow to cut figures here on the sand! Come here and show whether you're a man!"

When he came, she jumped up on him, wound her arms and legs around him, licked him in the face, bit his ears, kissed him, and whispered to him.

As they were lying on the sand later, he said, "You're the first human being I've ever met that I could talk to. If I could only bite you and eat you up so I could always have you!"

But she lay silent with her face touched by the moonlight so that her eyes glittered.

"Tell me one thing!" he asked. "Do you always go along when anyone asks you?"

"That depends if they're handsome fellows like you."

He looked at her sorrowfully, then hid his face against her breast, and said, "I'd like to marry you. With you I can talk."

She caressed him gently and answered, "How old are you?"

"Seventeen."

"I'm seventeen too," she said.

"Whom will you marry?"

"I shan't marry."

"Why not."

"Our sort doesn't."

"I know," he cried, jumping up. "If I'd marry you, you'd be willing!"

"Yes," she said.

"I'll show you," he said. "I'll show you," he exulted, throwing himself upon her and bursting into loud sobs.

"I'll show you, I'll show you!"

III

The following day Erik Nordhammer went to his class, but he hardly knew he was there. He did not hear what was going on around him; the sun shone upon him through the window, and he had an infinite sense of wellbeing. He thought of Laura and of the foreign harbors where he had been, of home and the life on shipboard, and of the future, which was a morning mist.

Then he was called upon to prove something on a blackboard, but when he got there he did not know what the question was.

The teacher, who sat on the dais and swung his stick, held him up to ridicule:

"Ahem, ahem! Nordhammer is a big man, he has seen the world, but he doesn't comprehend Euclid. He has a big frame and long legs, but he has a small and feeble intellect. There are many little men in the class here who haven't seen the world but who haven't brains as small as Nordhammer's. I think it would be a good idea if he chucked school for good and signed up on a boat, for he has a strong body and can do a good job carrying coal and flour. . . ."

Erik Nordhammer listened a while to the words of the hated instructor, but now he advanced, put his clenched fist under the other's nose and said coldly, "That's enough of you, you damned little Skåning! I've got my job. Goodbye to you and thanks for your kindness!"

With that he gripped the teacher, who became ashen-pale, gave him a good shaking, and in the midst of deadly silence strode out of the class.

He knew very well that now he could not return to school, and that was as good as having to start a new life. He realized too that now, by a single act, he had put himself beyond the pale; his comrades would avoid him, the story would pass from house to house, people would purse their mouths when he spoke to them, and the atmosphere around him would become so cold, so bitter, and so hostile that it would be unendurable—if he stayed. But he wouldn't stay; by his act of insubordination he had forced himself to the change.

Yet now that he saw the necessity before him, he saw all he should have to give up.

He was excited, he wanted to be alone and think the whole thing out, so he went up a high hill outside the city where no human being ever came.

There he sat on a stone and thought. He should, then, lose his warm room, his regular meals with good food, coffee in bed on Sunday morning, skating, ski-running, walks with girls of his age, dances, the sense of comfort in black dress-clothes, friendly words, jokes and laughter.

And what should he gain? Cold, discomfort, storm and wet, peril of life with slavish toil, dirt, want, and blows. In harbor there would be the fear of being decoyed into murder-holes, the risk of being robbed, uncertainty, loneliness. And when he should come back some day, he would be red, unkempt, and weather-beaten, with hands as stiff and hard as horn, tarry and hairy, his arms tattooed, perhaps with his nose broken by a knife-stroke, perhaps ragged and poor—or else he might never again see this town, which now lay beneath him so still and peaceful. But if he came back, what would his comrades be? Fine gentlemen in fine clothes, pale of complexion, with slender white hands, students and dance-heroes; men of books, who at the writing tables in their warm rooms earned an ample independence; gentlemen who could eat generously and delicately in restaurants, drink their coffee and punch, play cards and get married, become respected and rich, while he was roving like a homeless dog around all the nations of the earth. When he came back, they would not care to recognize him or take him by the hand; they would look with terror and repulsion at him as at a wild, unusual, and dangerous beast.

"You are swine!" he shouted to the winds, "snivelers, milksops, lapdogs, mothers' babies!"

Then the thought came that his mother was dead, his father old and sick and lame, his sisters young and undowered, he himself poor and alone in the world; and the whole thing was too much. He collapsed on the grass and wept over himself and his dismal fate, all the good things he must leave, the bad that awaited him; and he saw all the life before him as something cold, pitiless, hostile, and inevitable.

But when he had cried himself out, he felt lighter of mood; a sense of confidence rose up within him; he thought he could make this sacrifice just to be free; and then he felt strong.

He stood peering down at the city with his hands in his pockets. At last he suddenly burst out, "I'll be a man-sized man!"

Then he went quietly down the mountain to seek out his father and tell the old man his decision.

IV

Captain Nordhammer sat as usual in his big chair with a blanket round his legs, looking out over the harbor.

Erik went up to him and said, "Father, I've decided to be a sailor in earnest."

When he had spoken, he began to pace up and down the room. His father delayed long before he answered:

"If you had never been to sea," he said at last, "I should say 'no' and forbid you, for then you could not realize what a sailor's life means. But now that you've sailed and got yourself into a rumpus besides, I can't, my dear boy, forbid you, because I understand that there are stronger forces than I which have brought you to such a resolve. But tell me anyway: have you thoroughly considered what you're doing?"

"Yes," said Erik. "And I've got to do it whether I will or not, for I've taken a teacher by the collar and shaken him. I shall be dismissed if I stay."

"Ack!" muttered the old man, "this strange city, this strange city!"

He then turned to his son and said, "Come here, Erik!"

When the son came, the father took his hand, stroked it, and said, "I did as you did, and that was the reason I too became a sailor. We have

been seamen from far back, as you've seen in the
Bible; from the first name to the last it's all sailors. But my father said to me: 'Whatever you
are, don't be a sailor!' His father said to him:
'Whatever you are, don't be a sailor!' And I've
said to you, 'Whatever you are, don't be a sailor!'
But our blood is not calm yet. You'll have a
hard life, my dearly beloved Erik, but you'll be
a real man."

The old man was silent a while, caressing the
boy's hand. Then he went on:

"It's the will that makes the man, Erik. I'm
losing you now, perhaps for always. Perhaps,
yes certainly, I shall be dead when you come back;
or—what would be cruel and hideous—you may
go under. You may be shipwrecked. You may
fall out of the rigging. You may be washed over-
board. You may be stabbed ashore. But you
have will, and it's will that makes the man. It's
will that has made me. It's my will that has built
this house, it's my will that has created our home,
and it's my will that created you, my dearly beloved child. Remember all your life long, whatever may befall you, wherever you may put in,
whatever station in life you may reach, it's will,
Erik, and will alone that's the one important
thing. When I hear now what you've done, I
ought to punish you, but you did it on higher
grounds than mere disobedience; it was your will

that wakened in you, and therefore, Erik, I feel that I'm thankful to you for what you've done. For now I see that you're my son. After that others may say what they choose."

Thereupon the old man kissed with his cold lips the hot hand of his son. He then covered his eyes and was silent for a time.

Finally, his hand still before his eyes, he asked, "Is there maybe a girl in the affair too?"

"Yes," replied Erik in a low voice.

"Ah yes," said the old man, "it must always be so. Is she a pretty girl?"

"Yes," muttered Erik.

"Is she of good family?"

"I don't know, I expect not," said Erik. "She's a girl from the fair."

"What!" screamed the old man, staring at his son with wide-open eyes. "Are you crazy?"

"Forgive me, father!" said Erik.

"Oh," lamented the old man, rocking his head, "that too, that too!"

Erik freed his hand and began again his pacing of the floor. He was ashamed of having caused the old man such grief.

"Erik," said his father, "you'll have a hard fate, a hard fate."

"Yes," the son answered, "I believe it, father."

"You'll have the same fate as I, the same hard

fate as I. I too became a sailor because of a circus girl."

"Father!" cried Erik.

"Yes," said the father. "I shudder when I see this remarkable likeness between you and me, my boy. I seem to see your whole life before me."

"Come here, Erik!" he added, and took his son's hand.

"Though you won't be able to comprehend what I'm saying to you now, still hearken to the words of your old dad and remember them till you're old yourself. You'll come to see, Erik, that nothing will happen to you in life unless there's a woman in it. Nothing! If there isn't a woman, then nothing will happen that has any meaning for you. Whether it's ill or good, you must always be prepared that the real events in your life come with women. Women near or women far, but always women. You know I'm not a learned man, and I can't explain it; I can only tell you what I've lived and experienced.

"But don't fetter your heart to a woman! Never let yourself be mastered by them! Beware of them, for nothing on earth is so dangerous, so full of evil, cruelty, deceit, and baseness as a woman. But don't fear them either! If you're afraid, you are lost. Never forget that, whatever you do, you should always know how to free yourself. If you once get really into the claws of a woman, you are lost. If you train yourself to be cold and hard, you can command them as you command your sloop.

"You have one reliance that you don't know of yet. You're too young for that. But when you've been at the helm a few years, when you're standing lookout, when you hang in the shrouds as the yardarm goes under, you'll little by little get to know him. That is God. You needn't be any mollycoddle for that; you'll find no real seaman who isn't better acquainted with him than any priest you can name. But when you've once learned reverence for him, you'll never forget him again, and then you can always get yourself clear of trouble.

"Remember your dad's words, Erik: never shun a woman, but never let her get the mastery of you! Follow that rule, and you'll escape going under, as most others, as most of us others, have done."

Here the old man ceased and pointed to the door, as was his way when he was overwrought and wished to be alone. With a feeling of strangeness and terror his son stole out.

V

After supper Erik went to Laura, but he went

slowly and had entirely lost his zest. He thought of his father, and an expression of shamefacedness came over him.

"So," he thought, "the old lame man has been sitting imagining things about women, while he kept his eyes shut and rested in his chair like one dead. Wasn't he a rascal, teaching his son to despise and shun women like that, and he himself married twice!"

But was woman such a formidable power in life? He had never noticed anything but diffidence and playfulness in the girls with whom he went. Did they change when they were grown up? But if they changed, how did they change and what did they do? What had his father gone through, what had happened between him and his wives? What happened between all the men and women who lived in all these houses? That, he realized, opened a new door to him; but he felt himself insecure as a child in a dark cellar, a child whom some one has warned and frightened.

All he had thought of before had now lost its worth, and he realized that what had begun to suck him to itself was what everybody talked about: life.

Everything about him reeled, there was nothing to hold on to except the two things his father had said: "It's the will that makes the man;"

and "Never shun a woman, but never let her master you!"

But what should he will? And what was this about letting a woman master him?

Erik Nordhammer was completely miserable when he followed Laura from the fair grounds to her room. She lived in an old black shanty where she had a little low room with a curious smell.

The lamp shone darkly in the room, but as she sat astride him, a glow irradiated from her body with its slender waist and rounded breasts, the whole crowned by her head with its dark mouth, dark eyes, and dark coronet of hair.

There was something uncanny in her appearance, something of the witch and of the ancient goddess. There was something mysterious and untrustworthy.

And Erik Nordhammer asked, "Are you women bad?"

Sitting and sucking at a piece of candy, Laura answered, "Yes," and gave a confirmatory nod.

"Why are you bad?"

"I don't know."

"Are you bad too?"

"Yes, to be sure."

"In what way are you bad?" he asked.

At that she laughed. Then she leaned down and kissed him.

[308]

"You're talking nonsense," she said.

He sensed now that she was bad, though he could not be clear as to how.

She caressed him and said, "Your candy wasn't good. I like lollipops better."

As she said these words, his whole body grew cold, and he looked at her without saying a word, but he got up and put on his coat.

"Are you going already?" she asked indifferently.

"Yes," he answered shortly.

Then she came and clung to him, begging and beseeching him not to go.

"No," he said shortly as before.

"Then I'm done with you too," said she. "I'll go out and get another boy nicer than you."

"You can if you like."

"You haven't given me anything either, stingy," said she.

He took out a tenner that he had left from the summer and laid it very quietly on the table. When she saw it she threw herself on his neck, but he wrenched himself hurriedly loose.

"Schoolboy," she mocked him, with an indecent gesture that seemed customary with her. She then poured out a torrent of abuse, but Erik Nordhammer hastened out into the dark.

Drawing a deep breath he looked up at the clear starry sky, and it seemed to him that all the stars were laughing at him. Was that what the old man meant? Was it so that women were in the bottom of their hearts? The boy's head was in a whirl; he was afraid, at a loss, not knowing where to turn.

But this much he realized, that in two days he had so changed that he no longer recognized himself or his surroundings. In everything there was a hidden mystery, and in the same instant he had both perceived this and felt that from now on he was alone and should remain alone always.

VI

The days passed, Erik Nordhammer's vessel lay in the roadstead, and everything was clear for sailing. Then one misty morning the anchor was hoisted.

His sisters stood on the shore waving. His father sat at the window watching sail after sail set, and as the vessel gently began to get under weigh, he shut his eyes and murmured softly, "Adele, Adele!"

When Mrs. Nordhammer heard the name of Erik's mother, she went noiselessly out of the room and left the old man alone.

Off there Erik was beginning his life, and he was glad to get away, anywhere, but away, away!

ANNA LENAH ELGSTRÖM

OUT OF CHAOS

ANNA LENAH ELGSTRÖM (1882–) is at once a realist and a romanticist. Her humanitarian and pacifist sympathies have found expression in her stories of contemporary life, as in *Mothers,* a collection of short stories from which *Out of Chaos* in the present volume is taken. Her recent novel, *The Ant Hill,* is from the time of the World War, and tells the story of a woman who struggles heroically to keep the home intact, who falls a victim to temptation, but rises again. It celebrates the "great daily adventure" of the army of workers who move through the city streets on their way to work every morning.

The other side of Mrs. Elgström's authorship is a fruit of her romantic longing to clothe intense and vivid feelings in colorful garb and give them the perspective of distance. She has written stories from the Italian Renaissance and from the French Revolution. In the latter, her heroines are all daughters of the aristocracy, slender, indomitable figures, who pit their spiritual strength against a world of brute force.

Last year Mrs. Elgström visited America and, in collaboration with her husband, Mr. Gustaf Collijn, wrote *U. S. A. Life and Theatre.*

Anna Lenah Elgström

OUT OF CHAOS

SHE did not know where she was or how she had come there, but suddenly with a feeling of strained oppression she saw stretching before her the silent expanse of a great desolate square, gleaming in the twilight like a mysterious pool of turbid light between walls of stifling dusk.

She stopped, not daring to move—who could tell what might come out of the dark as it stood menacingly around the pale band of light?

So she lingered a long while, listening intently, but she heard only the dull throbbing of her own heart in the silence, which seemed to hold its breath in almost intolerable suspense. She did the same, though she did not know why she was afraid, yet for that very cause was filled with a more icy terror.

With eyes starting from their sockets she saw at last something crouching like a shadow, which stole out of the dusk and crawled questingly back and forth across the lighted quadrangle, sniffing about from one to another of the dark motionless heaps that blotched its surface. She stared at this enigmatical vision without comprehending it. And the unknown stared back at her, silent and empty. The dark globe of the world seemed ready to burst with its own inconceivable mystery.

The silence around her had, as it were, intensified into a dumb cry of horror. Her own mouth was open to voice it, but although teeming with fear, she could not utter it, could not comprehend what she saw.

With that the slinking shadow raised its crouched form and shattered the spell with a long-drawn howl of despair. And with its echo, which rang mournfully and drearily through the night, the meaning of what she saw rolled out before her like a hastily unfolded map.

It was *her* dog that was howling out there. And the dark heap into which, lamenting, he bored his nose—she threw back her head and shrieked with him, a piercing, protracted shriek, rising ever more madly as if it could never stop —the dark motionless thing that lay crumpled there—was her husband's corpse!

She clutched her head and felt the full incomprehensibility rise up again like an impenetrable wall around her, hiding the significance of everything.

Again and again all vanished into unmeaning emptiness; she could no more be sure on account of the void in her soul. Or was it perhaps reality itself which no longer endured, which had burst apart into its original wild malicious tumult on the day when war surged in over existence?

That day, she had come back from the neighboring village where she had hurried in the morning twilight to warn her parents of the enemy's expected attack, and when she turned the corner of the square, just as she had done now, she had seen it stretch its long gray-gleaming surface between the house walls; but from the place where her house stood she beheld flames, pale yellow in the bright blue daylight, streaming aloft toward the rosy heavens where the larks were singing . . . Then it was she had first felt the insane suspicion that existence had fallen asunder, that all reason, all laws had given way, and that insensible chaos had pressed in over the world with all its horror.

For she knew she had left her two-year's child locked up in the kitchen of that house which now had burst into flames in the glad summer day.

When she rushed screaming toward the fire, the soldiers threw down their leveled bayonets, as a storm tosses about sticks and straws, and reached the house just as its roof collapsed amid a billowing cloud of flames. At the same moment, in her mad rush, she ran into something on the ground, fell over it, and suddenly found herself looking into her husband's face, where

[315]

not his kindly eyes, his happy smile, but his red flesh, his bones kneaded into a bloody dough stared at her. Then it was as if an abyss of horror had swallowed her own brain and had spread out into a meaningless all-embracing void.

She looked at the red mask which had been her husband's face, and only a thing stared back at her—this unknown, incredible It.

She raised herself, suddenly perplexed and indifferent. Around her the massacre raved, shots rang out, women and children shrieked in death agony. But she stood on motionless with empty staring eyes, frozen by the incomprehensibility of it all.

Straight opposite her there chanced to be a confectionery shop, whose fine plate-glass windows, absurdly well-polished and gaily illuminated by the sunlight, glittered in uncanny sleekness on the desolation with the set uncomprehending grin of an idiot.

The Thing stared at her even from this—an expressionless white blur, a meaningless terrifying surface—her own face.

But this she did not grasp, she no longer grasped the meaning or coherence of anything, she was one with chaos, dissolved into its nothingness.

After that she did not remember much, only darkly that, like a drowning man before he sinks for the last time, she had come to the surface now and again and had indistinctly been conscious of herself.

Through her memory swept like shadows the long, long roads she had traveled with bleeding feet over endless desolate country, so monotonously pitted with shells and gashed by the dark bristling bands of trenches that, struggling on through their pale moon-landscape, she was tortured by the nightmare thought that she was always in the same place. And she was in such a hurry, hounded continually forward by the dreadful foreboding of something inexpressibly loved which was lost in this spectre world of shadows.

Nothing but shadows—shadows of dark shores against which heavy waves beat thunderously, shadows of steep paths winding up to the tumultuous clouds, lofty shadows of black cliffs around which vultures screamed, and gloomy shadows of deep autumn-red woods where the falling leaves silently covered bloody corpses with strange mutilated faces—an interminable shadow-woven jungle of ill-boding dreams, through which she vainly fought to win to a clear understanding of what was reality and what was not, ridden by a nightmare in a feverish dance that went around in a circle and ended in the same place.

Now she was back there, down in the ruins of her former home, and the blackened stones flew in all directions as she dug in the still warm ashes, working ever further down into the depths with her eyes fixed vacantly on the darkness, as if she would penetrate the abyss of existence, would dig herself down into the bowels of the earth to reach certainty. Certainty as to whether it was a dream or not, this precious agonizing hint of a memory that shimmered and then vanished amid the pictures of horror in her troubled soul.

Oh, that little delicate flower-like head, radiant as a little waxen-white lamp with light from heaven, that little tea-rose face, ever present in all wonder, in all fleeting laughter and tears, beaming with love as with the deepest, dearest secret of existence! Oh, those little arms stretched toward her, the tiny swaying hands so much like thistle-down, the little clear bird-calls to mother! She heard its echo through her heart, she tore wildly at the earth as if to create from that dead chaos all the precious, good and beloved that she desperately strove to remember.

If it was true, if it had ever existed, then there was safety, then there was light and knowledge, redemption—

But only ashes ran through her hands, and her heart stood still, her thoughts grew bewildered, as in the darkness she felt the silent sifting of all things to nothing between her fingers. Again it was as if she could not comprehend anything, her eyes grew more and more insane, more wildly she dug and searched on all fours at the bottom of the pit, like a dog tossing up clouds of ashes.

She was now so deep that the masses of earth threatened to crumble down upon her, but she paid no heed to this, only dug on straight down into the depths, as if she herself wanted to vanish down, down into that unknown which had taken her child and annihilated it in emptiness, obliterated it so that not the slightest trace remained, not the slightest proof that this wondrous beloved mysterious being which had been her all was other than a mocking dream, leaving *It* as the only reality.

Softly moaning, she raised her head and looked vacantly and desperately about her. It was already full day, and the same terror-striking joyous light—in which the world seemed to be paralyzed with bewilderment, staring at her in a hard white insane smile—illuminated the desolation.

Everywhere towered the same dead chaos of torn-up pavement, half-burned houses, and heaps of rubbish and corpses strewn about—a jumble of blackened beams hanging in the air in a fantastically woven network with twisted human limbs which were tossed about over the ground

[319]

in unnatural, grimly uncouth postures, so that they seemed to have congealed into a single mad revolt contrary to all law, against all human or divine order.

As far as the eye, or the thought, could reach there was no token of life, of reason, of anything humanly good and fair left out of this destruction. Now she knew it, knew that nothing remained to be saved or to save, no redemption from the nightmare without end. Her solitary moaning ceased, and all grew silent, petrified into a single unconscious indifference before its own incomprehensible enigma.

Chaos had unbounded rule in a spectre world of horror where anything was possible—the reality of the human world, as men had made it—

Then occurred the miracle.

Out of the petrifaction a little living child raised its tender head, whose bright golden hair gleamed in the sunlight. Over the dead chaos shone suddenly this little emaciated face, charming as a flower, with which the sunbeam played in golden and pinkish-blue shadows around the limpid dark child-eyes, eyes that behind all their helpless suffering and forlorn tears glistened with life's great sweet mystery.

Slowly and painfully, swaying with every step, it worked its way up through the labyrinth of blackened beams and broken foundations that formed its tomb. Like a vault of deadly peril they hung above the little tender life that wanted to get out. The fixed desolation around seemed to lean forward, watching with menace the fumbling effort of those small helpless hands.

In the endless paralyzing stillness the faint sounds of the stones as they fell from the little one's grasp seemed enough to waken Death, who silently opened his jaws.

But the child crept on. A narrow trickle of blood followed its steps, and it whimpered quietly, almost inaudibly, wearied as it was with suffering. But it lived, it rose on its little tottering feet and stumbled forward.

The fixed insane labyrinth was broken away bit after bit by the tiny living form, as it moved between stone-heaps and corpses. Over their dead immobility wandered the sweet radiant eyes of the child filled with helpless terror. The further it came, the more it tried as much as it could to restrain its tears and to go along as quietly as possible, so as not to break the silence and perhaps awaken one of the grim uncanny beings which seemed to slumber all around.

It understood nothing except that it was separated from its great beloved protection, which was called Mother, that it was no longer her little darling child and did not know where she had gone. But it was determined to find her, to cuddle up to her and not be so frightened any more.

The little underlip trembled more and more, but it controlled itself bravely—now was the time to slip by the most terrifying thing of all, that strange dark apparition which seemed to be neither asleep nor awake, as it became visible between the continuously billowing smoke-clouds from a deep pit that opened across the child's path. A couple of steps more, and the child saw that it was the ash gray figure itself which caused all the whirling dust.

Motionless on its knees in the bottom of the pit, black and gray from head to foot, like a statue of mould and ashes, the strange apparition dug hastily and half-unconsciously in the earth with its wounded blood-red hands. Wandering indifferently, the white insane eyes fell upon the child, which timidly sought to steal by. A second—then the mechanical toil ceased, the bleeding hands became still.

All was still for a moment as if in a single noiseless, motionless struggle to tear apart something, to remember, to understand—a final gigantic rigid weary effort, which seemed to be concentrated in the yearning look with which the mother down in the pit stared at the little bleeding, trembling form at its edge.

There it was—the sweet heaven that her womb,

her bosom had born and cherished; there shone
the light, the knowledge of whose mere existence
was to have saved her—it was reality—not a
dream.

Once more the same rigid trembling, which
passed like a convulsion through the motionless
world. But in vain, too late. As death cannot
grasp life, so the poor creature down there in the
ashes could no longer grasp whether this was
reality or dream, could not grasp anything.
Only horror, the great bright tears of horror
which ran along the little trembling child-face,
horror at her . . .

How could she have grasped that?

When the living had killed life, killed the man
and woman in humanity, killed humanity so that
only the Thing and its insensible terror were
left, and the mother frightened her child—what
was there left to understand?

Nothing—nothing—

Only two silent tears which rose up in the
petrified eyes as from the same ocean of pain
whose rim glittered in the child's wondering look.
They ran slowly down the maniac's tortured, now
hardly human countenance—the dying tears of
the last intimation, the last hope.

She turned her head away in anguish with a
last confused desire to spare, not to frighten.
With that she sunk back into the pit of ashes,

whose darkness received her as if it wished in pity to hide, in mercy to obliterate her and all of hers.

The light clouds of ashes which a tepid morning wind had begun to carry about laid themselves softly as a covering over the dead of the same doomed generation which had brought in chaos over the world.

Paralyzed they lay there, in a short while they would be hidden—soon just a dark layer in the earth—to be forgotten, perhaps in the end to be forgiven for the sake of their great suffering.

But away, past this, out of chaos, out into life, itself the new forgetting, forgiving life, went the little weeping child with the sunlight gleaming on its head.

SIGFRID SIWERTZ

IN SPITE OF EVERYTHING

THE CAFÉ OF TRANSFIGURATION

Sigfrid Siwertz (1882–) in his first book, a volume of poems entitled *Dreams of the Street,* emphasized the fact that his world was that of the city. His character as, in a manner, the laureate of Stockholm was shown when, a few years ago, he was called on to write the dramatic poem which was acted at the dedication of the new Town Hall, the pride of the city. It has, however, been fiction in which Siwertz has won distinction, and while his background is usually his native city or its environs, he frequently takes his characters out into the skerries, where he confronts the city man with the might of the open sea.

Siwertz's first two collections of short stories, *Margot and Other Stories* and *Circles* are both imbued with a fatalistic pessimism. His characters are in one way or another under the dominance of sex. In his later works he has acquired a more activist philosophy, and in spite of the often gloomy subjects, his belief that man can conquer his fate is apparent. His novels *The Reflection of the Fire* and *Home from Babylon* deal with events of the World War. *The Selambs* (translated under the title *Downstream*) is a picture of corroding selfishness as it was revealed at a time when the dregs of humanity were uppermost. It is regarded as the strongest book he has hitherto written.

Siwertz is an author in whom high intelligence and excellent craftsmanship are more evident than inspiration. He is never dull, and his inventiveness and skill in handling are especially noteworthy in his short stories. *In Spite of Everything* is taken from his first published collection, *Margot and Other Stories.*

Sigfrid Siwertz

In Spite of Everything

HE was to be a father, he who could hardly look after himself. Down in the little railway park, where he had gone to meet her, she had suddenly told him. A locomotive had been staring at him with its red-and-yellow eye and had broken the brittle silence between their words with its panting groans. And he had stood dumbfounded before his first experience involving life and death. But behind his anxiety was a faint, tremulous intimation of days when the child should be his joy and consolation.

Now they were sitting in his student room in the Quarter. He spoke a long while in order to reassure her, but he himself noticed how vague and helpless were his words. Agda sat looking out of the window at the neighboring poplars and their shadows on the old mossy tile roof. A high gable which faced them obliquely was illuminated with a dead, unnatural light, and the reflection of the crescent moon gleamed pallidly up from a pool of water in the street. There was a deathly silence, and he drew nearer to her.

Was she weeping? No. Suddenly her look seemed strange to him. She had become another being in the light of this new event. Yes, it was another woman who sat at his side, another woman whom he must seek to know and conquer.

He pulled down the curtains and lighted his lamp. How beautiful she was with the heavy mass of her bright hair knotted low and her neck slightly bent over the edge of her bodice. He stood before her and regarded her searchingly.

"Have you suffered much for my sake? I don't seem to recognize your eyes . . . Say something!"

She smiled absently.

"You are so young and nice, Erik, and this is such a warm, sad little room . . . I'm certainly a different sort from you . . . I don't feel a bit badly—here."

She began to loosen her bodice and shoe-laces. The strange woman began to loosen her bodice and shoe-laces in his room! Erik stole close to her and took possession of her with eyes and hands, and she caressed him in return. But there was pity in her caresses.

He kindled the fire to a big blaze and put out the lamp. She took off her last white garment and stood softly bowed with a warm restless light playing over her naked form. Erik caught his breath . . . he had never seen her before. She was remorselessly beautiful without a shadow of shame. No one could believe that this girl would be a mother.

She ran her hands gently up to her hair with a gesture that raised her breast and gave her body a prouder attitude. She let the loosened tresses glide through her fingers.

"Should you be vexed if I went away from you?"

There was something arrogant in her tone. Again he stole close to her. She accepted him in silence, her eyes closed, near yet remote. Her hands alone spoke.

In the following days Erik found in Agda a carelessness, a gaiety even, which he little expected. He felt that he was on uncertain ground, and had a dim foreboding that he was destined to suffer. He could not succeed in persuading himself that the change in her came from the fact that there were now two lives speaking through her mouth.

One evening he sought her at the office, but it was already closed, and her window was dark. Afraid of his solitary room, he dragged himself about, weary and helpless as a child.

Next morning Agda came up to his room, flushed and hurried. She stood in the middle

[329]

of the floor with her hat and coat on, adventure gleaming in her eyes.

"I'm going to America!"

Erik did not understand.

"America? But the child—where will you—?"

"As soon as I guessed how it was with me, I wrote a letter to some relatives in Chicago. They are rich and childless. I told them everything and asked if I mightn't come to them; I thought they might adopt the child. The answer has made me so happy—both for your sake and for mine. They had been wanting to adopt a child. They made only one condition—that the child should never know anything of its real father and mother."

She had been talking in feverish haste, and now was suddenly silent with a great questioning look at him.

Erik felt no suffering as yet. He thought he knew what she wanted to hear.

"You mustn't go—you should have told me everything right away. We can manage somehow here at home, get married as soon as possible—"

She wasn't listening. He felt that his voice had begun to tremble.

"Because I have a right in the child too, don't you see?—a right—"

She stood there, hard, unconcerned.

"Are you so sure it's yours?"

It wasn't badness—she was only a child; she was confused by motherhood. She did not realize what she was saying!

He started forward, caught her behind the neck with both hands, and kissed her neck and lips.

"You mustn't go, you mustn't!"

She let him keep hold of her. "Everything is packed, but I'm not going till day after tomorrow. We can write."

Finally he understood and let go of her, his face pale with impotent grief.

Then the door shut behind her, and she was gone without his asking where they should meet to say goodbye.

She was going away with his child—there was no way to stop her. He was helpless, helpless.

Erik tried to stay where he was and reflect, but the room stifled him, and he rushed out. He went up one street and down another without seeing or hearing, while he fought a silent, bitter fight with his pride. At length he came to her stairs, but his heart thumped, and his breathing hurt so that he had to take hold of the door jamb so as not to fall. All the letters of her visiting card danced before his eyes. No, he couldn't ring.

On the way home he saw Agda's large black

hat, but he shrank into a side street so as not to encounter her. He stopped at a cigar store window to see her go by . . . First came a boy with a basket on his arm, then an old woman, then a dog that cast a look up along the alley, sniffed at the corner, and slouched off with his tail between his legs. Now she would come. No, she did not come, she must have turned off.

In the evening he heard her step in the corridor. There was a knock; he did not stir. There was another knock.

"I know you're in—there was a light in your window. Open there!"

He sprang up and turned the key. She was quite calm, there was an atmosphere of coolness about her. She gave him her mouth to kiss, and smiled when he drew back.

"Think how it will be when I come back after it's all over!"

He knew she did not in the least expect to come back, but none the less felt a little comforted against his will. She drew him softly to her.

"Oh, how I long to see the ocean and the big cities over there!"

"But think a little of me and the child, the child . . . You're going to utter strangers!"

"Strangers, strangers—that's just what I

want. I can't go around here with a child. And then it's so stifling in the old familiar surroundings. I hate this town . . . Though I'm still ever so fond of you, you and your quiet room."

"How can you go away like this then?"

"I have to!" Adventure glittered in her eyes. "It seems to be easier to go if one knows there's somebody at home who's sorry."

"I have never known you. I can't understand you." Erik had a sudden intimation of what it was like to go into oneself in order to comprehend another person.

Agda clasped her hands over her knee.

"We're so different . . . I often couldn't understand you at all. I remember one evening by the window here; the sky outside was gray and heavy . . . you said something about quietness, love for what is near, poverty—it sounded so strange—beautiful but strange."

A thought flitted across her countenance, but vanished before a smile. It seemed to him like a grimace. Understand, understand! What does a woman understand? If she understood, how could one draw down the curtains on the stars and luxuriate with hands and limbs in her softness, forgetting one's thoughts?

Erik felt himself for a moment cold, malicious, and a trifle emancipated; but as soon as she was

[333]

gone, and he did not hear her speak, she regained her power over him.

Two days later he followed her down to the Stockholm Central Station. The train set off; he had a glimpse of her at the window waving her handkerchief slightly, and she was gone. He stood alone in the gray empty hall of the station till people began to stare at him. Then he sank down on a chair in the waiting-room. The loneliness was so thick and heavy about him that he could not so much as stir a hand.

It was but slowly Erik could teach himself to forgive and overcome.

Long months passed before he could remember without deep pain and oppression the tranquil charm of her gait and gestures, the bend of her neck, her smile as she let the black skirt glide down from her hips, all the thousand details which in mysterious combination fed his love and came to life within him when he whispered her name. There were times when he felt all the hot agony of life, when the strong imperative desire which awoke in him lay clutching helplessly at emptiness. There were other times when life shrank far away and spread great expanses of cold and darkness between him and her. Yes, everything seemed dead, sticky, loathsome now, since flower and fruit had been torn from him;

and he could lose even the diffident pride in his own suffering which is our last resource in misfortune . . .

But one morning when he awoke from his degradation and found that the daylight and his books once more attracted him, he felt also that he had become another man.

He went out in the late winter dawn.

The heavens hung dark and gray above the spires of the cathedral, stillness lay and dreamed in the treetops, the air was as though filled with pitying kindness and cool, chaste caresses. Far away across the plain the sky was a mild and sad symphonic prelude in violet-gray and transparent blue-green, where the stars had just dissolved . . .

He walked on. The high, wing-shaped walls of the Carolina * seemed to freeze under their thin gray hue. The frozen berries on the wayside aspens burned a strange red against all this white and gray.

He was conscious of a silent thankfulness. There was something new in him, something which was above both happiness and grief; his days would now pass like a cool wind.

Yes, there was now something in him which

---

* The main building of Upsala University.

was unassailable; in spite of all casual suffering, unrest, insensibility, a space deep within him would radiate with tranquil light. And he divined without fear that he would become yet more lonely, for from that time he was a force enclosed within himself; he was his own goal and his own meaning . . .

In that faith he lived on.

II

Evening had come.

The electric trains kindled their wandering lights, and the oily-smooth water between the Dam and the railroad bridge heaved slowly in dark violet. In the midst of a narrow red strip of light across the Malar the bronze signal lantern gleamed like a little green sparkling jewel. Above, no stars appeared.

The strip of light narrowed inexorably; night would soon shut its heavy iron-gray vault over the sorrowing waters out there.

Agda stopped a moment on the path around the Statue. She did not know what it was that welled up within her. Her thoughts fluttered hither and thither with restless wing-beats. She found no words, no outlet, she only felt an insufferable weight upon her limbs. If there was only some one who understood her, who could smile at her weakness, could speak terse and cool words to her. But she was alone.

She stood on the corner of a narrow side-street up in South Stockholm. Erik Vallenius lived there. She fought a silent battle with herself, as she had done so many times before, but it was impossible, she could not bring herself to go up to him.

So she took a carriage home.

In the deserted apartment out in Östermalm there was a dusty, stifling atmosphere, and all the windows were boarded up. The darkness of the great silent rooms frightened her. She lighted a lamp and two candles before the mirror in the bedroom and looked long into her own face. It was young, dangerous, without humility. She did not understand it; it was a mask that did not fit with her inner nature.

She undressed before the mirror, thinking all the while that she hated her neck and shoulders because they were white and soft, and because they belonged to him she hated.

Next day Agda started out again to visit Erik Vallenius. She wandered long amid the old dark shanties far up above Fishers' Harbor before she finally stopped in front of his number.

Two pale and silent children, who were sailing egg-shells in the little iron trough under the yard-pump, ceased their play to look at her with their large eyes. In the low windows on the ground floor were crowded all the pretty flowers that poor people grow, and between the four brown pillars of the porch cresses were trained in festoons along a network of strings.

Agda tried to deaden the rustle of her skirts, which seemed out of place here.

She then proceeded slowly up the old harshly-creaking wooden stairway with high shining newel-posts, and found herself up under the beams and laths of the roof. Erik's name was on the door, and she knocked hesitatingly several times.

"Go down a flight, if it's urgent."

His voice sounded strangely weak and far away. She dared not say who she was, but obeyed in silence.

Below, an old gray-clad woman opened the door and scanned her severely and searchingly.

"Who are you?"

Agda was bashful as a child at her own elegant costume.

"I've come from America. . . . I'm an old friend of Mr. Erik Vallenius."

"Doesn't the lady know he has been ill, poor man?"

"Ill?" Agda felt dizzy for a moment. "Can't I speak to him?"

The old woman went softly up the stairs and

vanished into Erik's room. After a while she appeared again and signed to Agda that she might come.

She entered a largish low room with a deep white window recess where white azalea blossomed together with amaryllis and some dark myrtle plants. Directly opposite this Agda could discern through a gap in a large tottering bookcase a bed which seemed in need of a wall to prop it. In the ceiling above was a damp space like the outline map of a mountain range. Agda took in all this with a quick, restless glance, after which she stole forward to the bed without daring to look up.

"I heard you were sick, so I wanted to come to you."

She hardly realized she was lying.

Erik lay white against the white pillows. His eyes were bright as formerly, though more sunken and prone to dwell longer and more sceptically on all they saw. His face showed neither surprise nor joy, he merely smiled pallidly out at the sunlight.

"Have you seen the ocean and the big cities now?"

Agda did not remember her former words. She was shy and uncertain under his calm gaze.

"You are so pale, and your hands are thin. Have you suffered a great deal?"

"A little at first on acount of you—you were mild and hard just as spring is—there was no merciful kindness in you. My illness—something with my heart—had only an external origin. I've just begun to succeed in making it something spiritual. There is in me a silent acquiescence toward everything—even toward death."

Agda sank down on a chair.

"I'm so unhappy too!"

He shut his eyes wearily.

"I don't know that it's a question of happiness."

She leaned gently down toward him with a hand on the bedpost.

"It would have been such a comfort to me to see you in different circumstances."

But he pursued his thoughts with something of the obstinate egoism peculiar to sick persons.

"Happiness—I dislike the word, I don't long for any happiness—but joy, that's different—joy is brief, but it's the deepest of all feelings."

Erik had long been living alone and self-absorbed. He continued, as though oblivious of her, to talk out toward the sunlight—about joy. It might come suddenly and upon slight occasions. It might be the expression of a face one met, the sunlight glittering on a gutter, a few tones of a piano from an open window, that transfigured the world. One walked with a lighter step, the heavens grew deep and radiant, the street resounded like a Wagner overture . . . Ah, joy—it was a kind of lightness, a kind of noble generosity toward the moment—one forgave life for being so barren and stupid.

Here he turned with a new smile to Agda:

"When I was young and unchastened, I spoke to you of sorrow, and you didn't understand. Now I'm speaking to you of joy, and assuredly you understand no better.—But you've grown more beautiful than you were—yes, you are very beautiful—and so elegant."

When Agda had heard Erik was ill, she had not merely been sorry for him. She had then hoped to find in him some one she could help, some one upon whom to lavish little attentions. Now she stood there blushing, shy and at a loss.

"Have you been dangerously ill?"

"Oh, I shall soon be all right again, though I've never thought I should live to be old—now I know . . ."

He sank back on the pillow. "But I think you'd better go now; I'm tired."

Agda took his hand.

"Mayn't I come again?—Won't you ask about the child?"

He did not answer. She went then, silent, submissive. When she was at the door, he called her back with an unsteady voice.

"I should be grateful if you'd write—write a little more of how things went with you and Edgar out there. I know most of what was in your old letters—that you'd married and that he's well and hearty. But write anyhow. I think it would be best for you not to come here any more —I'm not like this always."

"Mayn't I come and help you?" She pleaded with both eyes and hands.

He drew a deep breath.

"No, there's no need."

Agda went away with heavy steps.

She wandered back and forth on the streets, waiting for the boat which was to take her to her country house and her husband.

She wasn't to visit Erik Vallenius any more— Did he hate her? No, how could he do that? But he despised her; yes, despised. There was so much manly strength and firmness in his attitude, that she hadn't felt she was in the presence of an invalid. In the midst of her bloom she had become so small and humble before him, as he lay on the white pillow and looked out into far and silent realms which she could hardly guess at.

She wasn't to visit him any more—there was something in that which gnawed at her like self-contempt, which would some day become acute suffering, she divined. And she felt crushed and humiliated—like a servant. . . .

It was several days later, in Erik's room.

Agda had come silently slipping in through the open door.

She had to see him just once more; she had not been able to bring herself to write. He sat dressed at the open window with a book in his hand. The murmur of the streets and the harbor lived as a continuous grating note within the bright walls of the room. He laid the book gently aside.

Eager to find some excuse for her visit, she at once began to tell about her fortunes over there; she spoke rapidly, restlessly, with leaps over oud den digressions.

Being poor, she had been forced to travel as an emigrant, and she had strong and painful words for all the misery on board the great steamer out in the autumn gales. On their arrival they had been numbered on the back with chalk—her number was 38—and had been fenced off like cattle in various pens to be examined. She had had a horrible fear of being sent home again.

She had only had a glimpse of New York. In Chicago she had been cordially received by her cousin—he was a factory owner—but had been sent out almost immediately to a farm on the plains. And she had walked alone along the great billowing grain-fields, waiting with ever increasing anxiety for her child to come. When that was all over, she had been given a place in an office in New York; she wasn't allowed to stay with the child. There she had sat ten hours a day at her typewriter and rattled off letters direct from the dictaphone which sat like a helmet on her head and spoke the letters into her ears.

Agda was still a moment and turned away, tortured by what she was going to say.

"I saved as much as I could so as to come home . . . It was then I met Tom Ahrén . . . If it only hadn't been for that dreadful helmet it wouldn't have gone as it did . . . And then I knew so little about him. He had a good business, and I began to lead a life of indolence, far away from my real self, with his hard will around me like a wall.

"Two years went by. Then came a letter to say that my father was dead. I don't know what happened to me, but I felt ever so homesick and deserted in the midst of my luxury. The amusements I had longed for seemed as ridiculous as the bill-boards outside a vaudeville. And then I began to hate my husband—especially at table. We didn't talk much, but when he said anything, I compared his words with yours—I understood them now—and I could not answer.

"Well, so then we came back home here. We've been here a little less than a year. He buys houses and sells them at a profit. . . . You should see him when he takes out his pocketbook. For anything he can't take hold of with his hands he has a little dry laugh of derision; in that laugh is all his coldness and poverty of soul. He has surely never suffered, never had a gloomy dream. I didn't notice it so much over there, but now it's growing on him, growing at the expense of everything else; for me there will soon be nothing left of him but that laugh. When I don't hear it, I wait to hear it; and when I hear it, it cuts through me . . ."

Erik had risen from his chair and sunk down on a sofa, where it was darker. He now checked her wearily.

"Why do you tell me all this?"

"I don't know how to say it . . . it's such a comfort to be able to tell you about my life . . . it's as if it began to have a little meaning."

"Do you hate him really?"

"Yes."

"But you live together as man and wife?"

"No."

Erik felt to the tips of his fingers that she was lying. He shut his eyes and sat silent in the shadowy corner.

Agda glided to the window recess. In front of the house hung a little garden with bright red blossoms and lilac arbors rising above the narrow dark rows of broken-backed tile roofs. On the loosened moss-covered stones of the doorsteps below, a noisy crowd of children were scrambling, and two drunken workmen with carnations in their buttonholes embraced each other on an empty packing-case in a little black hole of a yard. Beyond was the water and the city with the strong sunlight of late summer upon it . . .

This then had been constantly before his eyes for a long time. Agda divined how tranquilly his life slipped away, how different it had been from hers. Her eyes filled with tears; she glided down to him and took his hand forcibly.

"You mustn't despise me!"

Erik gazed searchingly into her face.

"Why have you come here, what do you really want with me?"

"My life has been so restless and confused . . . You must help me, talk with me. You know more about me than I do about myself."

"You've been reading, I think you said."

"Oh yes, I wrote for the books I saw on your shelves. There was so much I got a glimpse of there, but when the intoxication had passed, the old burden weighed me down again, and I couldn't see any escape. . . . You must help me."

"How can I help you? You won't understand me."

"Tell me something about your life in the past years! You smile almost all the time, but your eyes are so sad. Hasn't it been hard to be all alone?—for I know you've been alone. Tell me!"

"My life?" Erik made a motion toward the book-case and shook his head, as if she had asked for the impossible. But then he seemed to recollect.

"Alone, you said— Loneliness isn't so hard to bear for a man who has taught himself to love life in its entirety: people and things, perhaps most of all things. He who doesn't hear too many empty words, to him everything begins to speak: the light, clouds, lamps, trees. If you have ever listened to their mysterious whispers, you know they are not far off and indifferent. Out of the turmoil of a thousand contours gradually emerge one's own features—lost in the outer world; one rediscovers oneself and reposes there magnified in the certainty . . . It's like being borne on through a blue endlessness—I am inwardly one with all that is, all that was and is to be; I am all that in which I seem to move as an indistinguishable and evanescent part."

Erik rose and walked back and forth in the room with moist, radiant eyes and small feverish spots on his cheeks.

Agda followed him with her gaze, kindled by his emotion, but with her thoughts struggling in the depths, unable to rise to any clarity.

She then kissed him in farewell.

It was as if something of his soul had flowed into her. When she mounted the drawbridge, she felt a man's faculty of comprehending everything and feeling its nature in an instant. . . .

Across the shore of Kungsholm the evening brooded a menacing red, as it is only above a factory district, but around the church spires of Norrmalm the glow lingered more pallidly, as if in fear that no one had seen its beauty. Under her feet was the Old City with roof upon roof, chimney upon chimney out into a deep evening-blue perspective, where the star-seed of the lights was still thin and pale. Agda shivered at the thought that every stone, every beam, every tile, everything she now embraced in a swift glance, was formed with toil during long hours by human brains and human hands. Her thought labored painfully and helplessly to lift this to the light of an ultimate meaning, but it could not, and she passed on with an oppressive weight on her breast and limbs.

A month later Erik and Agda visited Upsala together.

They walked a long time in silence along the small streets up in the Quarter, whence they had glimpses of the plain in the background like a bright blue band. The air had an autumnal stillness above the asters of the garden terraces, the dahlias still defied the night frosts with their dusky glow. There was no wind in the hanging gold of the birches.

Agda stopped in front of the little yellow house where Erik had lived.

"Shan't we go in and see your old room?"

Erik went in to find out from the landlord whether it would be all right.

Oh yes, the student lodger hadn't come to Upsala yet.

Up in the room which used to be his the dust lay soft and gray on the old furniture, but the walls were covered with drawings from *Aphrodite* by Pierre Louys.

"Poor fellow!" laughed Agda, but Erik went to the window and looked out at the old poplars which raised their deep, still unfaded verdure above the roof opposite. Under his hands were the holes he had bored with his pen in the edge of the table when he was tired and could not think any longer.

[349]

Agda sat down silently. In her look was a prayer that he would come to her.

"No, come away—I can't stay in here any longer!" His voice sounded broken.

As the twilight came on, they went out from the town. The plain was a vast enfolding melancholy. In the distance an avenue of maples drew its dim streak of gold across the dark hill ridges.

He stood still and took her by the arm.

"It was my pride to rest in myself without a hold on any one else. I believed so firmly in my strength. 'Solitude' I said to myself, thinking of something great, deep—What have you done to me now, what will be the years I have left to live? . . . I know your failings, your deceit, your hardness when you think yourself secure, your heavy and helpless emptiness when you are alone; and yet I live only in you, all my dreams are in you. . . . I hate you."

He kissed her long with trembling lips.

And she gently lifted his hand to her breast.

THE spring was already more than a promise. The chestnut buds lifted themselves up as large as the clasped hands of a baby over the glittering gray-white asphalt of the boulevard, and inside the café the shadow-patterns of the window curtains lay like beautiful lacework on the sun-yellow sand of the floor. Men in their shirt-sleeves leaned over the green cloth of the billiard table, and the reflection of the rolling balls was repeated far into the unreal perspective of the smoke-blue mirrors. But to-day one's gaze was unwilling to lose itself in these eerie corridors of dream, where the last echoes of the light die away in the hovering distance. Their world was too much a manufactured, a deliberate mystery in this benevolent sunshine, in the artless and blessed spring season. Nor did one lose oneself in following the balls' motion in those graceful and stimulating geometric fantasies which are commonly the chief pleasure in the game of billiards. Looking at the green cloth and the balls, one seemed to see cool spring grass —a wide meadow with red and white flowers. There must be one somewhere between the hills— far away from Paris.

At the table beside me sat four old men drinking their wine. The air was very still, and the smoke which rose in straight pillars from their pipes formed a majestic ethereal dome about their gray heads. But they were very silent and serious; almost sad, I thought. This surprised me, for surely the spring sun must feel good to tired limbs and senses.

But then all at once there was life in the sunlight that shone amid the blue smoke. Yet another old man had glided in through the mill of the swinging door. He was deeply bowed as he walked, and his long white beard brushed his vest between the folds of his unbuttoned coat. He seemed emaciated, for the coat hung in wrinkles around him.

One of the tottering brotherhood beside me— a little man with very wide trousers and a black, snoring stump of a pipe that seemed to have struck root between his teeth—arose on the instant, raised his hands and declaimed with a loud voice:

"Stand up, fellow members, and make room for Eugene Auguste Armand Delavigne, greengrocer of the Rue des Saints Péres. He has fought with death and come out victorious."

The newcomer saluted with a little tired nod, reached with thin and tremulous hand for his pipe—number 29 in the glass cupboard above the cues—and sank down among his old friends with his head against the same dark spot on the wall where it had rested before during the many slow-rolling years of his life. From what was said I heard that he had lain sick the whole winter and was now come back for the first time to his club café. I could not take my eyes from him as he sat there with the sun on the thin white tufts of his hair.

My first imagination took a little journey into the melancholy of the past winter. I saw the thousand wrinkles about his lips and eyes as meshes of the net which death invisibly spins around us. And the street suddenly gave forth a hollow reverberation out in the stabbing light.

But with that the old man smiled—his first smile of recognition to the faithful brotherhood and the waiter, Napoleon, also known as the Ship of the Desert, who with a nod of special respect came toddling out on his flat feet and immediately served the customary drink. All the wrinkles in the worn face became merry—the meshes of fate were loosened a moment. I saw the mercifulness of oblivion in the halo around the features over which death had breathed.

My ancient unknown friend did not speak much. His eyes rested long on everything. Old men's glances often do so, to be sure, but in his was a special expression of shy love without rest-lessness or demand. His eyes loved all things and were apart from all. It was as if they raised things into a cooler atmosphere. The light became clarified from dwelling in his gaze.

Yes, the commonplace objects of the café became all at once more beautiful from the fact that he beheld them. His nearness gave a glory of quiet consecration even to the heads of the others. When one of them silently raised a glass to his mouth, it became a significant act of worship in the sanctuary of this man's thought. At the table opposite me were a gentleman and lady. They were young and handsome. Bread lay on the shining white cloth between them. . . . And he took the bread, broke it and gave to her saying . . . What? . . . I did not hear. But it must have been, "I love you."

So everything seemed in the light of the old man's gaze. He helped me to accept the gifts of every day with deeper thankfulness, without any weakness or shunning of that which awaits us all. The time became for me one of those silent and delicate feasts of contemplation which are among the best gifts of our life.

I felt that death need not be anything shadowy and hostile, which roams outside the border of life, but something which life embraces and presses to its bosom like a weaker friend.

Let not the thought of death come as an unbidden guest, for its kiss and promise make you

rich and ardent.   Mortality is the secret perfume
of beauty.   It is through its mortality that everything is immortal.

So I thought over my white wine on a Sunday,
when the chestnut trees were budding in the city
where men have perhaps succeeded best in making something beautiful of their limitations.

MÄRTA AF SILLÉN

THE GOLDEN CIRCLE

MÄRTA AF SILLÉN (1899–   ) is a daughter of Kammer-
herre Joseph af Sillén. She has published a volume of
poems, *When the Sap Rises,* and some short stories.   She
is married to Major Erik Ribbing, a direct descendant
of St. Birgitta.

Märta af Sillén

THE GOLDEN CIRCLE

HE stood holding the letter in his hand. He did not, however, read it for a long time. Instead he gazed fixedly at the little, light, glittering object which lay in the folded sheet. It was a small bracelet, a woman's bracelet, one of those diminutive gold chains that one sees so often on the wrists of young girls, and that are not too insuperably dear for poor young men to buy.

He sat down and laid it on the table in an even circle, smoothing out all its irregularities with an almost pedantic exactitude. But still he could not get on with the letter. To be sure, he knew what was in it. The little gold hieroglyphic before him was enough, since for the initiate who knows how to interpret it a hieroglyphic may contain an extended meaning of great importance.

His thoughts went back to the time when he had given it to her. It was in the spring about two and a half years ago. So it was, for their romance, like so many others, had taken its beginning at that season and, as far as romance went, had not differed much from the average.

[359]

He had even been so banal as to propose in a park on a bench in a side arbor, where for the moment no promenaders were in sight. In the air there had been a feeling of spring, but no sign of it on the ground, except for the plucky snowdrops which peeped up from the black, damp soil.

It was the Northland's romance, as so often happens: a little shy, a little cool, filled with expectation and longing.

He could still see her clearly before him as she sat on the bench with sparkling eyes and the little blue-chilled cheeks, for she had put on a new spring dress for him—the little idiot! But although she was freezing, she would not get up and go. She was warmed by an inner fire, like the trees, like the frost-bitten snowdrops.

So they had become secretly engaged, as secretly as possible. They were in no hurry to inform the world, and the world which would have known of it was not so very large and would not have thought it as unusual, as wonderful, as romantic as they themselves did.

It was to be an engagement of the protracted sort, long and patient as the Northland spring, long and patient as such an affair could be only in the North. He was to study and work, and then travel and study further. He felt sure of getting a scholarship. People had great hopes of him as an architect. He would some day build churches and palaces and beautify the city. As they walked through the streets and across the squares, he showed her all that he wished to make over, and she on her part was all eyes, ears, and wonder. They would travel together, for travel was now his heart's desire, and hers too.

It was a week later that he had given her the bracelet. On that day it seemed that spring had come in earnest. As by a stroke of enchantment everything had begun to sprout, and the air was like wine.

It was again in the park that they met and there that he snapped the slender bracelet around her wrist. With that he suddenly took the notion of dragging her in to a goldsmith's and having him solder it together. Now the chain was shut and could not be opened. Neither could it be pulled off over her wrist; that he saw to carefully.

Afterwards they sat down on a bench. He drew off her glove to see how the gold chain looked, and kissed the place where her pulse beat.

Then he pointed to the bracelet and said, "Do you know what that is?"

"What it is? It's a bracelet, I should hope; a bracelet that I've got from a person I don't care about in the least."

"Yes, but it's something besides. It's a circle."

"Um—yes. To be sure. Well?"

"And what is a circle?"

"As far as I know it can't be anything else but a circle," she responded.

"It is a symbol of eternity. For the circle, as you see, has neither beginning nor end."

"Oh, and it's a golden circle too," she continued. "But we've all had a beginning, though, haven't we?"

"Yes, but then the circle was open. Now it's soldered."

"Listen to me, little one," he went on in a more earnest tone. "If you should ever regret our engagement—let us merely assume the possibility—if you should ever change your mind, just send this back, and I shall understand. It would be a symbol, for you appreciate that in order to send it back you would have to destroy the circle, to break it by violence. Why should there be scenes and long explanations? I've always detested that sort of thing. This token will be sufficient. But it will also be irrevocable."

"Hark to what you're saying!" she had cried impetuously. "Such a thing is inconceivable. I know of course I might go to a goldsmith and say: 'Clip this off!' And then he'd take a pair of pincers, a pair of hard, brutal pincers. I can hear how it would sound. Clip!—Done!— Short, cold, and brutal. So dreadful! You must admit that you don't believe any such thing ever would happen. You wouldn't dare—"

No, no, he wouldn't dare—of course not. And so they had laughed gaily together again. After that they had gone through the park arm in arm in the open light of day. And yet only a little while before they had felt so terribly strange!

It was less than a year later that the accident had occurred in which she had strained her back.

First had come despair, terror that she would be taken from him—that she would become an invalid. Then when she grew better followed the glad assurance that she would recover entirely. The human mind is prone to see everything in extremes. The middle degree, which is neither black as night nor red as sunrise, then comes along stealthily, as gray and cold as winter twilight.

The doctors pronounced that she would not be an invalid. But they also informed him that neither would she ever be like a person in full health. She would never be able to work like others, never be strong enough to make severe journeys; she would always have to be treated carefully. Although—here they shrugged their shoulders—one could not be certain; remarkable things sometimes happen.

There was not cause enough for him to leave her—nor did he wish to. The vital, restless force that groaned within him he suppressed into silence. It was an unworthy, an inhuman impulse.

Lately, however, as he had sat by her bed and talked about the future—with a cheerfulness that was perhaps a bit constrained—she had smiled very sadly. It was at no castle in the air that she was looking, as he now knew, but at a gray granite house of reality, perhaps a lifelong sanatorium.

And now he was sitting there, staring at the bracelet. The gold circle lay before him—unbroken!

He unfolded the letter carefully and read. The contents were brief and simple: "Beloved! I am sending back herewith the bracelet you gave me, the irrevocable token!

"One has time to think in a year's illness. It was yesterday that the frightful struggle came upon me. All that was selfish in me screamed aloud and tried to drown what really loved you.

"At that moment I made a violent gesture with my hand. And—the gold circle slid over my wrist. There it lay on the sheet and glittered. I looked at it a long while, as at a miracle; then I looked at my hand. With that I understood. Illness has made my hand so thin—. Realize how it is then: no goldsmith has needed to clip with his hard pincers, but illness has made my hand so thin that the chain slipped off of itself.

Dearest, I now send you back the gold circle—
unbroken."

There followed several lines of thanks for the
past and of wishes for a happy future for him.
There were even a few sportive lines.

But he could hardly see to read them for the
mist that came over his eyes. He could hear so
plainly how she had said: "And it's a golden
circle, too."

SCANDINAVIAN CLASSICS

IV. *Master Olof, by August Strindberg*

An historical play, translated, with an Introduction, by EDWIN BJÖRKMAN

V. *The Prose Edda, by Snorri Sturluson*

Translated from the old Icelandic, with an Introduction and Notes, by ARTHUR GILCHRIST BRODEUR   Price $2.00

VI. *Modern Icelandic Plays, by Jóhan Sigurjónsson: Eyvind of the Hills and The Hraun Farm*

Translated by HENNINGE KROHN SCHANCHE   Price $2.00

VII. *Marie Grubbe: A Lady of the Seventeenth Century, by J. P. Jacobsen*

An historical romance, translated, with an Introduction, by HANNA ASTRUP LARSEN

VIII. *Arnljot Gelline, by Björnstjerne Björnson*

A Norse Epic, translated by WILLIAM MORTON PAYNE

Price $2.00

IX. *Anthology of Swedish Lyrics, from 1750 to 1915*

Selections from the greatest of Swedish lyrics, translated by CHARLES WHARTON STORK

X & XI. *Gösta Berling's Saga, by Selma Lagerlöf*

The English translation by LILLIE TUDEER, completed and carefully edited. Two volumes

XII. *Sara Videbeck (Det går an), and The Chapel, by C. J. L. Almquist*

Translated, with an Introduction, by ADOLPH BURNETT BENSON

Price $2.00

XIII. *Niels Lyhne, by J. P. Jacobsen*

A psychological novel, translated, with an Introduction, by HANNA ASTRUP LARSEN   Price $2.00

SCANDINAVIAN MONOGRAPHS